'The Jenson Rose Trilogy'

Jenson and the Dreamers

By

Alan Hendrick

www.publishnation.co.uk

'A book is a dream that you hold in your hand'

- Neil Gaiman

Follow me on this Dream:

Facebook   - Alan Hendrick
Instagram   - alanmhendrick
TikTok   - @alanhendrick1

Prologue

Some say when the time comes, their desire is to leave this world quietly in their sleep. And many are comforted by this relief, their loved ones dying peacefully in their beds. A sense of tranquillity, transcending from this world to the next. But what is the other world? Is it really a heavenly place where we can spend the rest of our days with other passing loved ones?

'See you in the next life.'

Is there even such a place? What if we were wrong after all these years? And what if our belief in a "so called" God diminished?

According to estimates, there are some 4,200 different religions in this world. So which one is the correct one? Should we believe in Christianity, Hinduism, Buddhism, Islamic beliefs, or even any of the thousands of others? Are these such beliefs even true, or are they causing war and destroying us all???

~Albert Einstein quoted in his New York Times Obituary on April 19, 1955,

"I cannot imagine a God who rewards and punishes the objects of his creation…..Neither can I believe that the individual survives the death of his body, although feeble souls harbour such thoughts through fear or ridiculous egotism."

What if Einstein was right, and we began to believe that our universe consists of just two worlds connected, our world 'Earth' and our 'Dream World'? And what if our matter excels between these two worlds? So, when we sleep at night, our souls travel back and forth to the Dream World allowing us to dream?

Therefore, what happens in our Dreams affect us in our real life. If we injure ourselves in our Dream, this alters our bodies. From a simple fall, a cut, or even a burn mark, whatever we endure in our sleep, it appears physically. So as the myth that once was is now true, if we die in our sleep, we die in our reality. And our souls are not taken to a heavenly place full of kindred spirits. They are simply lost in this Dream World forever!

A new disease called the 'Dream-death disease' is plaguing a widespread of people, causing an upsurge in deaths whilst sleeping. People are starting to believe in this "Einstein belief". And as a United World, we have set up an organisation called 'Stem Industries'. A government funded organisation created to find a cure for this killing disease.

Some believe in dark forces from the other side, 'Evil Demons' killing us in our sleep, but nobody knows for sure.

Evolution has somehow come up with a way to combat this Dream-death disease.

'Dream-drifters' - 'Drifters' have evolved with the ability to drift in and out of peoples dreams within this Dream World in the human form. They can escape this death by fluctuating from dreams.

'Soul-searchers' - 'Searchers' are not as powerful, but they can search for each other in this Dream World. Siblings and blood tied relatives who can help each other.

But some believe the most powerful of them all are the 'Non-dreamers'. Non-dreamers cannot dream. This phenomenon has somehow skipped them, a glitch in the system if you like. They can never die in their sleep because their souls never reach this other world to dream.

Stem is in search of 'Non-dreamers', and believe they are the key to finding a cure. In the beginning 'Non-dreamers' did come forward to help, but experiments proved fatal. Because of this, 'Non-dreamers' have gone into hiding, keeping a low profile and evading capture at any cost. This secrecy will buy them time. But Stem forces are getting stronger, and not a day goes by without 'Non-dreamers' being taken.

Ever since these deaths have been happening, each human has been stamped with a serial number, an identity. And every day, numbers are picked out at random, and those unfortunate, will be taken by 'Stem' to be tested on. So, if your dreams and nightmares do not catch up on you, 'Stem' eventually will!!!!

Chapter 1

15 years ago –
The Beginning of the Dream-death disease.

The crying screams of a new-born were becoming increasingly tiring for Stephanie. She didn't seem old enough to lap this new experience up in her stride. At the tender age of sixteen, she was still finding it an overwhelming struggle.

A sudden disruption from her slumber, she rolled back her eyes before glancing over at the illuminated alarm clock, which read 3:06am. Her committed obligation dwindling as she lay there questioning her next move. But the cries were like sharp needles scratching at her skull. She knew she had to move.

With one huge intake, she quickly exhaled all the anger and pulled back the covers to go tend to her son.

'Shhhhh, please be quiet Davrin,' she begged.

Her hands, like shovels, scooping her long black hair away from her face. Her fingertips sweeping each clump in behind her ears. She leaned forward, allowing the top half of her body to fold. She reached into the cot. And cradling her son, she lifted him out, placing him up against her chest,

'You cannot be hungry. You're not due a feed for another hour,' she said, lightly stroking his back whilst softly shaking his little fragile body.

Stephanie turned round after hearing her bedroom door creak open, revealing a dark shadow in the doorway. Just then, the light switched on as her mother, Margaret, stepped in.

1

'Is everything ok Steph? Here, give him to me,' Margaret instructed whilst holding her arms out and pressing forward. Margaret wasn't one to wait on replies. 'You go and make up his bottle.'

'But I only fed him shortly after midnight,' Stephanie replied.

'And what time is it now?'

'It's a little after three.'

'Have you checked if he needs a change?' Margaret suggested.

And as Stephanie handed over her screaming child, Margaret realised why this tiny bundle of joy was crying.

'He's all wet,' she said, one hand pressing underneath and feeling around, recognising the dampness in his nappy. The other hand continuing to tap him on the back.

This was not a scorning report from Margaret, for she knew it was unfamiliar territory, something Stephanie had never experienced before. It was exposure to motherhood, a transfer of guidance passed down from generation to generation, something her mother had bestowed upon her. And now it was her turn to wield this knowledge,

'You go on and get him his bottle,' she instructed. 'I'll get him changed.'

'But he's not due another feed yet,' Stephanie barked.

'Ah sure he's a growing boy, trust me...when I get him changed, he'll be hungry. And don't worry Steph, you'll get the hang of this soon enough.'

Stephanie didn't say a word. She withdrew silently, but her body language suggested otherwise. She stormed out past her mother. Her hand, taking hold of the door and swinging it shut. Her frustration showing as she left the screams of her baby behind.

Slightly more bearable, and masked behind the closed door, the supressing cries were fading. But they still called out.

2

Shallow howls like tiny torments, edging in her brain again as she climbed down the stairs.

Stephanie was annoyed at her mother for interfering, but she had misjudged this as a patronising jab. And this assessment soon changed before she had even reached the bottom step. The negligence of not knowing why her baby had been crying began to eat away at her. The harsh reality consuming her as she stepped into the kitchen. But the affliction soon dissipated, transferring to an appreciation of having her mother around. And then guilt set in from her tantrum. The slamming of the door was unjustified. Another slip-up she would later apologise for.

She clicked the switch on the wall. And with it, the light provoked a warm sensation as the country kitchen greeted her, the old-fashioned kitchen she grew up in, the heart of the home. Fond memories began to flourish, something she knew Davrin would soon experience. She smiled to herself. The gratitude of her mother's assistance took hold of her heart, squeezing it and pumping the affection all around her body. For some grandmothers would begrudge being woken up five nights in a row now, but not Margaret. She seemed to enjoy every minute. A woman in her fifty's, having renounced her childcare duties years ago, but now, another baby to wreak havoc. A crying infant to evoke confinement. But Margaret embraced it all. It somehow rekindled a spark in her life. A spark that had been extinguished a year ago from the passing of her husband.

Filling up the kettle and placing it back onto the heating coil, Stephanie clicked the switch. She began to scoop out some formula powder and drop it into the bottle, before taking a seat and waiting for the vibrations to sound.

The rumbling of the boiling water alerted her. She had only sat down minutes previously. Her eyes sluggishly returning to reality. She had somehow managed to drift back into a light slumber. Her elbows, each resting on the table as her head sank deep into her palms.

Rubbing her eyes, she began to summon every ounce of energy. Her excessive yawning proved how tired she was. She wondered if she would ever get a handle on this. A fatigue weighing her down with every yawn. Quicksand gnawing at her feet, eagerly trying to pull her under. But she whooshed herself away from the table, the chair legs squeaking in protest. And standing up, with a stubborn determination, she shuffled across the tiled flooring, proving to herself that she could do this.

Stephanie knew motherhood would be tough even before she had her baby. She finally gave in to the stares and comments, and the falsity behind the smiles. She knew people were talking about her. News spread like wildfire. And with it grew more suspicion and fabrication. For her consensual lovemaking quickly turned sour. And stories of her sleeping around soon tainted the accuracy.

Truth be told, there was only one person. And the father of her baby was also a miner. He had been staying with his aunt and uncle for the summer. His cousin had introduced him to Stephanie, which in return, fuelled a summer romance. And this brief encounter resulted in Stephanie losing her virginity and becoming pregnant.

Consequences caused that family to pack up and vanish, leaving a town to revel in the shock and disgrace of a fifteen-year-old girl. And because Stephanie had "willingly participated" in these actions, no repercussions had been taken.

Town folk seemed to disregard the fact two people had fallen in love. For they simply focused on the "disrespectful" behaviours of an underage child. And their branding and judgemental eyes never accepted the impact this had on an innocent, naïve, fifteen-year-old; the result being a mental breakdown.

Instead, they stewed on the gossip of how it all happened. But what they failed to realise was that this young girl's heart had been broken into more than one piece. For not only had she buried her own father that summer. She had also lost her first true love. Deep wounds she would carry around with her forever, and a baby to remind her everyday of what she had lost. Her heart shattered into tiny pieces, never to be assembled back together again. For Stephanie never saw this boy again after the news broke. His family simply condemned the idea of keeping this baby, suggesting a child would ruin their lives.

They pushed hard on an abortion, insisting it would solve the problem. But Stephanie's mother Margaret disagreed. She was a woman of the cloth, a holy woman who was truly against the idea to terminate the baby. And communication between both families quickly broke down.

Margaret assured Stephanie things would get better. She was a believer. And no matter how popular this 'Einstein religion' was becoming, she believed God had a plan, and that his mysterious ways would always work out for those who believed in him.

And as her husband (Stephanie's father) had died that summer from cancer, Margaret understood this baby to be the miracle that could get her little family through the grief and pain of his passing.

'Now. All done my pretty little green-eyed boy,' Margaret said as she clicked the last under button of her grandson's garment.

She lifted him up from the bed just as she heard the footsteps of her daughter.

'Here's your mother now with your food,' she added whilst kissing him on his soft forehead.

'I'm sorry Mum.' Stephanie said.

And there it was, the awaited apology.

'No need to apologise. You're tired and snappy, we both are. I'll feed him if you want to go back to bed. You look exhausted.'

The thought had crossed Stephanie's mind. Maybe a few extra hours of sleep would help. But even though it was a tempting offer, she knew she had to kindly refuse.

'No, I'll be fine Mum, you've done enough, but thank you.'

Stephanie simply smiled and held out her hands to take her baby. It was her turn to palm off any opposition.

'Are you sure......I don't mind?'

'No, honestly Mum, I'll be fine. You already do too much.'

'Okay then,' Margaret surrendered.

She handed over the baby and watched her daughter sluggishly stroll past. She could see the fatigue weighing her down.

'How have you been sleeping Stephanie?'

'Ok I suppose.'

Stephanie collapsed down on the chair beside her bed. She gently edged the bottle into her son's mouth just as he began to suckle aggressively.

'God, he must have been hungry,' Margaret said. A light chuckle in her statement as a grin took hold of her face. 'You sure you're coping with everything?'

'Yeah. It's still a lot of getting used to. A little tiring, but I'll get there.'

'And what about those nightmares?'

'They're not as bad anymore. The voice comes and goes, but I haven't heard it in a while. Hopefully, whatever it was, it's gone for good. But it did seem so real. God only knows I suppose.'

'We all have demons to fight with in our heads,' Margaret began, emphasising that these "demons" were decisions we must all face. 'But we cannot let them win. God challenges us every day. He makes us stronger. And he has given you one of his little angels to help make you stronger. I am so proud of how you are handling everything Steph.'

'Thanks Mum,' Stephanie exclaimed. 'And thank you for all of your help. Now go get some sleep and we'll see you in the morning, won't we…..yes we will.'

Stephanie began shaking her head at her little baby as if talking to him.

'Ok then, I'll see you both in the morning. Goodnight!'

And with that Margaret stepped out of the bedroom, taking one last look behind her before gently closing the door.

'Your Nan is right.' Stephanie declared, looking down at her baby. 'Those demons in mummy's head are all gone. She's not going mad….no she isn't. She's gonna look after you….yes she is….you're my beautiful little boy!'

Stephanie began humming her favourite lullaby, allowing each note to soothe any strain. And after a short while, her eye lids began to dip. This easing hum had not only relaxed her baby, but she too began to recline comfortably. And little by little her eyelids reduced even further, eventually closing and remaining shut as she fell into a peaceful slumber.

'Stephanie?' A call resounded as she slept.

'Steeeeppphhaaannnniieee?' The chilling echo repeated itself.

The voice was back. The demon inside her head had returned.

'Steeeppphhaannnieeeee, I need you. Its time!'

Chapter 2

Margaret suddenly woke to the sound of her grandson's screams again. Her head had only hit the pillow when she began to snooze, no reservation to drift into a deep sleep.

Just like earlier, she clicked on her bedside lamp and checked the time on her watch. It read 3:36am. She had not become distressed this time, for she knew her grandson had only been changed and fed. She simply figured these cries were her daughter's inattention to wind him.

She pulled back the covers and routinely stepped into her slippers. She snatched her dressing gown at the end of her bed and threw it over her nighty.

Without hesitation, she continued towards Stephanie's bedroom, a clockwork motion she had become accustomed to.

She could hear Stephanie's mumbles alongside the baby's cry.

Now standing out in the hallway, a screencast of her daughter's panic entered her mind. Visions of her scrambling around with her baby, confused, and not knowing what to do next. Margaret smiled again. Her head nodding with amusing discontent as she entered.

'I know you have everything under control, but I just wanted to check on you and……'

But that was as far as Margaret could get. She stood in the doorway and froze. Her eyes widened with concern. She was shocked. Her grandson lay there on the floor. His wiry body wriggling like a worm beside his mother's feet. But Stephanie remained still in her chair.

Margaret's body engaged auto-pilot. She rushed over to her grandson. Her focus remaining on him as she called out her daughter's name. But Stephanie never flinched. A continued linger loomed and Stephanie's mumbling picked up momentum.

'STEPHANIE?' Margaret called out again.

Her concern deepening as she reached Davrin. He must have fallen from her lap.

'STEPHANIE, WAKE UP!' She instructed.

'STEPHANIE, CAN YOU HEAR ME?'

But still no reply.

Margaret reduced her posture to kneel at Stephanie's feet. She reached over to pick up her grandson. Her arms fully extended and just moments from cradling his fragile body when suddenly, another pair of hands came swooping down and grabbed hers. The speed was snappy and the grip firm. Margaret immediately became afraid. The hold on her wrists seemed too strong to be her daughters. She had never imagined Stephanie capable of such strength.

She screamed from the grasp. It was as if her wrists were slowly being crushed,

'STEPHANIE, YOU'RE HURTING ME!' She squealed.

No response.

'Stephanie please! You're hurting me.'

Again, no response.

'I'm sorry Stephanie!' She begged.

And with that, the release came.

Margaret shot back. Her wrists too sore to break her fall. She lay there on one side, her shoulder arched with just enough support to see what was happening.

Stephanie retreated calmly, re-adjusting herself into the seated position she previously held. Her mumbling continued.

'STEPH?' Margaret called out. A fear now in her plea.

9

No reply.

'STEPH! Wake up please!' She cried.

Her grandson's screams becoming less of a priority. Her focus had shifted towards her daughter.

But Stephanie remained seated and poised in a comfortable but sturdy position, perhaps ready for another attack.

Margaret didn't know what to do. A sense of isolation chilled her bones as the fire pulsated in her wrists. She hesitated, but equally, she knew she had to do something.

Her joints burned with the pain. Her hands throbbed. But she knew she had to move.

She crawled over to the end of the bed and began to pull herself up, the bed frame supporting her position.

She stood up. Her posture resting with reserve.

She cautiously tip-toed around to the other side of the bed. Her eyeline never leaving Stephanie's body.

Stephanie remained still, her eyes straight ahead and fixed towards the bedroom door.

Realising Stephanie was not watching her, Margaret arched her leg up onto the mattress and continued her journey, cautiously crawling across the bed.

Carefully hanging over the drape, she snatched her grandson up into her arms, strategically choosing the angle for immunity. She didn't want to be clawed at again.

Now seated on the bed, her body nestled into the headboard as she watched her daughter. But she was afraid to move. Stephanie's body began to twitch. This caused Margaret to flinch, wrapping her arms around Davrin, as if holding him in a protective layer, shielding him as her eyes scanned the room to conjure her next move.

She began to drag herself back across the bed, one arm remaining tightly around the baby whilst the other supporting her weight. The burn penetrating her wrist with every move. Her gaze never leaving Stephanie. And off the bed she slipped.

She charged towards the door. But just as she reached her escape exit, a voice spoke,

'What are you doing with him?'

But even before Margaret could turn around, she knew that this was not her daughter's voice. It felt dark, a sinister like question. The chills slowly crawled down her back, like tiny ants eating away at her backbone. She suddenly froze again, afraid to take another step, and holding the baby securely into her chest.

'Whoever you are, please don't do this,' she answered. 'Stephanie, are you there?'

'Yes Mum?' Stephanie answered.

This time the voice did sound like her daughter's.

Margaret slowly turned around. The look in her daughter's eyes instantly brought a state of bewilderment. It was as if Stephanie had just woken up.

'What in god's name is going on?' Margaret demanded. Her tone abstained certainty. She began to question everything.

But Stephanie immediately got up from the chair and proceeded over towards her.

Margaret's impulsive step-back surprised Stephanie. And as she shielded her grandson from his mother, a stalemate standoff pursued.

Margaret looked frightened.

Stephanie too halted with caution,

'What's going on?' She asked.

'I don't know Steph, but something isn't right!'

'I, I must have fallen asleep,' Stephanie declared.

'No. No Steph. It was more than that. You were mumbling and then you spoke.'

'I don't remember mum. I must have been talking in my sleep.'

'No Steph. This wasn't you!'

'Of course it was me.'

'It wasn't you. It was something else.'

'But it had to be me. I don't understand?'

'You let Davrin fall. And you left him there. Something is wrong Steph. I don't know what it is, but something isn't right.'

'What are you saying?' Stephanie requested. 'Look mum, it is me, Stephanie.'

She extended her arms, hoping her mother would respond. But Margaret flinched again.

'I'm sorry Steph. Maybe it's to do with this new Einstein religion? Perhaps it's something about the Dream World when we sleep. But it wasn't you who spoke to me.'

'But mum, it had to be. It's me, Stephanie, your daughter.' Stephanie arms were slowly weening towards her mother. 'Who else could it be?'

'I think we need to get you some help. That voice you have been hearing in your head while you sleep. I feel as if it spoke to me tonight.'

Stephanie stepped back. Her reaction displayed a horrid confusion. Just moments earlier her mother had said how proud she was of her, but now, this praise had somehow suddenly been ripped away. And the frightened look in her mother's eyes brought a certain indication that something was clearly wrong with her.

'I am so sorry! I don't know what is happening to me?' Stephanie yelped.

She cupped her hands up to her face and slumped onto the edge of her bed. She started to rock back and forth, her worry becoming evident.

'What is wrong with me?'

'Oh Steph,' her mother acknowledged.

A caution in her approach as she moved towards her daughter.

She sat down beside her and held out one arm. She softly placed it against her daughter's back, not quite knowing the reaction she would get. Her other arm still edging away, strongly securing her grandson,

'Don't worry Steph, we will get you help,' she added. She began to feel her daughter's pain. And the fear soon evolved into sympathy.

'Why me?' Stephanie pleaded. The weight of the world against her.

'There has to be an explanation. I hear this sometimes happens to women after they have a baby. It's called "Post Natal Depression". Maybe it's that?'

Margaret knew this was never the case. It was far worse than that. She felt she had to say something. Her daughter was crumbling in front of her.

'Try not to worry, we'll get you some help.'

'You said something spoke to you, but it wasn't me?' Stephanie questioned. Her eyes grasping at her mother for reassurance.

But Margaret hesitated. Her lack of response spoke volumes.

'Mum?'

Still no response.

'Mum?'

Margaret was trying to remember the voice. But her mind now fighting with the fatigue. Her memory blocking out what had just happened. She paused, trying to second guess the whole situation.

'I don't know,' she said, now questioning her own sanity. 'Maybe it was you, I'm not sure. Yes, it was you. Who else would it have been? I'm sorry Stephanie. I don't know if I'm coming or going.'

Stephanie's body relaxed. This was the reassurance she needed.

'You were scaring me there for a moment.'

'I'm sorry Steph. Don't mind me. I'm probably just imagining things as well. People are really beginning to take

13

heed of this Einstein movement. It's putting the fear in everyone. We must not abandon the church, for God will watch over us all. I think I'm just exhausted. We both are. We could both do with a good night's rest. Don't mind me.'

'What a relief,' Stephanie muttered, 'You scared me there for a minute. You nearly had me believing in something strange.'

A relieved laughter escaped from Stephanie's mouth as she hung out her arms to take her baby.

But Margaret hesitated again. Something held her back from handing him over. *Had this all been a mistake? She thought.* But then the fire returned. She looked down and saw the claw marks on one of her wrists.

'I tell you what, why don't I take him in with me tonight so you can get some sleep? And then we'll talk in the morning. How does that sound?'

Stephanie wavered. She was considering her mother's offer. But before she could reply, Margaret interrupted.

'Right well that settles it. You are not at your best, so you get back into bed and I'll take him into my room. All you need is a good night's sleep Steph. I'll take work off tomorrow so you can get a lie in, okay?'

'But I couldn't...'

'Ah ah, enough said, I'm not asking you!'

And with that Margaret began walking towards the bedroom door.

'Thank you mum. Thanks for everything.'

'Isn't that what I'm here for?' Margaret responded. Her back still shielding her grandson from the chill behind her. She couldn't turn around. She couldn't quite look her daughter in the eye.

And just like that, she left the room, leaving a darkness behind.

Chapter 3

The morning sky had woken Margaret without even a
whimper from her grandson. Feeling blissful at having had
some sleep after the events of last night, she felt as if she was
ready to face the world. She quickly deemed last night to be
some horrible nightmare.

She glanced across the sheets, flinching at the unruffled
covers. A sudden sickness dropped to the pit of her stomach
like a dead weight. Her grandson was missing.

She mulled over her movements from the early hours of the
morning, but this was cut short as she abruptly shifted herself.
She hung her legs over the edge of the bed and slid her feet into
her slippers. She didn't have time to stay there contemplating.
She felt something was wrong.

She reached over and aggressively took hold of her dressing
gown. She began to question her thoughts once more, a
distraction which led her to re-adjust the sleeves of the cotton
fabrics.

*Maybe Steph came in earlier and took him downstairs for a
feed, she thought.* A kind gesture from her daughter perhaps?

'Steph?' She whispered, slowly opening her daughter's
bedroom door.

Stephanie was nowhere to be seen. The covers lay
untouched. Margaret observed the bedspread as if it were the
inside of an unspoilt hotel room. But further confusion took
hold as she glanced across, noticing that the cot was in a
pristine condition also. It was as if Stephanie had spent her

morning tidying. But it was too early for this action. Something just didn't feel right.

Margaret continued downstairs.

She checked the front room. Nothing. She stepped into the kitchen, yet still no sign of her daughter or grandson. She figured the answers would reveal themselves inside the cloakroom. The buggy would always sit in amongst the coats. And if they were missing, then her daughter had surely gone out for an early morning stroll with her baby.

A satisfying feeling overwhelmed her as she began to open the cloakroom door, for she knew her daughter liked to occasionally nip out and get some freshly baked croissants from the local market. Perhaps a weekend surprise for all her mother's hard work?

But this excitement did not last long. She opened the door, and there it was staring right back at her. The buggy standing upright and leaning in amongst the draped jackets.

'That's strange,' she said aloud. 'The buggy is still here and so is her coat.'

Panic quickly set in again. And Margaret immediately shuffled over to the house phone.

Reaching it, she began to dial Stephanie's mobile number.

Placing the phone up to her ear, she waited as every dial tone bellowed, each ring bringing with it an added alarm.

Squinting over at the kitchen clock, Margaret could just about make out that it was a quarter past nine in the morning. She began tapping her fingers gently against the counter-top and nodding her head as she remembered on numerous occasions, reminding her daughter to put a voice mail on her phone.

Unable to leave an urgent message, she hung up. One more attempt before all communication was lost. She redialled, and again, nothing but a phone dial calling out.

16

She set the phone down on top of the counter, preventing a disconnect, and continuing the ring as she dashed upstairs.

Reaching the landing she began to hear the faint call from her daughter's phone. The tones coming from Stephanie's bedroom. Margaret poised herself. She stepped in and looked over on the locker. No sign of the phone. She carefully stood still and began to listen for the sounds.

She gently crept over to Stephanie's bed, as if stealth would prolong the noise.

She could still hear the faint ringing. And vibrations tingled the soles of her feet as she stood beside the bed.

Bending down and reaching her arm in under the bed, she startled herself. She felt a damp patch underneath.

She began to tremble. She didn't know why, but she got a sudden sense it was blood. Her breaths began to deepen as she cautiously reached in further. And tilting her head sideways, she was able to see what it was.

Releasing her gasped breath, she took hold of her grandson's baby bottle and pulled it out beyond the spillage of milk.

'I must be going mad?' She said aloud, just as the vibrations stopped.

She then noticed her daughter's phone. And relief set in when she heard the front door open.

'HELLO?' Stephanie's voice sounded from downstairs.

'STEPHANIE, IS THAT YOU?' Margaret shouted.

She leaned forward against the bed. Her hands throbbing as she exerted the pressure to pull herself up. A memory of her daughter came flooding back. A flashback of when she had latched onto her wrists. And looking down at each wrist, Margaret could visibly see the puncture marks in each arm. Puncture marks that were made in anger, by her daughter.

'MUM?'

'STEPH, IS THAT YOU?' Margaret hollered back. A quiver in her reply.

'YES. WHO ELSE WOULD IT BE?' Her daughter exclaimed.

And as Margaret stepped out onto the landing, she could see her daughter threading carefully up the stairs with her baby all wrapped up in his blue blanket. It was the very blanket she had knit for him when he was born. This emotional attachment prompted any concern to perish within the ruffles of the blue fabrics.

'I was so worried about you two. Where were you?'

Margaret's response had a humour to it.

'We went for a walk, didn't we,' Stephanie retorted, answering her mother yet speaking to her baby as she cupped him up into her chest. 'Breakfast is downstairs on the counter.'

'I could do with a cup of coffee, maybe something stronger to ease these nerves,' Margaret explained.

She gave a nervous chuckle. But Stephanie never responded. She walked past her mother and stepped into her bedroom, shutting the door behind her.

Margaret instantly felt a shiver. Something was odd. Even after the inconsiderate closing of the door, she could not hear her grandson.

She questioned the lack of cries from the slamming of the door. But still, no sound from Stephanie's room.

She stood there in total silence. No mumblings or reassurance had come from the other side of the door. And thinking deeper into it, Margaret hadn't seen her grandson in the arms of his mother. Stephanie had somehow made sure he was sheltered from her view.

'What in hell's name is going on?' Margaret muttered.

But unwilling to provoke any further suspicion, she shook her head and began to descend the stairs.

The sweet taste of that much needed cup of coffee and perhaps a croissant with blackcurrant jam etched inside her mind, allowing her thoughts to solidify with her saliva. This was something she figured would shatter her madness and bring back normality.

Stepping into the kitchen, she glanced over at what she had hoped were the lovely croissants. She had imagined them waiting for her on the counter. But instead, there happily lying flat out on his back, was her grandson. He seemed to be amusing himself, playfully wriggling his arms and feet whilst staring up at the ceiling.

'What in hell's name is going on?' Margaret repeated.

She quickly rushed over to stop her grandson from falling off the countertop. Looking down at this cute innocent baby, she pulled him as tightly into her chest as she could. Nothing would wedge them apart now.

Immediately stepping over to the house phone to call the doctor, a loud rap impeded her decision. It was a knock on the front door.

Curious, yet alarmed, she briskly walked over to answer it.

She opened the door. And there, standing in front of her, were two male police officers, and another female officer coming up her garden path.

'Is everything ok?' Margaret asked, a stern guise on her face as she held onto her grandson even tighter.

'Hello Miss Belshaw, I'm detective Fielding. I'm afraid we have some rather disturbing news. We have a witness that confirms your daughter was involved in something really disturbing. Is she home?'

'Yes, but I don't understand?' Margaret asked.

The detective never gave any further explanation. Margaret's hesitation had caused the uniformed officers to barge their way in past her.

'Where is she Miss Belshaw?' The detective asked.

But Margaret didn't say a word. She couldn't. The shock of it all had finally taken its toll on her. She stood there frantically watching on as they began to search her home.

'Can somebody please tell me what in God's name is going on?' She called out as the officers proceeded to ascend the stairs.

Margaret knew it was only a matter of moments before her daughter would be intercepted.

'A murder and kidnapping investigation in underway, and we are understood to believe that your daughter, Stephanie Belshaw, has some sort of involvement.'

And that was as much information as the detective was willing to give.

'This has to be a mistake?' Margaret questioned, but not fully committing herself to her own statement.

She immediately scaled the stairs after the officers.

Reaching the top, she could hear some sort of commotion in her daughter's bedroom.

Still clutching onto her grandson, she charged for her daughter's bedroom. But she was blocked by one of the officers.

'I'm sorry I cannot let you go in there,' he said.

'But that's my daughter. I have a right to know.'

And with that Margaret flung her grandson into the officer's chest.

She entered the room and stood at the end of the bed. She could see Stephanie calmly sitting in her chair. It was the same position she held last night, and both officers stood over her, trying to talk to her.

Stephanie just sat there staring straight ahead as she clung onto the blue blanket. It was as if she was mollycoddling her baby.

Under any other circumstances, this would have looked like a protective hold, but Margaret knew her grandson was outside with the officer. A rush of blood suddenly surged to her head. Her feet gave way. Her body dropped as she clung onto the bed frame.

The female police officer charged towards her as the detective remained firmly beside Stephanie.

'Please take her out of here!' Detective Fielding demanded as the female officer turned round and began to escort Margaret out of the room.

'What in God's name happened?' Margaret begged.

But the officer outside handed back her grandson. He then stepped into Stephanie's bedroom with the others, leaving Margaret outside on the landing. The door closed behind them.

Margaret began to sob. She leaned back and slid down against the wall, falling to the ground. She then began to shake her grandson's fragile body as he too became upset.

Suddenly, a commotion erupted inside the bedroom. This sparked further panic from Margaret. But she couldn't move. The fear and panic of it all caused a numbness to take over her whole body. She remained there, sitting on the ground, and cradling her grandson for comfort.

The bedroom door abruptly opened. Detective Fielding stepped out first. The other two officers followed as they aggressively held onto each of Stephanie's arms, escorting her downstairs.

'Stephanie, what's going on?' Margaret called after her, still clutching her calm grandson into her chest.

'It's ok Mum, I've done it. She told me I had to do it and now they're gone.'

'Who's gone?' Margaret questioned. A sudden shiver causing her body to freeze even more.

'It has begun! She wants to come into our world from the Dream World!'

'Is it that voice in your head?' Margaret questioned.

But Stephanie never answered. She had already reached the front door and was being ushered outside into one of the police cars.

Margaret didn't know why she hesitated from following her daughter down the stairs with the other officers. But something made her wonder back into Stephanie's room.

She looked over at the blue blanket lying on the bed. She didn't know what was inside, but knew she had to find out.

She quickly moved straight over to it, one hand clutching her grandson, whilst the other lifting the bloodied end piece.

She became frantic.

'You cannot be in here Mrs Belshaw,' Detective Fielding cautioned as he approached her with a notepad in his hands. 'Please, you need to leave this room. We cannot allow any evidence to be tampered with.'

'But nobody has told me what happened?'

'I'm afraid I cannot comment as it is now a full homicide investigation.'

'A what?' Margaret rasped.

'A young couple's home was broken into earlier this morning and their lives were taken as they slept in their bed. Their baby vanished from their home.'

But that was as far as the detective could get. He didn't continue. The bloodied blanket lying on the bed exposed the brutal ending to his detailed account.

Margaret shook frantically. She was lost for words. Her chest stung. Had she heard the officer correctly? Had her daughter been involved in all of this?

'That blanket, covered in blood, it is a....' but that was as far as she too could get.

'I know you must have a lot of questions yourself, but for now Mrs. Belshaw, will you please come downstairs with me.'

And as they reached back out onto the landing, two people in white overalls came marching up the stairs, heading for her daughter's bedroom.

'Oh my dear grandson Davrin, if God is out there, may he watch over us now.'

Chapter 4

Jenson Rose is a normal 15-year-old boy except for one fact; he has never dreamt. As a young boy, he tormented his parents. His constant questioning why he wasn't like the other kids, envious of those who dreamt. But John and Sarah Rose kept it a secret from the outside world and told Jenson to do the same. They said he was special. But the truth behind this was that they feared for their son's safety. If Stem Industries got hold of this information, their son would be taken away from them, just like other 'Non-dreamers', and forced into testing which could possibly kill him.

Jenson's parents wanted to keep him safe for as long as possible. When he was old enough, they explained the situation to him. It was a family secret they had to keep hidden for fear it would end up in the wrong hands.

After finding out, Jenson wanted to be like everybody else, so in order not to be taken away by Stem Industries, he began making up dreams. He wanted to fit in with society to avoid Stem's domination.

But Jenson knew it was only a matter of time before his number would come up in the system. Someday Stem would come for him, resulting in crucial testing, possibly fatal. It was only a matter of time before Stem would find out his true identity.

Looking in the mirror, his hazel eyes and handsome reflection stared back at him. But Jenson never took any heed of his aesthetics. He never understood how attractive he was.

And his mind blank from the night before. A dreamless sleep etched with a tranquil darkness. No pictures or reincarnated memories to cause regret. No questionable truth behind any recent dream. His mind, like a bare canvas, ready for the day ahead.

He began styling his short brown hair with wax-filled hands, shaping it into a messy upward position. He continued to whistle the tune to his favourite pop song when he heard his mother calling from downstairs.

'Jenson? Come on, get down here and have some breakfast before you go to school, and get out of that mirror!'

Jenson wasn't a vain teenager. He just liked to look after himself, and because of this, his parents would tease him from time to time. In fact, Jenson, although he seemed quite confident, sometimes lacked self-confidence. Not many people noticed this. They assumed he was a self-assured teenage boy because of his good looks.

'Yes Mum, I'll be down in a minute,' he said, washing the residue of hair wax from his hands before drying them.

He headed back towards his bedroom. Already dressed in his grey trousers, white shirt, and navy jumper, he just needed the tie around his neck, the uncomfortable restraint, reminding him every day of the ownership his education had on him. It was nothing like the authentic Gryffindor tie Harry wore. Not a speckle of scarlet or gold in Jenson's story. His tie blending in with the navy consistency. And the overall snugness of the uniform, revealing how little his parents had. In fact, most people were living on pay cheque to pay cheque. Taxes steadily increased every year since Stem Industries was formed. The wealth and power of this organisation had left most people surviving on the scarce resources, something Katniss Everdeen was only too accustomed to. Her Capital replaced by Jenson's Stem Industries.

Having completed the overall look, Jenson picked up his schoolbag. And throwing one strap over his shoulder, he walked over to his locker, over to the glass of water and tablet pouches. Snapping one tablet out of the pack, he popped it into his mouth and washed it down with a mouthful of water.

'Morning,' he said, running down the stairs and brushing past his father, John, who had already eaten his breakfast and was on his way upstairs to complete his morning ritual before work.

Jenson didn't get his looks from his father. Jenson was a thin, strikingly handsome boy with dark hair and dark eyes, while his father was ruggedly handsome with a stocky build and receding grey locks to accentuate his blue eyes.

'Relax there Jenson. If you got up a little earlier...'

'Yeah yeah, I know dad.' Jenson retaliated. 'I would have more time. It's a work in progress.'

Jenson had been too familiar with this statement. And having heard it so many times, he kept moving, sliding past his father, and continuing down the stairs.

He rushed across the hallway and continued into the kitchen. His mother was standing over at the counter making the lunches, whilst his sister, Robyn, was sitting at the kitchen table.

Robyn too had the dark features like Jenson. The only difference was, she had long, dark brown wavy hair. They got their looks from their mother who had sallow skin, cropped brown hair and distinctive hazel eyes.

'Morning,' Jenson said in a muffled tone whilst cheekily grabbing a slice of toast from his sister's plate. He quickly shoved the whole piece straight into his mouth to conceal the evidence.

Robyn immediately looked up from her plate with her puppy dog hazel eyes.

'MUM?' She shouted, trying to get her mother's attention.

'Jenson!' Her mother mouthed without even looking up from the counter, knowing quite well that her son was pestering his sister.

'Shhhhh,' Jenson hissed, holding one finger up to his mouth. 'I won't walk you to school if you say any more,' he added. And with that, he shoved another piece of her toast into his mouth.

'I'm nearly ten,' Robyn retaliated. 'Mum said I can walk to school on my own.'

Robyn snatched the last piece of toast before Jenson could get hold of it. She took an eager bite from the end and dangled the remains, as if taunting him with the win.

Their mother was listening to every word,

'Not now honey, we said we'll see about it when you are ten.'

Robyn's proud grin quickly turned into a sulk. Her elbows stubbornly dropped to the table as the piece of toast weaned in her hand. All life had been taken from the toast, just like her expectation of walking to school by herself. She had lost this battle, and Jenson's smirk childishly supported his triumph.

'It's not fair,' she huffed.

'Life's not fair!' Jenson whispered.

~~~

Jenson stepped out through the front door just as Robyn ran past him, brushing her school bag intentionally against his waist.

'Byyyeeeee,' she grunted as she got out the door first.

'Robyn, make sure you wait for your brother,' her mother scolded, throwing a jacket at Jenson. 'Put this on her and make sure she doesn't say anything. You know what I mean?'

27

'Yes, of course I do,' Jenson snapped. His reply was that of a disgruntled teenager. He was fed up with the constant reminders. 'She's not stupid,' he added, following his sister out the door.

'JENSON?' His mother scolded as if Jenson had done something wrong. She snatched the cuff of his jumper moments before he could make his exit,

'You know what Stem do to Non-dreamers? Your sister has been exaggerating her dreams again. She's getting carried away. Her friends will soon be asking questions, and if word gets round…'

'Yes Mum, I know, I've got it,' Jenson snapped.

He shrugged his arm back from his mother, perhaps a little too aggressively, and followed his sister out.

'HANG ON ROBYN!' He instructed, an anger in his tone which also showed in his walk down the garden path. His demand not really connecting with his sister as he tried to catch up on her.

'ROBYN?' He called out again.

Jenson quickly caught up with his sister. But before he could say anything, she turned round and began to speak hastily.

'Can I tell you now? Can I tell you now? This is the best one yet!'

Jenson threw the navy jacket his mother had given him on top of her head.

'Okay, okay, you can tell me now, but first, put on your jacket.'

'But how come you don't have to wear a jacket?' She asked cheekily.

This was more of a statement rather than an ask. She was already awkwardly putting on her jacket, completely forgetting about her statement. And what she also failed to recognise was the fact she already had her schoolbag on her back.

Jenson dropped his schoolbag on the ground to help Robyn put on her jacket. He rarely wore jackets, even on days as cold as this autumn one, so she had a point.

'When you get to my age, you can choose if you want to wear a jacket or not,' he said, adjusting her jacket. Another one of life's teasing moments from Jenson, proving he was the dominant sibling.

'Can I tell you now, Jenson?' Robyn asked, forgetting all about the jacket.

'Okay, go ahead, you can tell me now.'

Jenson's eyes rolled.

'This is the best one yet,' Robyn began. 'I told mum I was like Supergirl flying around and I saved a cat from falling off a huge tree and the dragon nearly got me, blowing his fire all over the place. Lucky for me he didn't catch me.'

Robyn was smiling now with a cheeky grin on her face. She wasn't quite sure how her brother would react, but she was proud of this one.

'Not bad, not bad at all. Your imagination is getting better, but I would leave out the flying dragon, Robyn.'

'But it's the best bit.'

'But if you say you escaped a dragon, other kids in your class mightn't believe you. Your dreams must be realistic. Some people don't wake up from there's, especially if they come across a dragon. There is magic in every dream, but yours go beyond that. You exaggerate too much. You cannot let anyone know you made this up. This is our family secret. Okay?'

Robyn nodded. She understood Jenson's instructions. She, like Jenson, did not dream and, because of this, Jenson told her it was best not to let anybody know. If she wanted to be like everybody else, then she would have to think up realistic dreams and fit in.

Grabbing her gently by the arm and turning her around to face him, Jenson calmly but firmly repeated himself,

'You cannot tell anyone, you hear me? Promise me you won't tell anyone?'

'Yeah yeah, I promise.'

'ROBYN!' Jenson demanded. He could see the distant look on her face. 'Look at me and promise me! This is for your own good.'

A short pause confirmed Jenson's seriousness,

'If you tell anyone and it gets out, people will think you're different and because you're different they'll think you're weird. Stem will come and take you away. They'll take us both away.'

Robyn looked shocked. She peered into her brother's eyes but seemed too afraid to speak.

'I'm sorry Robyn, but it's just what we have to do, okay?'

'Okay,' Robyn replied, finally getting the message.

~~~

Jenson watched as Robyn ran to meet her friend, Anna, at the main entrance to Clarets primary school. He wished Robyn were a little older. That way he could watch her more closely in his school. But Robyn waved goodbye and disappeared in amongst the crowd of kids all bustling to get inside.

This amused Jenson. The excitement of kids wanting to go to school. An excitement that would soon dissipate when they got to secondary level. A rush that would subside and transform into a lingered approach at the school entrance, never really wanting to proceed.

He continued his walk towards his school building, which was located right beside hers. But just before reaching the main doors he heard his best friend, Ethan White, yelling behind him.

'Hey, Jenson! Hang on!' He shouted, whilst shoving the remainder of his cereal bar into his mouth and jogging up to meet him.

Ethan was slightly smaller than Jenson and of a heavier build, an indication of his comfort-eating habit. He had short brown curly hair and blue eyes. His family were wealthy and lived on the other side of the neighbourhood—the more expensive side—but he wasn't a snob. His dad worked for Stem. In fact, he was the CEO of the company, and everybody knew it.

Truth is, most kids were afraid to befriend Ethan because of his father's status in Stem. And when Jenson's parents found out who he was many years ago, they too were concerned about their son's friendship with Ethan. They considered Jenson would let his secret slip, resulting in Ethan telling his father. But somehow Jenson proved that staying friends with Ethan would have no effect. And being close to him somehow disguised him even further. His secret was safe as he flew under the radar.

Still to this day he has never told Ethan, even though they're best friends. Jenson did and still does believe that Ethan can be trusted, but just not with his biggest secret. For fears of him accidently spilling it into the wrong hands were too great a risk to take.

Jenson's parents soon felt at ease with Jenson being so close to the 'White' family. He seemed camouflaged, becoming part of their own, shielded from any suspicion. The truth, Ethan's father wasn't around that much. In fact, Jenson couldn't remember the last time he had seen him because of the long hours he worked. They never spoke about him, and Jenson never brought his name up in any conversation. And as he was rarely at home, Ethan didn't have much time for his father anyway.

31

Ethan's mother was the principal of the primary school which Robyn attended. She was nice enough but liked the finer things in life. Her greatest pleasure was to attend social events where she could show off her status and wealth. Jenson had only met her a few times on one of his rare visits to their home. She, like her husband, always kept busy and never had too much time for Ethan either.

This parental neglect caused Ethan to gain weight, but also allowed Jenson to get closer to him, compelling their friendship even more so.

'Nice shoes,' Jenson commented as Ethan approached wearing a brand-new pair.

But before Ethan could reply, they both got distracted by a commotion at the side of the school.

Heckling and jeering shouts of 'Hey freak', 'Weirdo' and 'Faggot', all came from Joey Williams and his posse of bullies.

Joey was a well-built boy. He was taller than most and had a quick tongue with a vicious temper. His brown hair was always shaved tight at the sides, with whiskers of longer strands, an indication it was never a professional job. And his clothes were not of the best quality. He was renowned for having less than most, but whatever he needed, he somehow managed to get, and often at the expense of others.

Jenson had a small run in with Joey many years ago when he started school. But as soon as he became friends with Ethan, Joey somehow backed away and never gave him any trouble. This protection added to the fact Jenson wanted to remain friends with Ethan. Everyone knew that Ethan's father was a powerful man who worked for Stem; all the students were afraid of his connections and Jenson allowed this stature to elevate his acclaim.

Joey and his posse were chanting offensive words at Davrin Belshaw. Davrin was a quiet boy, roughly the same age as Jenson as they were all in the same class. Davrin had a distinctive look about him. He had jet-black, shoulder-length hair, and always wore skinny jeans with combat boots. He had a kind of gothic look about him, but what intrigued Jenson most about him was his unusual green eyes.

Davrin kept to himself, but Joey never really allowed this freedom. His decision to torment him increased daily. Jenson felt sorry for him, especially being a victim to this intimidation before. He had tried to convince Ethan to befriend Davrin, to offer the same protection he was allowed. But Ethan refused. Ethan felt Davrin was 'too weird'.

Jenson just had to go along with this decision. He was too afraid to do anything to help Davrin. He was too worried that, if he did, it would turn Joey's attention towards him. Or worse still, he could lose Ethan's respect and the safety that came with it. Jenson wanted to remain unnoticed, so he had to just keep his mouth shut and fall in line.

Davrin held his head down as he walked past the bullies who were taunting him. He too became a victim of the tax increase. And being poor also, this could have been something Joey should have related to, a connection you would think would have allowed them to join forces. But it didn't matter. Joey somehow had it in for him.

Davrin's schoolbag was hanging over his shoulder when Joey barged into him, preventing him from getting past. This sent Davrin crashing to the ground just as the school bell rang.

'You're lucky the bell rang. See you in class, queer!' Joey remarked.

His sneer causing laughter amongst his posse, like a pack of wolves howling in the spoils of their kill.

'Come on,' Jenson said, gesturing for Ethan to come over and join him.

'I don't think we should…'

But before Ethan could finish his sentence, Jenson had reached Davrin and was extending his hand to help him up off the dusty pavement.

Ethan followed cautiously, making sure nobody else was around to see him with Davrin.

Davrin accepted Jenson's kind gesture, but without making full eye contact. He simply uttered a 'thank you' and shoved his cracked iPad under his arm. He quickly scarpered off into the main building.

'You're lucky Joey didn't see you do that,' Ethan said.

'I don't care. I'm sick of them. They're bullies, and something needs to be done.'

'What? By you?'

'I don't know, but enough is enough,' Jenson replied. 'Maybe if the three of us stick together?'

Ethan's pause confirmed his reluctance to do this.

'But you know everyone is afraid of your dad?' Jenson said. 'They won't say anything to you.'

'Come on, let's go before we're late,' Ethan replied. He was never so eager to get into school. This mere mention of his father had caused him to change the subject.

Chapter 5

In her classroom, Robyn was sitting beside her best friend Anna. She had just told her about her dream when they heard a knock on the door. Their teacher, Miss Ward, had only managed to get up from her seat when two Stem soldiers opened the door and walked straight in.

'We're looking for serial number A1096254,' one of them said abruptly.

Miss Ward looked down at her logbook. But soon recovered the gaze back towards her students. One of the younger boys in her class gasped after hearing his number being read out.

'Robert?' Miss Ward said, looking concerned as the timid boy stood up rubbing his serial number on the top of his arm.

No sooner had Robert stood up, had the Stem soldiers taken him by the hand and escorted him out.

A brief silence engulfed the whole classroom, displaying suspicion if he would ever return.

'Do you think he had a better dream than me?' Robyn asked, not quite understanding the severity of Stem's visit and the invasive testing.

'I don't care. I don't believe you anyway,' Anna replied, turning away from Robyn. 'I think you're a liar and you're always exaggerating your dreams so you can be the best.'

Her harsh tone broke Robyn. She was jealous of her, especially of the fact that Robyn had never been hurt in any of her dreams. Anna, on the other hand, had come into school with a few knocks and bumps in the past and even worse.

'I mean, you're just so lucky, flying beside a dragon and not even a scratch,' she said.

Anna looked down at the burn mark on her hand which happened in a dream a few years back, a burn mark that would always plague her with flashbacks of the nightmare.

'You don't have to be so mean about it,' Robyn replied.

'GIRL'S BE QUIET DOWN THERE!' Their teacher shouted. 'HAVE YOU NO CONSIDERATION?'

Miss Ward was a nice teacher, so this seemed out of character. Her stare lingered. The warm twinkle in her blue eyes had gone. It was now replaced with a cold rage. She looked cross. And her erratic scratching had caused her high bun to dwindle, losing its proud red structure as if collapsing to one side.

Some of the kids were afraid of her, and others liked her because of her mothering charm. But this charm had just snapped, its grip lost, and was now falling off the bracelet that held it all together.

'Can I go to the toilet please, Miss?' Robyn asked as she stood up and started to walk toward the classroom door, even before Miss Ward had given her permission.

Miss Ward didn't say anything. She noticed Robyn's quivering lip. Her stern appearance softened.

Robyn began running as soon as she opened the classroom door, not quite shutting it properly.

Miss Ward could see this, so she stood up instantly but calmly as not to alarm the other children.

'Right, out with your homework boys and girls, and have it ready for me when I get back,' she instructed.

She left the room in search of Robyn.

~~~

Opening the main female bathroom door, Miss Ward heard a subtle sob from behind one of the cubicles.

36

'Are you okay in there, Robyn?' She asked, knocking on the cubicle door, and pressing her ear up to listen.

'Yes Miss, I'm okay.'

'Robyn, please open this door so we can talk. You can tell me. What's wrong? Is it Robert? Hopefully, he'll come back from Stem.'

'No, it's not that. I can't tell you Miss,' Robyn explained, 'I can't tell anyone, I'm not allowed to.'

Miss Ward started to get worried. She knocked harder on the door.

'Robyn, please open this door.' Her voice a little sterner now. 'You can tell me. I promise I won't tell anyone.'

Robyn sniffled. She looked up from her seated position on the toilet. Her knees carefully shielding her body as she tucked them high into her stomach. A cubicle door only separating them.

Miss Ward was her favourite teacher and she always said if she had to have a second mother, it would be her. *Maybe I can open-up and tell her? She thought.*

She slowly slid open the lock at the back of the door and immediately sat back down on the toilet seat.

Wiping the tears from her eyes, she watched on as Miss Ward pressed the door open and entered.

'It's okay, Robyn,' she said, stepping a bit closer. 'You can tell me petal.'

'I can't Miss, I can't tell anyone.'

'You can tell me. I won't tell a soul.'

'But Jenson said Stem soldiers will come and take me away if I tell anyone. And Anna hates me now. I'm weird. I'm not like everyone else, and I hate it.'

'Don't worry, you're safe here.' Miss Ward confirmed. She reached her hand over and cradled Robyn's shoulder. 'I promise I won't tell anyone, cross my heart. Now what's wrong?'

37

~~~

Sitting at his desk and leaning on one hand with his head tilted, Jenson was staring out through the classroom window. His gaze drifting off into the distance. He imagined what it would be like to leave this mundane history class and to be swept away by an imaginative daydream. He wondered what it would be like to escape this reality, even just for a moment.

Like Robyn, he got frustrated at times because he was not like everybody else. But he was older than Robyn. He understood this 'abnormal feeling' a little better. He knew it was necessary. His conclusion was not negative at all. It was quite positive in fact. For one, he knew he would not experience this 'Dream-death disease', and two, maybe he was different for a reason, a reason he hoped to one day find out.

Joey, the school bully, was sitting two rows across from Jenson. His arms were folded on top of his schoolbag as he lay slouched over his desk. His head resting on this newly formed cushion. This was his midday ritual, and for everybody, including the teacher, it was somewhat of a relief.

Joey always argued with his history teacher, Mr Murphy, saying things like, 'But it's in the past', and 'Who cares Sir?' These arguments became so tedious, monotony had truly set in, and with everybody. So, eventually, Mr Murphy got fed up with Joey and simply decided not to care anymore. He gave up teaching him and settled for an easier life instead, allowing him to have his nap.

This was the only break Davrin got from the torturing torments of crumpled pieces of paper flying across the room when the teacher's backs were turned, not to mention the abuse he received in the hallways throughout the day.

'Mister Rose?' The teacher shouted from the top of the class.

'Yes Sir?' Jenson replied, turning his head from the window.

'Can you answer the question, Jenson?'

Jenson looked up at the screen. He began to frantically search for something he could latch onto, some clarity, a word even, anything to provoke attentiveness. He needed an answer, but he had been caught off guard, paying no attention whatsoever.

'Emmm,' he mumbled, dipping his head, and trying to sort out the scrolls on his own iPad.

Halfway down the screen, he gave up; he had hesitated for far too long.

'Sorry Sir, I wasn't listening.'

'I know that.' Mr Murphy replied as some students began to giggle. 'Give it over,' he added, looking across the classroom. 'As I was saying…'

But before he could finish, Joey's body began to tremble, knocking his schoolbag to the ground.

Jenson turned sharply, as did everybody else in the classroom. They all looked on in pure fright as Joey shook. His head slipping off the desk as his face began to turn purple.

He fell to the ground. His convulsions increased as Mr Murphy scurried over to help.

Jenson caught a glimpse of a green light in the corner of his eye. He turned to the direction it was coming from; it was Davrin Belshaw. He was sitting there in his seat, staring right at Joey. Jenson had to have a retake. He was trying to understand what was happening. Davrin's eyes were illuminated. But the strange thing was that Jenson seemed to be the only person in the room to notice this. All the others were still fixated on Joey.

He quickly glanced back at Joey. The convulsions continuing. And then, when he looked back at Davrin, this time Davrin's eyes were closed.

Suddenly, Davrin opened his eyes again, as if he had only woken. His glowing green eyes were a normal green now, their colour somewhat fading. Jenson was confused. He didn't know what had just happened. And then he heard his teacher's voice.

'Are you okay, Mr Williams?' The teacher asked, helping Joey up from the ground.

Joey had somehow come round from his seizure. He lifted his head in full view of the class. A squeal left the mouth of the first onlooker around him as he brought his hand up to his nose, smearing the liquid that was running from it. It was blood—his nose was oozing blood.

The whole class erupted into a simultaneous ball, shrouding them in complete suspension around the event. Nobody quite believed what they had just seen.

Jenson's attention was drawn back towards Davrin. Davrin too realised he was being watched, and in turn looked back at Jenson. Both boys had a brief stare-off. They appeared to be just as surprised at each other by what had just taken place.

Suddenly, this staring match abruptly ended as Joey began shouting across the room, his blood-stained finger pointing at Davrin.

'That freak! He was in my dream. He hit me with his iPad.'

'Settle down, Mr Williams, he couldn't have.'

'But he was Sir. His iPad floated in the air and came straight at me, smacking me in the face. He didn't even touch it. It was him. He's a freak!'

Davrin began to panic. An anxious gaze hit him as he stood up from his desk. Leaning down, he quickly grabbed his schoolbag and shuffled the contents of his desk into it. His eyeline never leaving Joey. He then picked his iPad off the table and hurried towards the classroom door.

'Mr Belshaw?' The teacher called out.

But within seconds, Davrin was gone. The classroom went silent.

Chapter 6

Opening the front door, the aroma of fish slapped Jenson straight in the face, causing him to pause briefly. He could smell his mother's home-cooked dinner, a normal occurrence when he came home from school on a Friday.

Robyn suddenly appeared, running out of the kitchen. She must have heard the front door opening.

'Hey Jenson,' she said. Her face beaming with pride.

'You must have had a good day?' Jenson replied.

'Yep, I had a brilliant day. I have to tell you something though.'

But before Robyn could finish her sentence, their mother interrupted, calling from inside the kitchen,

'If that's Jenson, will the two of you get washed up for dinner and tell your father to get ready as well.'

'OKAYYY,' Robyn yelled.

Jenson brushed past her and started to walk up the stairs.

'But Jenson?'

'We'll talk later Robyn. You heard mum. I have to get ready for dinner.'

'Okay,' Robyn replied. Her head dipping, and saddened by the rejection, she walked towards the living room to call her father for dinner.

~

Night had fallen when Jenson came into the kitchen wearing a white t-shirt and a pair of dark blue jeans.

'Hey,' he said, dragging his chair out from the table.

41

'What kept you?' His mother asked, implying he had been late home from school.

'Sorry mum, I should have called. I just got carried away,' he replied, thinking of what had happened in history class earlier that day. 'Myself and Ethan we went for a milkshake after school.'

His mother smirked,

'Well you better eat your dinner,' she stated, smiling at Robyn. 'Here, will you give this to your brother.'

She handed the plate over to Robyn.

'You okay son?' His father asked as Jenson dug his fork into the kitchen table.

Jenson snapped out of a trance and saw that his fork had slightly edged a mark in the wooden table.

'Sorry,' he muttered, rubbing his finger against the indent, hoping to smear the trace clean. 'I was miles away.'

He immediately dropped the fork as Robyn placed his dinner down in front of him.

Eventually they were all seated and tucking into dinner.

'How was everyone's day?' Their father asked as he put a fork-full of food into his mouth.

Nobody answered. They too, had their mouths full.

'You seem in an extra special mood,' he said to Robyn. 'Anything nice happen?'

Robyn turned towards Jenson eagerly, as if awaiting his approval to speak.

Jenson wondered what she meant by this action. He had forgotten all about their conversation this morning and his mind was elsewhere. He had forgotten that she wanted to talk to him when he arrived home.

Their mother looking at the pair of them in bewilderment,

'Everything okay with the two of you?' She asked.

'Yes,' Robyn blurted out, 'can I tell them Jenson, please?'

Jenson didn't know what she was going on about. And the day he had had, he didn't really care.

'You can tell them what you like, I don't care,' he barked.

'Now Jenson!' His father commented.

'What? I don't care. She can say what she likes.'

When Robyn received this confirmation, she started to speak. And as her story unravelled, Jenson realised why she had been so anxious to speak to him.

She spoke for ages, throwing in words like 'secret', 'weird', 'told my teacher', and 'she promised to tell nobody'. She spoke continuously while everyone at the table sat there in silence, listening to every word.

When she finished her story, Robyn's mother dropped her knife and fork onto her plate. The chiming against the dish indicated how angry she was. She turned to face her son.

Jenson just sat there, dumbfounded. He couldn't believe Robyn had given her secret away, their family secret. And so easily. Especially after their conversation this morning.

'Jenson?' His mother snapped. A disappointment in her eyes. 'I told you to make sure she didn't tell anyone!'

Jenson was speechless.

'JENSON?' His father called from across the table. 'Your mother is talking to you!'

Recollecting himself, Jenson began to speak.

'I did tell her. We spoke about it this morning, on the way to school.'

This back and forth arguing went on for a few minutes until Robyn started to cry. Her hyper-enthusiasm was now replaced with a howling guilt.

'It's okay Robyn,' her mother said. 'Your brother should have...'

'SHOULD HAVE WHAT?' Jenson demanded. His patience no longer present. 'It's not my fault she can't keep her big mouth shut!'

JENSON!' His father shouted, dropping his knife and fork firmly onto his dinner plate. 'You two need to stay off the radar. What have we told you?'

'I can't believe you think this is all my fault!'

'We did tell you to keep an eye on her.'

'I can't control her 24/7. This is not my fault.'

Jenson pushed his chair out from the table,

'I don't even like fish anyway,' he snapped, throwing his knife and fork down onto the table.

And with one last gesture, he threw his napkin down. The white material slowly falling, signifying his surrender. All communication was lost. Jenson knew he would never win this negotiation. He retreated to his bedroom.

Robyn's mother turned to see her daughter crying, her hands clasped across her face, hiding herself from the commotion.

Sarah reached over and removed her daughter's little hands, placing them in hers. She began to speak,

'Please don't be upset Robyn. This is not your fault. We just had a little disagreement with your brother. We love you both so much, and when Jenson calms down, he will apologise. He'll tell you the same thing, okay?'

Robyn gradually composed herself.

'But he said I have a big mouth. He hates me. Everyone hates me!'

'Don't mind him, he was just angry and didn't mean it. I'll see Miss Ward on Monday and I'll straighten this out with her. It'll all be okay.'

'Please don't go to see Miss Ward,' Robyn begged. 'She said she wouldn't tell anyone.'

'Don't be worrying, okay? You just finish your dinner like a good girl, and your father will go up and talk to your brother when he's finished eating his.'

Sarah looked over at her husband and immediately picked up her knife and fork, trying to resume the calmness that had existed before Robyn's revelations.

~~~

Placing his knife and fork gently onto the middle of his spotless plate, Jenson and Robyn's father got up from the kitchen table. As he walked past his wife, she put her arm out and touched his wrist.

'Go easy on him John.'

'Don't worry,' her husband replied, mainly to reassure Robyn who was looking up at him. 'I'll just have a good boys chat,' he added, smiling down at his daughter, and winking at her.

'See Robyn,' her mother began. 'Everything is going to be fine. They'll have a quick chat and then we can all go inside and watch a movie. I got some nice treats for us to eat.'

Robyn nodded.

John was on the first step of the stairs when he heard a rattling noise against the front door. He paused for a moment. But brushing it off, and assuming it was a gust of wind, he continued. A few more steps up, he stopped. There it was again, another rattle.

He turned around and climbed back down. A curiosity taking hold. But he didn't have much time to investigate. Suddenly the door burst open, and a group of uniformed men barged in, their guns pointing out in front.

'WHAT THE....?' He shouted, as he attempted to run back into the kitchen.

He had only managed to get a few feet across the hallway when he was shot twice in the back with tranquiliser bullets.

He immediately dropped to the ground at the entrance of the kitchen.

His wife ran over to his body, screaming his name.

Within seconds, she too, instantly dropped to the ground beside her husband. Two tranquiliser darts sticking out from her chest.

Robyn remained seated at the kitchen table. She froze with fright. She was petrified. Even though her body couldn't move, her facial muscles reacted. It all happened so fast. She began to scream, not quite sure if it had been a warning cry, but it was all she could do. She looked down at her parents, their bodies, both lying unconscious on the ground. But her screams didn't last long. She received the same punishment, dropping forward and slouching into her dinner plate as a tranquiliser bullet jutted out of her neck.

Chapter 7

Jenson was lying on his bed when he heard the shouting and frantic screams of his mother and sister downstairs. He immediately jumped up and sprinted out of his bedroom to the top of the stairs.

He stopped abruptly in disbelief when he saw the uniformed men invading his home. His shoulders tightened. His eyes focusing on everything around him as he arched across the staircase to find his family.

He immediately noticed his father's shoes and realised he had somehow been reduced to the ground. Jenson recognised these men; they were Stem soldiers.

He was scared. He didn't know what to do. His hands jammed into the banister as his body positioned itself. He was getting ready to run.

Then, without warning, one of the soldiers shouted up at him.

'UP THERE!' He yelled, shooting a dart at Jenson who reacted just in time.

Jenson swung round the banister and dropped to the landing floor. He landed on his backside, watching, as the dart embed itself into the wall.

He clung to the carpet, his hands uprooting his footing. He picked himself up and instinctively dashed back across landing, and ran into his bedroom, immediately locking the door behind him.

His body was shaking uncontrollably. But the adrenaline kept him moving.

He ran over to the window. He swung it open and climbed out without any hesitation. It was as if he had done this before. But he hadn't. The adrenaline had notably taken over. And again, without any delay, he jumped down into his mother's prized rose bushes. Only wearing his dark blue jeans and white t-shirt, his body seemed to take the brunt of the lengthy brambles.

Scrambling out of the bush, his body stinging from the rose thorns, he looked up.

He saw a uniformed man looking out from his bedroom window, his eyes homing in on Jenson, his gun aiming fire. But Jenson didn't pause. And despite being hurt from the fall, he sprinted away as fast as he could, his dry socks soaking up the moisture from the damp grass.

Suddenly a buzzing sound echoed past as Jenson realised his luck. He had just escaped the soldier's target.

At the bottom of his garden, he stretched up and took hold of the top brick. He quickly hurdled himself up onto the wall and threw himself over, landing in his neighbour's back garden.

He awkwardly picked himself up, holding onto his leg. His body now realising it was injured, but he kept running.

He reached the fencing and hopped over onto the next street. He was terrified, but he knew he had to keep moving.

Running across the deserted street, he suddenly heard a sound of an engine.

To his right, he saw another soldier, dressed in black, on a motorbike driving up the road towards him. But Jenson immediately took cover behind a car.

The soldier drove by with no attention towards him. And as soon as the bike turned the corner and disappeared, Jenson ran for it again.

He had now reached the entrance to the park. Thankful he had lost his followers, and thinking he was safe, he grabbed the railings to jump over. But just as he did, somebody grabbed his leg.

Jenson instinctively kicked out and loosened the hold. This caused him to fall over the railing and land on his side awkwardly.

The soldier, feeling the blunt of Jenson's kick stumbled backwards, but only momentarily. He then continued forward again.

Jenson got to his feet, but the air was knocked out of him. He wanted to move but couldn't. He struggled to catch his breath.

This delay caused the soldier to close in on the gap.

With one leap, the soldier jumped over and ran towards Jenson, charging him to the ground.

A short grapple ensued, but the soldier was too strong for Jenson. He was now on top of him, trying to pin him to the ground. But Jenson was fighting rigorously to free himself from the clutches. He struggled desperately to free himself. For Jenson knew that once he was pinned, there would be no escape.

The soldier proved too powerful. He eventually restrained Jenson.

Jenson was exhausted; it was game over.

'GET OFF ME!' He shouted.

He figured this was his last hope, but a plea bargain would never work. Then to his surprise, the soldier suddenly dropped his body. His whole weight came crumbling down on top of him.

Jenson managed to roll the dead weight off. And as the soldier dismounted, Jenson could see a dart sticking out of his neck.

Confused, he looked up and saw another soldier, the one dressed in black, the same man who must have been driving the motorbike earlier. He was standing there on the other side of the railings with the tranquiliser gun pointing at him.

'STOP!' He shouted.

This hesitation brought confusion. Jenson didn't know why he was spared. But he knew this was his last chance to escape.

Maybe luck was on his side and the tranquiliser dart missed the intended target, or maybe it was never meant for Jenson. But either way, Jenson didn't stop to consider this. Rolling around in the ankle-length grass, he gave it his all, his last attempts to dodge another soldier.

Getting to his feet, he began to sprint once more. He scarpered for the trees, and reaching them, he felt another bullet whizz past him.

'Come on, come on,' he whispered to himself as he fumbled in between the trees, his heart beating so fast.

He had realised his luck was back when he reached the other side of the park.

Hopping over another railing, he adjusted himself to his surroundings and instantly realised where he was. He was only a few minutes away from Ethan's house. And even though Ethan's father was possibly in on this, Jenson figured Ethan would not have known. Going there was his safest bet. Afterall, he had nowhere else to go.

~~~

Outside Ethan's swanky home, Jenson got out of sight. He hid down against the concealed perimeter and waited. He crouched down in the dark, thinking of what Ethan's mother would say if he came banging on their door at night, wearing a rose torn blood-stained t-shirt and no shoes. Nonetheless, he felt safe for the first time since leaving his home. And this was backed up when he peered in through the iron gates, noticing both cars were missing from the driveway. He just sat there trying to gather his thoughts. He needed to rest but he also needed to keep moving. His breaths were deep and the sweat beads dripping from his forehead proved how far he had come.

After a few minutes, he reached down to retrieve his phone from his pocket. He was thankful he had automatically put it there when he heard the commotion from his bedroom.

Taking it out, he noticed a crack on the front screen. Hoping it was still working, he swiped the screen and typed in his pin code. He searched for Ethan's number and dialled,

'Hey Ethan,' he whispered, 'are you home? Okay, cool, come round to the back door. I'll explain it all.'

But before he hung up, he asked his friend one last question,

'Are you alone? Okay, see you in a minute.'

Jenson had scaled the wall of Ethan's fortified home. He was hiding around the back when he saw the rustling from behind the curtain of the patio door.

A light switch illuminated the back garden just as Ethan revealed himself, pulling the curtain across and opening the door.

He stepped out. A puzzled look on his face. His gaze motioning around the whole garden trying to find his friend.

Jenson had never been happier to see him. He quickly approached Ethan who looked just as scared as he did.

'What's wrong Jenson?' Ethan asked.

Jenson scurried past him and into the house.

They were now in the lavish new kitchen that Ethan's mother had just gotten decorated, but this was no time to be admiring it.

'Thanks, Ethan,' Jenson stated as he began pacing the kitchen floor. 'I'm so sorry but I have nowhere else to go.'

'Calm down, Jenson,' Ethan replied. His hands waving in the air, instructing his friend to slow down.

It was only then that he noticed Jenson's blood-stained t-shirt and no shoes.

'What happened to you? Did you have an accident?'

'It's Stem,' Jenson explained. 'They took Robyn and my parents.'

Jenson noticed Ethan seize up. For he knew Ethan didn't agree with the work his father did at Stem. But being so afraid of his father, he simply chose to ignore what was going on, throwing a blind eye over it all.

'I don't understand Jenson. My father knows you. He's met you before.'

'I'm not sure if he was there. Maybe he doesn't know anything about it?'

'But why would Stem be after you?'

'I don't know.'

But Jenson lied. He still couldn't tell Ethan the truth.

'Do you want me to ask him?' Ethan offered. 'Maybe it's some sort of a mistake?'

But Jenson noticed how tense Ethan had become. He knew Ethan was probably too afraid of his father to ever mention it. But even though this night had been thrown into chaos, he was appreciative of the gesture.

'Thanks Ethan, but please don't say anything for now. From what you've told me about your dad, I don't want you getting involved. Just wait and see if he says anything to you.'

'But Jenson, what are you going to do?'

And with that Ethan stopped.

'Wait, that's my mum, she's home.'

The noise of an engine pulling up outside alerted both boys.

'Shit, I have to go,' Jenson declared.

'Wait, Jenson, it's only my mum, she can probably help?'

'No, please. I'm sure she's just in the dark as you are. I don't want things to get worse. I have to go.'

'But Jenson, maybe it's all some sort of a mistake. She can call my dad and…'

'NO! Please! Maybe something is happening in Stem that your father is unaware of. I don't want him getting hurt as well. I have to go.'

Jenson lied with this suggestion. After all the stories he had heard about Ethan's father and how high up he was in Stem Industries, he had a gut feeling that his father had some sort of involvement. He believed Ethan was just oblivious to Stems abduction attempt. But he didn't want to tell the whole story, the story about Robyn and her teacher, the story of why Stem would be after him. He figured Ethan would never trust him again. He needed Ethan. The only solution he had was to make sure Ethan didn't say a word, even if it was short lived. It would give him enough time to escape into hiding, just like other Non-dreamers, providing there were any left. He needed to keep Ethan quiet until he had a plan. But where would he go?

'So you think Stem are keeping things from my father?' Ethan asked.

'I'm not sure,' Jenson answered, 'but I will try and find out. So please don't say anything.'

'I won't,' Ethan replied, now feeling his whole family could be in danger if he did. 'Here, take these,' he ordered as he ran to the back door, picking up his new trainers and giving them to Jenson.

'And take this too,' he said, scurrying over to one of the stools and throwing Jenson his grey hoodie. 'Be careful, Jenson.'

'Thanks Ethan,' Jenson replied, acknowledging his help. 'And please don't say anything to your parents. I'll find out myself what's going on. I'll call you when it's safe. Promise me you won't tell anyone you saw me?'

'Yes, I promise. But I'll try to find out if my dad knows anything, on the QT of course. Oh, and take this—just in case.'

Ethan rummaged through his grey tracksuit pockets, and taking out a handful of notes, he placed them into Jenson's hands.

'Thanks Ethan, I know I can trust you,' Jenson said leaving through the back door, just as Ethan's mother came in through the front.

~~~

Jenson was scared. He hid in the shadows, trying his best to stay out of sight. Sleep was the last thing on his mind, but he knew he had to find some sort of cover to get some rest.

He approached the gates of his school and stealthily snook around the back, hoping to hide there for the night at least. He knew nobody would be around as it was closed for the weekend.

He sat down in a doorway at the rear of the school.

Taking out his phone he noticed that the battery was down to 24%. He switched it off. He wanted to save the battery life, but he also grew paranoid about any track and trace methods Stem might use to find him.

Lifting his hood up over his head, he pulled his knees tightly into his chest and placed his hands around them. He began to weep. The thought of his family being captured broke him. Sitting there alone in the dark doorway, he soon cried himself into a dark dreamless sleep.

Chapter 8

Robyn suddenly woke. She realised she was tied up with tape stuck to her mouth. She knew she was in a large jeep, but not knowing whose jeep terrified her. She tried to yell when she saw her parents, their unconscious bodies lying beside her, but the tape prevented her from making any noise. She wasn't sure if they were still alive. The tears, streaming down her face as she tried to understand what had just happened.

Eventually, the vehicle came to a stop. Robyn began to hear muffled voices outside. It was dark, with only a tiny light entering from a vent, so she couldn't see anything. The jeep started to move again and drove on for another little bit.

Unbeknownst to Robyn, they had just entered the Stem building. She then heard the noise of two doors opening and slamming shut again. The voices sounded once more, but clearer this time, and closer. The back doors of the jeep suddenly opened, revealing two Stem soldiers, the same uniformed men that had entered her home.

They reached in and grabbed her father, dragging his lifeless body out. Then, a minute later, they returned and did the same with her mother. Robyn was trembling with fear. She couldn't understand why these men were taking her family, and with such force. What did they want with them?

'Hello Robyn,' a stranger said. He appeared from the end of the jeep.

This man was not dressed like the soldiers. He was wearing a black suit with a white shirt and black tie. Robyn was confused. She had never seen this man before, but yet, he knew her name. She could see his face, but she wasn't too sure of his age. As a nine-year-old, she found it hard to distinguish between ages. This man looked about the same age as her father, she felt, though maybe not as old because he didn't have as much grey in his hair.

'Get her out,' the suited man instructed. His soft 'hello' quickly changing into a harsh demand. And Robyn became more frightened.

The soldiers leaned in to grab her out. But unlike her parents who were unconscious, Robyn tried to put up some sort of a fight, twisting and shaking. She attempted to scream but the tape restricted her from doing so, dampening the screams, and turning them into muffled echoes.

The suited man spoke once more,

'Don't put up a fight Robyn, it won't help you,' he said, gesturing to the two soldiers. 'Put her in through there,' he ordered.

Robyn was strapped into a chair, preventing her from any further struggle. They wheeled her body over to an elevator. Once inside the lift, everything went quiet until they reached the designated floor.

As they wheeled her out, she quickly glanced around.

She was in a big room, just like the science lab in her school, only fancier and a lot larger.

The two soldiers wheeled her over towards a beaming light stand. Robyn didn't put up much of a fight this time. Strapped in a chair, she knew she had no chance of escape.

Another man came towards her and moved a big shining light over her head. She just about managed to see his long white coat before she was blinded by the light's glare. Unable to see anything else now, she closed her eyes and started to sob.

'This will only hurt for a bit,' the man in the white coat said as he took up a needle and punctured her skin.

Robyn felt a sharp sting in her left arm and before she had a chance to react, her eyes closed. She fell unconscious.

Chapter 9

Jenson woke to the sound of a dog barking. It was morning but he didn't know what time it was. Daylight had broken and he could hear the birds chirping in the trees. He forgot where he was for a moment. But then the horror returned.

He opened his eyes fully and surprisingly honed-in on a brown and white boxer dog, standing no more than five feet in front of him. This dog looked so adorable, standing there observing him. But when it realised Jenson was awake it started barking viciously. It looked to be waiting on Jenson to make the first move. Jenson was startled. All he could do was sit there and stare back at the dog. He grew afraid. He was weapon-less against this animal.

Adjusting himself gradually into an upright position and hoping not to alarm the dog any further, Jenson cautiously got to his feet.

The boxer dog lowered its head as if getting ready to attack. Its loud bark quickly changing into a low resonating growl. Jenson, no weapons in hand, and nowhere to hide, clenched his fists. He was ready for the attack.

He was fearful, but he had no other choice.

Then suddenly, a man's voice called out from around the corner.

'Here boy! Meatloaf! Here boy!'

With that, the dog instantly retreated its growl and turned his head away. Jenson was still in shock and continued to arm himself as best he could, his fists still clenching tight. But he too, turned his head to look in the same direction as the dog. They both watched on as a man approached.

Jenson recognised him; it was Mr Ward, the caretaker of both his school and his sister's. He was a small broad man, possibly in his sixties, with red hair and a ginger beard. Jenson often saw him around the school, as did most of the kids who took great satisfaction in heckling him because of his huge gut and Viking appearance. Mr Ward looked shabby. He walked towards them draped in a knee-length dirty brown coat, tapping a long branch-like-stick off the ground. This relief allowed Jenson to loosen his fighting mitts.

Even though Jenson had never sparked up a conversation with this caretaker, he was so pleased to see him. He hadn't decided on an explanation, he was just so relieved to see the owner of this dog before it savagely attacked him.

'Hey Meatloaf, what did you find here?' Mr Ward asked as he came closer.

The dog stood there, shaking his tail, and feeling proud that he had found something for his owner. A huge change from their earlier encounter.

'Hey kid, what are you doing hanging round here so early?' Mr Ward asked.

But before Jenson could answer, Mr Ward had another question backed up and ready to go.

'I've seen you around. You go to this school, don't you? Did you sleep here?'

Jenson didn't quite know what to say but knew he had to say something before Mr Ward would call for help, or worse still, set his dog on him.

'I'm sorry,' Jenson replied, 'I...eh... I slept here, yes.'

Instead of trying to think of an excuse, he believed it was too obvious to lie, so why not tell the truth, that bit of it anyway.

'Look kid, don't be apologising to me,' Mr Ward said as he approached.

He then got into a sit-down position beside Jenson.

'Do you mind?' He asked, but never waiting on Jenson to reply. It was more of a rhetorical question. 'Aaaaahhh, that's better, my knees aren't what they used to be.'

Wardy meticulously sat down and reached out a hand to shake Jenson's,

'My name is Jim. We've never really met have we. There are so many kids, I never get the chance to talk to them all. Anyway, people call me 'Wardy'. What's your name?'

Jenson felt the power of his handshake. It was strong.

'It's Jenson Sir, Jenson Rose. Nice to meet you.'

'Oh, how rude of me,' Wardy expressed, stroking the jaw of his boxer dog as he sat in front of the pair. 'This is my best buddy, Meatloaf. I named him after a famous singer—don't know if you've heard of him?'

'No, I'm sorry, I don't know who he is,' Jenson replied.

A sudden ease came over Jenson as Meatloaf began to lick his hand, the hand that was shaped like a brick and ready to attack earlier. But now, resting on his knee, the muscles began to retract. This seemed to be a completely different dog to the aggressive one that had just woken him.

'Ah it was before your time, I'm sure.' Wardy continued. 'Meatloaf was a singer. Anyway, how come you stayed here last night. Nobody looking for you?'

'My parents think I stayed in my friend's house,' Jenson replied, feeling a kind of guilt for lying to this friendly man. 'I just had an argument and ran out, but it was late. I didn't want to ring my friend to stay at his.'

'Can I ask you a question?' Wardy asked.

Jenson hoped it wasn't anything too personal because he was beginning to feel uncomfortable, the lies, the torment of it all. He just nodded, cautiously waiting on the question.

'Can you fix this argument?'

'Yes Sir, I hope I can.'

'Good. I'll let you in on a little secret of mine,' Wardy admitted. 'I had a fight with my father many years ago. We never fixed it, and now, well, it's too late. I ain't gonna get that chance again. It's probably the biggest regret of mine, and I have to live with that for the rest of my life. So, please, do me a favour, don't make the same mistake I did.'

Jenson could have broken down there and then. He had had a fight with his parents, and even though it was a silly one, it was still the last conversation he had with them. He just about held back the tears.

'Yes Sir,' he said, 'I promise.'

At that precise moment Jenson let out a groan.

'What is it kid?' Wardy asked.

'Aaaarrrrgggggghhhhh!'

Jenson couldn't speak. He was in agony. A sudden pain had come from nowhere. His head was bubbling with pressure. It was excruciating.

'Hey kid, what is it?' Wardy asked again, now even more concerned.

Jenson was still unable to reply.

Wardy quickly got to his feet.

'Wait here kid, I'm just going to get some help. My daughter will know what to do,' he explained. 'You stay here boy and watch him.'

His instructions clearly intended for his dog, Meatloaf. And off he hobbled around the school corner and out of sight.

Jenson sat there for a few minutes, trying to understand where this pain had come from. He was in so much discomfort he couldn't think properly. He simply lay there, curled up in the foetal position on the school step, both hands cradling his head hard, as if trying to squeeze out the pain.

Meatloaf didn't understand what was going on. He started to make an odd howling sound. His concern showing.

60

Then it dawned on Jenson; he had not taken his medication the previous night, and he was due to take another one this morning. He had always taken his tablets, twice a day, and from as far back as he could remember.

He managed to sit up and lean against the door, taking some deep breaths in.

A short while later, the pain seemed to ease, and as it did, he remembered Wardy had gone off to look for help.

Even though he was lightheaded and dizzy, Jenson managed to get to his feet. He didn't want to draw any more unwanted attention to himself. He figured he would chance going on the move again. He needed to stay hidden and out of sight. He couldn't be seen.

Just as he started to walk off, Meatloaf let out two single barks.

'You're a smart boy,' Jenson said. The barks were obvious orders for him to stay until his master returned. 'I have to go,' Jenson added, 'STAY Meatloaf—you stay there and wait for Wardy.'

With that, Jenson walked away. He turned to face the opposite school corner. Within seconds he was gone.

Meatloaf stood there, his head eagerly waiting for his return. But Jenson would never come back. He was on the run again, but where would he go?

Chapter 10

'Good morning,' a voice spoke as Robyn began to wake. She was still in the same chair and in the same room as before, but this time the harshness of the light overhead was reduced. She could see clearer.

'Please take some water,' the voice insisted as her seat was adjusted into an upright position.

This stranger immediately fed her some water from a white plastic cup. Robyn automatically took rapid sips, causing her to spill some down her chin.

'Sorry, my fault,' the voice spoke again, and whoever this man was, he began wiping her chin with a rough white paper towel.

Robyn focused her eyes round the room. Everything seemed to be white, white walls, white computers, white desks. *Where was she? She thought.*

Gradually able to focus in on the figure, she watched him. It was a man. He wore glasses and had brown hair that was thinning on top; he was nearly bald in fact, which made him seem a lot older. He looked a bit silly to Robyn.

If it were any other circumstance, Robyn would have laughed and asked what was wrong with his hair. But in this situation, she had no humour to add.

'Hello,' he said, greeting her as he sat by her side in his white lab coat.

Robyn shyly looked up at him. Even though her mouth was free of tape, she was too afraid to speak. She was too afraid to scream. Also, this man seemed a lot friendlier than the suited man she had encountered the night before.

'It's okay,' he continued, realising Robyn was afraid to say anything. 'I'm not here to hurt you. We have to do a few tests on you. I'll try and make them as painless as I can.'

Robyn nodded.

'You remind me of my daughter,' he said, smiling and gently rubbing his hand through her hair, removing any stray strands from her face.

Robyn flinched; she considered this action to be creepy.

'My name is Tom. I won't hurt you. I won't let anyone hurt you. I'm just going to take some blood,' he explained.

He turned to the table behind him and lifted a big syringe and a cotton bud.

Robyn realised he was probably the white coated man from last night, the same man that stuck something sharp into her arm, which caused her to sleep, when she first arrived.

She began to tremble.

Lifting her short-sleeved pink t-shirt, Tom wiped the cotton bud against her soft skin before throwing it in the small white bin at his feet.

'This will only hurt for a moment,' he said as he inserted the needle and drew blood.

Robyn titled her head forward to see what he was doing. And when she saw the blood, her head fell back.

The white room blurred into an even more white. She passed out again.

Chapter 11

Jenson had walked about a mile when his migraine had completely faded. Now able to think again, he decided to phone the one person he knew would help him.

'Hey Ethan,' he said, feeling ill-at-ease. Jenson was a little stubborn. He never liked asking for help.

'Hey Jenson, are you okay? I've been worried. I sent you messages. Where are you?'

'I'm okay. You didn't tell anyone about me, did you?'

'No.'

'Good!' Jenson answered. 'Did you find out if your father knew anything on the QT?'

'No, sorry Jenson, he didn't come home 'til late last night.'

Even though Jenson had only spent one night alone, he longed for a friendly face he could trust. He paused for a few seconds and then it hit him.

'Would you be able to meet me?' He asked, feeling reassured at Ethan's response.

'Yes, of course. Where?'

'Plaza? In about twenty minutes? And please don't say anything to anyone. You're the only person I can trust right now. Please come alone.'

'Sure Jenson, you have my word. See you then.'

Walking towards the Plaza, Jenson was in two minds. Was it a good idea to meet up out in the open with an abundance of shoppers? Could this be a crafty scheme, or was it a ridiculous move? Questions began to float around in his head like tiny jigsaw pieces, some fitting neatly whilst other segments proving too difficult. Their sharp edges unsuitable for the puzzle, a challenge Jenson was sceptical about. A game he was uncertain to ever complete.

Did Stem have his profile? Would they have taken a picture from his home, a picture leading search parties to his capture? Jenson didn't have the answers to these questions. But there was one thing he was sure of. He would find out soon enough.

It was the usual busy Saturday morning at the Plaza. The car park was full, with vehicles and pedestrians everywhere. *Surely it would be impossible to be picked out from this crowd, he thought.*

But paranoia set in. His momentum grew to an erratic march. Adopting an excessive safety precaution, his eyes began roaming, spreading far and wide. The suspicion had consumed him. It had consumed everything in sight.

The main entrance came into view. A raw nerve brought about a fumbling. He increased his pace. His hand pressing against his forehead, rubbing hard. The fidgeting produced a creasing of the brow. His hand enduring this position to camouflage his face. An attempt to conceal his identity from the prying camera's.

Adhering to his own suspicious belief, he made haste through the main glass doors. He felt alone. He needed a familiar face. But in a busy shopping centre, this luxury was something he could not afford, not right now. He needed to escape the crowd.

He darted straight for the public toilets.

A deep fear of getting caught weighted on his mind as he spotted a cleaning trolley lying idle outside the toilets, all stacked with the weekend supplies.

He stalled. He knew the cleaner was inside. But where else could he go? He had to get out of sight, and quickly.

The desire to avoid this situation was strong. He knew he had made a mistake in coming here, but he also knew he couldn't back out now. His anxiety levels reaching an all-time high, but he needed his friend.

He continued. And just as he reached the door, a uniformed man leapt out from behind it.

'Apologies, I didn't see you there,' the man admitted.

Jenson struggled to maintain eye contact. His lack of reply brought about some scepticism.

The cleaner watched him quickly squirm past without speaking. Luckily for Jenson, this teenage display of insolence was only too often an occurrence for this weekend worker.

Jenson stood over at the sink. His arms heavily placed down against each edging. An emptiness washed over him as the whole room filled with silence. He had time to think.

A grimy and desolate face stared back at him in the mirror. In need of some encouragement, he turned on the tap and splashed some water over his face.

Suddenly the toilet door opened. Jenson was no longer alone.

His whole body ceased. He turned off the tap and steered himself towards the cubicles, scurrying inside the nearest one.

Jenson locked the cubicle door. His lips began to quiver, releasing a lasting breath. A response to his reprieved confinement. The pressure had suddenly subsided.

Nature had called long ago, but Jenson never allowed the urge to rebel. Soon he was in full flow, the splashes vibrating against the ceramic dish. Loud turrets echoing and releasing a composure. He felt safe in here. For the first time, nobody could see him. He was hidden from harm's way.

Finishing up, he heard a toilet flush. It was the cubicle beside him. Only now realising he was never alone, Jenson paused. He listened. The door gently creaked open in the cubicle next to him. Yet whoever it was, they had left in such a hurry.

Jenson then heard another person outside his cubicle. Whoever it was, must have slipped in whilst Jenson was peeing. He could hear the trodden footsteps along the tiled flooring, just as a phone rang out,

'Did you find him?' The voice asked. 'Is his name Jenson?' The voice continued. 'Okay, wait there. I'll be straight out. And don't let him out of your sight.'

A strangled cry of panic restricted Jenson's airwaves. A Stem soldier inside the toilets?

Mental bargaining took over Jenson's mind, conjuring anything he could to get him out of this situation. If a Stem soldier was already here, then there must be more outside? How did they know he was here?

Ethan? He was the only person he had spoken to. Did Ethan know what was going on? His best friend? Had he betrayed his trust and led them here? Or was it a simple coincidence?

Jenson knew he had to get out, and quick. His plan vanquished. Now, a sitting duck, surrounded by his enemy.

His phone unexpectedly beeped. It was a message from Ethan,

[Hey Jenson, where r u?]

Jenson didn't respond. He couldn't believe he was going on the run again, just when he felt safe.

He held down the button and switched his phone off. Knowing these soldiers would have had every exit covered, his options diminished. There was only one way out.

More people entered the toilet. Like a revolving door, they came and went. But Jenson sat there hiding. His thoughts focusing on how to escape. Then suddenly, he remembered the trolley outside.

He waited until the toilet emptied. And now, seizing his moment, he opened the cubicle door and started to walk towards the over height windows. But just as he got there, he heard the main door open again. It was too late for him to climb up without being seen.

A stranger came in past the partition with a newspaper bundled under his arm. Jenson nodded before dashing back to his cubicle. He was trapped. And whoever this stranger was, he stepped into the end cubicle and locked the door.

Jenson stood still, listening. His coyness allowing him to hear even the faintest of noises. A ruffling sound emerged from the cubicle. Shortly followed by a rigid crease. A pair of jeans hissed as the brass zip separated. Jenson recognised the sound of dismantling trousers and somebody dropping the seat to get rid of solid waste. He needed to take advantage of this, and quickly.

He burst out of his cubicle and bolted for the exit.

Without delicacy, he pulled back the door and peered out. He grabbed hold of the idle trolley and wheeled it towards him just as another passer-by advanced.

'Sorry, the toilets are closed for a few minutes,' he stated. The approaching man now turning into a confused spectator.

With the doorway congested, Jenson retreated into the room. Strategically picking up the small bin nestled in against the wall, he continued towards the high set window.

He overturned the bin. No time for evaluation, he centred himself on top of the bulging frame. His weight now concerning. The foundations buckling underneath, but he had to keep moving. He stretched up and pressed against the restricting hatch. The narrow opening in sight, he hung onto the ledge and pulled himself up.

His muscles aching. His lungs depleting. But the adrenaline offset any defeat.

Without hesitation, he squeezed through the opening and threw himself over, landing hard on the concrete outside. Another unpleasant drop, but this time there were no rose bushes to shred into and break his fall. This time the air had not depleted from his lungs. And this time he was at an advantage.

He weaved in and out amongst the established cars, avoiding any suspicion by cloaking himself and crouching behind every vehicle, eventually nestling in behind a silver car.

He immediately looked up. He could see two Stem soldiers standing over by the main entrance.

Suddenly, one of the soldiers peered over in his direction.

Jenson immediately withdrew against the bodywork of the car, dropping down behind the aluminium panel. His back leaning against the cold metal, weighing up his options. His eyes scouring the car park at the ready for his next move to reveal itself. A convoy of cars impeding the exits, he couldn't see the escape routes from this cowering position. He needed to get up.

Poking his head toward the window, his eyes bulging to gaze out through the glass. But he could no longer see two soldiers. One of them had disappeared.

A sudden fear caused him to panic. And adopting an erratic approach, he managed to relocate himself about six cars away.

He glanced back over to where he was hiding. A soldier came into view, swinging round against the silver car. His mannerism presenting confusion as he signalled a false alarm to the other soldier. He must have seen Jenson.

Following this signal, Jenson witnessed the disappearance of the second soldier. He was no longer standing over at the glass entrance to the Plaza. He flinched. Suddenly a firm hand dropped down and struck him hard on the shoulder.

Chapter 12

Jenson's whole body filled with dread. His heart pumping faster; he felt numb. Had all his dodging efforts finally come to an end? Was this the biggest mistake he had made, coming here?

He cautiously turned to see a smaller figure hovering over him. It was a girl. She was not much older than him. She had dirty blonde hair and blue eyes. It was a face he had never seen before in his life.

'Come on, follow me,' she instructed, tilting her head rapidly to one side. 'I can help get you out of here—but stay down,' she added, taking her hand off his shoulder, and making her way through the vehicles.

Jenson didn't have a clue as to who this stranger was. But he felt his luck had returned. He had no other choice but to follow her. Any place was better than here.

She escorted him to the outer edge of the car park.

Jenson practically fell against her as she came to an abrupt stop. Not a Stem soldier in sight as the motorbike greeted them.

'Here, put this on,' she ordered, straightening up and throwing a spare motorbike helmet towards him. It was as if this dark covering had been planned.

Jenson followed her instructions and put on the helmet without question.

Now on the bike, she gestured him to hop on the back.

'Get on! I'll explain it all later. But for now, we need to get out of here.'

She revved the engine.

Jenson hopped straight on. Not knowing where he was going or who he was going with, he sat back and held onto the hips of this stranger.

Exiting the car park and shrouded by the tinted helmet, he glanced back, taking one last look over his shoulder.

Two Stem soldiers reconvened at the main glass doors. For now, Jenson had escaped. But for how long?

He let out a huge sigh of relief and held on tight.

~~~

Driving out of the city felt like an endless weight lift. The cool breeze treated every ache Jenson had like a fresh antiseptic spray, conserving any injury. He almost lost all track of time.

Eventually coming off the main carriageway and taking a few side roads, the bike came to a sudden halt. They reached the corner of a narrow junction.

A signpost stood ahead. Its pylon reclining and in need of repair. The sign's appearance had faded somewhat and was on the verge of falling off its mast. It was filthy. Jenson couldn't read it, an indication nobody had visited this place in quite some time. A deterioration he was unfamiliar with.

They took another intersection and continued driving. Wilted grasslands aligned either bank. Both sides of the road brown with rot. And within minutes, passing the sheltering trees, a small 19th Century church building came into view.

The grey stone building with large colourful mosaic windows instantly took Jenson's breath away. It was something he should have recalled from his history class, but he never remained focused enough to do so. It was mesmerising even without the rejuvenation of its forgotten charm.

The number's attending church had declined steadily over the years. People had lost faith because of the 'Dream-deaths'.

71

Jenson's parents were amongst these; for they questioned why men, women and children would pray to a false god at night to never wake up in the morning. Was there even such a god listening to these prayers?

The smooth road swiftly transformed into a gravel runway as they drove up the driveway of the church.

They came to a sudden stop. The engine faded.

'Come on, you must be hungry,' the stranger declared.

She removed her helmet, revealing her blonde locks again. She dismounted the bike and turned to face Jenson, allowing him more time to recognise who she was. But still, her deep-blue eyes gave nothing away.

Jenson took off his helmet and waited behind the bike.

For one, he hadn't a clue where he was, so running wasn't an option and, secondly, even though this girl had just saved him from a sticky situation, he wondered how she knew him and what she was after.

'Are you coming?' She asked.

Jenson hesitated.

'Suit yourself,' she added. A retaliation proving successful to Jenson's withdraw.

'WHO ARE YOU?' Jenson called out.

But this stranger didn't answer. Her body language signified disregard. She continued walking towards the church. And Jenson's delayed response allowed her to disappear inside.

Chapter 13

Two beautifully carved wooden doors stood in front of Jenson as he stepped up to enter the building. Even though the church was mesmerising, it was rundown, seemingly abandoned.

Upon entering, he got a strong musty smell.

The building called out in despair, as if it hadn't been cleaned in a long time. It was dusty and dark with shards of light cutting through the stain-glass windows, forging a colourful mosaic scene inside of this dilapidated setting.

Jenson gained ground and followed the stranger up the middle aisle, passing rows of benches either side, some broken, whilst others barely managing to hold onto their structure.

He took a deep breath. His repressed words all aligned, ready for the interrogation, when suddenly a voice bellowed from behind the altar.

'Well, if I had of known we were having company, I would have cleaned the place up a little.'

'Don't mind him,' the girl instructed. She turned towards Jenson and held out her hand. 'I'm sure you have a lot of questions about what's going on. My name is Chloe, and this is my brother, Callum.'

Jenson extended his hand and shook hers.

'I'm Jenson, Jenson Rose,' he responded.

The dark figure stepped out of the shadows and into the stain-glass light.

It was a boy. He looked the same age as his counterpart, and with identical features. The same deep blue eyes but with a dark blond shaved head. He wore a shabby black hoodie, similar in design to the grey one Jenson had on, just a lot more worn, and a pair of black combats with black boots.

As he got closer, what struck Jenson most was the scar on his left cheek. He wondered how he came to have such a big scar on his face. Possibly a bad dream of some sort, or maybe an accident on his bike? Jenson had seen another one parked up out front. But now was not the time to familiarize himself with unimportant questioning.

'Who are you and why am I here?' Jenson asked. His bewilderment echoing around the church.

'We should be asking you the same question,' Callum answered. 'Why is Stem after you?'

'Here—catch!' Chloe said, throwing Jenson a bar of chocolate. 'Come on, we'll explain it all—well, as much as we know anyway.'

Catching the bar of chocolate, Jenson sat down on an unbroken bench.

Callum and Chloe also withdrew to the second tier of the altar.

Chloe began to talk.

Jenson listened carefully as he unwrapped the bar of chocolate and devoured it. Only now, realising how hungry he was.

'As you might have guessed, myself and Callum, we're brother and sister, twins, well, triplets...'

Chloe pausing for a moment,

'Our sister Carly, she passed away when we were young. She died from the Dream-death disease.'

Jenson turned his attention to Callum who had raised his arm and was now gently rubbing his sister's back.

'Sorry,' Chloe apologised. Her response evoking a sadness inside her.

74

'We haven't told this story in a long time.' Callum interjected. 'We're 'Soul-searchers', or 'Searchers' if you like. Do you know what that means?'

'Yes,' Jenson answered. 'Searchers' are people who dream the same dream?'

'Not quite,' Callum replied. 'We can meet up in the same dream. We're blood tied because we're related. It's a bond. We can search for each other within the Dream World. But we didn't know this when the Dream-deaths began. And by the time we did understand what we were, well, by then it was too late.'

'Too late?' Jenson asked.

'We were only six when our sister Carly died. Shortly before she passed, I remember her telling me she kept seeing a monster in her dreams. She said it was following her, waiting for her to sleep. I thought she was just trying to wind me up. They always teamed up against me.'

Callum's statement reignited a forgotten childhood memory of the three siblings quarrelling. He grinned, nudging his sister, who looked up with an uncertainty in her smile.

'I'll never forget that night,' he continued. The memories came flooding back. Something he had shut out for a long time.

'We had just come back from visiting our grandparents. The three of us were arguing in the back seat. It was only our dad. Our mother, she too lost out to these Dream-deaths. She was one of the first. Our dad was different after that. He was angry a lot. Looking back now, I understand. But we were only kids. I remember you Chloe, you ran upstairs while myself and Carly ran out the back. We were playing on the swings. We always competed against each other. Silly games. But I beat her this time. Carly lost. I remember her getting into a strop. She stopped her swing and hopped off. She threw hers back into mine. I was so mad. My swing tangled up in hers. I ran up after her, and do you remember when I barged into your bedroom?'

Callum's eyes shifted towards his sister,

'Do you remember?' He prompted.

'Yes,' Chloe answered. 'I stood in front of her to protect her from you.' Her mouth revealing a faint satisfaction.

'That's right,' Callum agreed, 'and you didn't even know what had happened. You would have always protected her from anything. No matter what.'

He paused.

'We were sent to bed early that night. I suppose we deserved it. But I remember waking up. Well, I thought I woke up. I heard scratching at my door. I was scared. If only I had of done something sooner. But I was only six. After the scratching stopped, I felt strange. I realised I had somehow woken up in Carly's dream. It was her. She was scratching at my door. She was trying to hold herself onto my doorframe. She was afraid. She was all alone. She couldn't hold on any longer. She was dragged the rest of the way along the landing and down the stairs.'

Jenson glanced over at Chloe. Her sniffling confirmed how tough this memory was.

'I'm sorry, we haven't spoken about this in a long time.' Callum explained.

'No, please, go on,' Chloe snivelled.

'Are you sure?'

'Yes.'

'Okay. Well, I remember how cold it was, how cold the floor was.' His blank expression adding to the suspense.

Callum's eyes locked towards Jenson's, but only for a second. He didn't allow too much time for pity. A lifeless stare, recreating the night, remembering just how cold it was. Now defeated in the pain and sorrow. He continued,

'It was like ice blocks under my feet. And there was a chill in the air. The wind, I could hear the howling wind outside. I just knew something was wrong. I remember grabbing my bedside lamp and pulling it so hard. The cord snapped out from the wall. And when I reached the top of the landing, I saw what it was. It was some sort of a creature, a demon, dragging her down. A dark demon with skinny bones, but also long and sharp.'

Callum raised his hand up to the big scar on his left cheek,

'I guess I wasn't quick enough,' he said. His lip puckered. 'It was all true. Carly's story of this monster. She was trying to tell us. She was trying to warn us, but we didn't listen. We didn't understand. I had woken up in her dream. I ran so fast down the stairs. And I used my lamp. I smacked this thing, whatever it was. I hit it so hard in the face. It let Carly go. I can still hear the squeals from it. They still ring out in my head from time to time. I remember it like it was yesterday. I had to hold onto my ears. It was so loud. And then that's when it hit me. It sent me flying across the hall. I smashed into the wall. I fell hard, and my face was throbbing. I couldn't do anything. All I remember after that is the demon's face. It was staring at me. It just stood there watching me, with its black eyes. It was like looking into a dead soul or something. I couldn't move and the blood was pouring from my face. And then I saw her being dragged outside by her hair.'

And that's as far as Callum could get. His head dropped. A final bow to put an end to his nostalgic nightmare.

'Oh Callum,' Chloe acknowledged. 'You did everything you could.'

'Were you there?' Jenson asked, now looking at Chloe.

'I was too late,' Chloe answered. 'I did somehow get into their dream, but it was too late. I remember being woken by the cries of an animal. That's what I thought it was until I ran down the stairs. I saw Callum lying unconscious. Blood all over his face. The front door was wide open. It was pitch black outside. I hesitated to go look for her. I panicked. I knew she was outside, but it was so cold. I couldn't see anything. I knew Carly was out there, I could feel her, but I was too afraid.'

Callum's head lifted,

'It's okay Chloe, you were a child. It was okay to be afraid. I was afraid.'

Jenson instantly realised that both siblings had forgiven each other. But with that came a deep blame from within. Each owning up to their unattempt, and their actions leaving a hole inside, something they could never let go of.

'Yes, but you tried to save her,' Chloe responded. 'I just stood there. I didn't do anything.'

'You were in shock Chloe. She was gone. There was nothing we could have done. And if you had of went outside, it could have taken you as well.'

Callum's hand reached out to grab hers.

'I'm sorry,' Jenson quietly said, feeling saddened at their loss but also uncomfortable at how upset they had both become.

'No, it's us that should be sorry Jenson, the last thing you need now is for us to be giving you our sad story,' Chloe muttered. Her hands now wiping her eyes.

Jenson had heard stories of this happening, dreams with consequences. But he had never heard anything so vivid and terrifying.

He didn't mean to change the tone or sound selfish, but he needed to know why he was brought here,

'Why did you help me? Has Stem anything to do with this?'

'You're welcome.' Callum said sharply.

'You see Jenson,' Chloe began, squashing Callum's response. 'Our father, he worked for Stem Industries. And when our mother died, we stayed with our grandparents a lot. Eventually we lived with them full time while our father worked. He worked so many hours. Sometimes we wouldn't see him from one end of the week to the next. His days and nights spent in the Stem labs. But when Carly died, well, he, he never really came to terms with it. I think every time he saw us, he just pictured her. Then one day, he left for work and was never seen again. Soon afterwards they found his umbrella down by the docks. We didn't quite understand it until we were old enough. Our grandparents explained it to us properly. They said he still loved us even though he jumped into the river and drowned. He killed himself. They said he wasn't a well man.'

Chloe had a distant look on her face.

'But now,' she continued, 'we don't believe any of it. He worked for Stem and that's where the trail goes cold. I don't know if you're aware of what Stem really do? But they take people to be tested—studied on—they are looking for Non-Dreamers, and people who have abilities in their dreams, Dream-Drifter's, Soul-Searcher's, people like us, who can help them find a cure. A cure to prevent us all from dying in our dreams, but it's not as simple as that. They make it out as if it's a routine experiment, but it's not. Most of the people who are taken are never seen again. And they fob it off as wanting to save the world. They make it out as if it's our duty. We think our father knew something. He knew something bad was happening and he probably tried to stop it. And that's when they had him killed. Our grandparents were suspicious at first but then they stopped asking questions. They were older. They feared it would endanger us all. They said Stem could easily make us all disappear, just like our father. We know our father wouldn't have left us like that. We believe that Stem made it look as if he took his own life.'

'I'm so sorry for everything you have been through,' Jenson said. 'But how do I fit in in all of this? How do you know about me, and why did you bring me here?'

'We're here to find answers,' Chloe started. 'We ran away from home. We still check in on our grandparents, but we haven't told them the whole truth. We just said we needed time away. I know it's bad, but we needed to disappear for a while.

We need to find answers. They send us some money, but they don't have much, because of Stem. So, I suppose hiding out here makes that money last longer. I know it's not ideal, and I know we're going to hell for lying to them, but....'

Chloe shrugged her shoulders.

'So you lied to your grandparents to find out why Stem killed your father? You do know how dangerous Stem are, don't you?' Jenson questioned.

'Yes, and so do you by the looks of last night!' Callum scolded.

'What do you mean?' Jenson asked. His tone barking a hint of accusation. 'How do you know about last night? Were you two there?'

'Please calm down Jenson,' Chloe insisted. 'We were at Stem Industries last night and Callum followed one of their black jeeps. It drove straight to your home.'

'I did try to help. But you just ran off,' Callum responded.

'I don't understand,' Jenson questioned.

'I followed you on my motorbike when you ran from your house. Stem soldiers were chasing you. I saw one of the soldiers on top of you, in the park. You kicked him off you, but he jumped back on top of you. I saw his tranquiliser gun on the ground. He dropped it when you kicked him. You would have been captured if I hadn't of shot him in the neck.'

'So that was you who shot the soldier?'

'Sure was,' Callum replied. A satisfaction staining his face. 'I even got a nice souvenir out of it.'

He stood up and walked over towards the altar table.

'So that was you I saw on the bike?'

'Yep,' Callum replied, lifting his prized possession out from behind the altar table. 'And here it is,' he said, holding the gun in the air while polishing the barrel with the sleeve of his hoodie.

'But you tried to shoot me, after you shot that soldier?'

'I did, yes, because you wouldn't listen. I had to do something. I told you to stop. I figured you would have realised I was trying to help you, especially when I shot the soldier who had you pinned to the ground. It was over, you were done for. Was that not a big enough hint? I told you to stop but you just kept running.'

'What did you expect?' Jenson probed. 'I've never seen you before in my life. And anyway, you had a black helmet on. Stem soldiers broke into our home and captured my family. I had to run. I didn't think somebody would try to save me. I don't even know you.'

'Well now you do. And you're welcome!'

Callum's smart reply forced Chloe to interrupt again.

'Okay, so that now leads us to you and your family,' she said, moving the conversation along. 'Maybe we can help each other?'

'Yeah, why is Stem after you?' Callum barked.

Jenson was reluctant to answer, but after finding out Callum had given him a helping hand in his escape last night, and now Chloe, saving him back in the Plaza, he figured he owed them an explanation, even a share in his story at least.

'I'm a 'Non-dreamer' and so is my sister,' he declared.

'What?' Callum demanded. 'I thought there were only a few of you left. Why aren't you in hiding?'

'So it's true?' Chloe gasped. 'Non-dreamers really do exist? I mean, we've heard stories of them, but we've never met one before. I presumed Stem found them all.'

'Have you ever been experimented on?' Callum asked.

But before Jenson could acknowledge his statement, he abruptly raised his hands to his forehead. This caused panic. His grunting began to bellow throughout the church.

'What's wrong?' Chloe asked, watching him gasp in pain.

'It's...arrrrrghh...these pains in my head. I just started getting them this morning...arrrrghhh...I haven't taken my tablets.'

Chloe stood up from the altar step, brushing the settled dust off her backside.

'Can we help?' She asked.

'What tablets?' Callum added.

'Thanks, but I don't think so. I take these tablets, but they're at home. I can't go back there.'

'I'll go,' Callum offered. 'Just tell me where they are?'

'No, it's too dangerous,' Jenson replied.

'Don't worry about me,' Callum said, snatching his biker jacket.

Chloe was silent; she was thinking. Then, just as Callum's jacket clung to his shoulders, she spoke,

'No, Callum, you can't go. 'I'll go.'

Callum began to laugh.

'So I can't go, but you can?'

His laugh exaggerated.

'Yes! Stem are looking for Jenson, and most definitely have his house guarded. So the last thing you want is for another teenager—a hot-headed one at that—who's around the same age as Jenson, trying to break into his home; they'd think it was Jenson. They could easily capture you and question you. They would never suspect a girl.'

Callum's laugh dwindled. His silence flourished. He knew she was right.

Without waiting for a reply, Chloe put on her black biker jacket.

'Right, so that settles it. Jenson, where are your tablets?'

82

Chapter 14

Callum returned to the church after seeing his sister off. He continued past Jenson without saying a word, quietly reaching for the altar table. He began to rustle around.

Jenson gauged the silence. A discomfort loomed.

'Here, catch!' Callum said, throwing a bottle of water towards Jenson. 'I don't know if it's cold enough for you but as you can see, we've no fridges here. Should help with the headache though.'

'Thanks! And thanks for your help.' Jenson replied. He realised he had not thanked Callum for his assist in saving him last night. 'Will she be alright?'

'Don't worry, she'll be fine. She's not stupid. She is related to me after all! She has a knack of talking her way out of anything. Believe me. I've witnessed it too many times.'

'How old are you both?' Jenson asked, now unscrewing the lid of the water bottle. Is it legal for you to drive those bikes?'

'We're sixteen. And what is even legal these days. The helmets cover our identities anyway. We know what we're doing, and we've been doing it for a while now.'

'I'm sorry about what happened to your sister,' Jenson said.

Callum didn't respond.

'What does this demon want, the one who took your sister? Why was it after her?'

'These demons exist in our Dream World. I suppose anybody that dreams can be killed by one. Some people believe these demons are trying to kill 'Searchers' and 'Drifters' because we can somehow travel further into their Dream World. Our 'matter' and 'souls' somehow gives them strength and power in their world. It maybe helps them live. I'd say it makes them stronger?'

'So that's why people are dying at night? These things are killing them in their sleep, to get stronger?'

'That's what we believe. You must feel lucky you're not one of us, hey?'

'Yeah, I suppose so,' Jenson shyly answered.

Not only had he never experienced a dream before. He had been totally taken aback by the mere mention of a demon massacre being the cause of all these dream deaths.

~~~

Driving towards Jenson's house, Chloe noticed a red-haired woman walking down the driveway. Donned in a formal suit, she looked suspicious. Chloe continued her steer.

Casually passing the house and leaving an unsuspicious exertion in her wake, she glanced back using her wing mirror. The chestnut stranger had abruptly stopped at the end of the driveway. Her posture shifted upright as she stood beside the car. It looked as if she was speaking to somebody. Her position exuded authority. The car emptied, and a Stem soldier revealed himself just as Chloe turned the corner.

Knowing now that the house was being watched, Chloe decided to drive to the next street. Perhaps entering in through the back would be a better option? She had to be as inconspicuous as she could. She needed to get into Jenson's house unnoticed.

The rattling of the engine dwindled. Chloe dismounted the bike and took off her helmet.

Without reservation, she ascended the driveway.

She tapped on the door. No answer. She knocked again. Still no answer, so she continued around the side. Her plan had worked. The illusion of having a relationship with the resident was implemented. And checking around the back would give any nosey onlooker the satisfaction of no concern.

She quickly scrambled around the side of the house, with one last check for any prying eyes. The coast was clear. Throwing herself up over the fence, she landed down the other side.

Inside the housed perimeter, she continued along the edge of the garden and climbed over the wall. Little did she know, it was the same wall Jenson had jumped the previous night.

Her unflawed approach led her straight to the back of Jenson's house. Standing there, still in stealth mode, she retrieved a pin from her pocket.

Immediately wedging it into the keyhole, she began twisting it until she heard a click. The door unlocked. She entered.

The house was quiet, but a noise called out in the background like a faint chatter. It grew louder as Chloe continued out into the hallway. She began to hear the muffled voices talking from outside the house. She couldn't make out what was being said but she knew who it was.

She rapidly dashed up the carpeted stairs and went to the second bedroom on the right; the directions Jenson had given her.

She entered the bedroom, but just as she did, she heard the front door below open. She froze.

Pausing for a second, she held her breath. She listened. The muffled voices were now clearer and more distinct. They were now inside the house.

Tiptoeing over to the locker, Chloe prayed for solid flooring. She saw the pills where Jenson had said they would be. She snatched the pouch from his locker.

Suddenly, she heard the voices and footsteps again. The chatter below echoing and disturbing the silence. They began to follow Chloe upstairs onto the landing. She was trapped. Standing over Jenson's locker, her eyes scouring the room. She knew it was only a matter of seconds before they would enter.

The bedroom door opened. The male voice spoke,
'See, nobody's home.'
Chloe's lips pressed tightly against each other. Her eyes closed. The fractured light dimmed. Hidden inside Jenson's wardrobe, her body hardened, cementing into the rigid scaffold. She waited. Time stood still. But she knew she wouldn't be able to hold her breath for much longer.

But just like that it was all over. They left just as quick as they had entered.

The fear eased as Chloe let out a silent gasp. The gust of air sent a warm relief around the internal structure. The voices had been cast from the room and into another. And the darkness now brought a satisfying relief.

Her ears pricked as she listened more intently. But she couldn't make out exactly what they were saying. It seemed as if the red-haired woman was being brought around the house for an inspection. Chloe then heard the footsteps retreating down the stairs.

She crept out of the wardrobe and tiptoed over to Jenson's window.

Standing behind the curtain and shielding herself from view, she peered out.

Just then, she heard the front door slam. She watched on from above as the Stem soldier and the flame haired woman sauntered down the pathway.

Knowing her surroundings were clear, she went on the move again.

She glided down the stairs as smoothly as she could, her back pressing against the wall and her eyes constantly searching below.

She moved towards the front door and darted back out towards the kitchen.

Believing the coast was clear, she reached for the handle. Opening the door, she slipped out just as quietly as she entered.

'HEY YOU!' A voice shouted. 'What are you doing here?'

Chloe didn't know what to say; she stood still and watched the man advancing, his hand edging towards his hip holster. Apprehension in his stance alarmed her. He secured the grip of his gun.

Chapter 15

'Are you deaf?' The soldier asked. He proceeded towards her. His footsteps strong and bold.

Now standing right in front of Chloe and pressing firmly down on his gun, he observed her. His eyes scrutinising her sudden appearance.

Chloe's eyes refused to make direct contact with his. Her stare homed in on his gun. A gun she recognised. It looked identical to the one Callum had stolen the previous night.

'I said, are you deaf? What are you doing here?' The soldier repeated. His patience dwindling.

He stood a good two feet taller than Chloe. She felt a slight intimidation, but knew she had to say something, and quick.

'Oh, sorry,' she managed to finally say. 'You just startled me, that's all. I didn't know anybody was in.'

'What are you doing here? How did you get around the back?' The soldier asked.

'I just called round to see Jenson. I just live in that house there.'

Chloe pointed to the house that backed onto Jenson's.

The soldier stood silent and followed her direction.

'I always just hop the wall.' She continued. 'We've been doing it for years now. I haven't seen him since yesterday at school and he's not answering his phone. We were supposed to meet up for a school project and, well, he never showed up so I came here. I was just looking in the window and you startled me. My mother always tells me not to be so nosey.'

Chloe began to giggle but continued,

'I just can't help being nosey, you see ever since I was a little girl, my mother would always say…'

Becoming irritated by Chloe's rambling, the soldier interrupted. One hand still grasping towards his gun while the other one waving flippantly.

'Okay, that's enough,' he said. 'I don't have time for this. If you hear from Jenson, will you let us know? He just got himself into a bit of bother and his parents are worried. We need to find him. So if you see him, you ring us immediately, you hear?'

Chloe took the card that was offered.

'Yes, of course, thanks,' she said. Her heed convincing the soldier she was oblivious to what was happening. Her acting applaudable and giving no reason to doubt.

She took his card and began her strides towards the end of the garden. But only taking a few steps, she turned back around.

'I saw a woman out front, through the back window. She had gorgeous red hair. I'm thinking of dying mine. Do you know who she is, or if she's still here so I can talk to her, find out where she got it done?'

'You should listen to your mother,' the soldier said. 'She's right. You are a nosey little bitch. It'll get you into trouble one of these days. Now get out of here before I drag you back to your mother.'

'Good luck with that one,' Chloe whispered sarcastically, 'my mother died years ago.'

Her voice, too low to be heard. And a sudden misplaced humour in the irony of it all. But her plan to find out who this woman was had failed.

'Oh, did you say you had Jenson's phone number?' The soldier asked.

'Yes, but he's not answering, and I left my phone at home. Do you want me to call around later to give you his number?'

'No!' The soldier responded, a little too eagerly. He didn't want to see her again. 'Just ring the number on that card. Give it to them.'

'I will. And if you see Jenson, will you tell him Jennifer was looking for him?'

The soldier disregarded this comment and proceeded towards the front of the house.

Chloe looked down at the card before scaling the wall. Steadily holding it out, she recognised the Stem logo.

~~~

Callum pulled back the sleeve of his hoodie to reveal a white watch with a damaged face.

'Three o'clock,' he muttered, rolling his sleeve back down.

He walked to the front of the church and looked out through one of the cracked stain glass windows. He muttered again, this time a bit louder, returning to the altar,

'Where is she?'

His pacing began to unsettle Jenson.

'I'm sure she's fine. Like you said, she'd talk her way out of anything.'

Just at that moment, the sound of a motorbike pulling up alerted both boys. Jenson was lying on a bench. His headache had now passed. His anticipation taking over as he sat up eagerly and swung round to look at the big wooden doors.

Callum sprinted down to the doors just as Chloe walked in. She hadn't time to say a word. He hugged her tightly, and then slapped her on the shoulder.

'What was that for?' Chloe rasped.

'What kept you?'

Chloe didn't say a word. She reached into her pocket and pulled out the pouch of tablets, waving them in the air.

'Eh Maybe these!' She said, proudly sauntering up the aisle with a satisfying grin on her face.

'What happened?' Jenson asked.

Chloe sat down beside him and handed him his tablets,

'Where do you want me to start?'

The boys were silent as they waited for her to have a drink before she explained what had happened. She swallowed the mouthful of water and began,

'Well, first, I got there and there was this red-haired woman in a suit leaving your house. A Stem soldier sat in a car which was parked right outside. I think they have some sort of surveillance on your house. And when I got inside, they came in....'

Chloe didn't even get a chance to finish her story before Jenson interrupted her.

'That's it! I should have known it was her all along,' he said, before popping a pill out of the pack and throwing it as far back into his mouth as he could.

He reached over for the water bottle beside Chloe. He picked it up and swigged enough to wash down the tablet.

'It was staring me in the face all along. Robyn told her yesterday in school. She's Robyn's teacher, this red-haired woman. Her name is Ward, Elizabeth Ward. She must be in on it. She must be in there, in Robyn's school, watching the kids and picking them out one by one. Gaining their trust and then handing them over to Stem. What a set up? What a bitch!'

Jenson paused and then another thing hit him.

'Call me Wardy,' he said. He got to his feet. 'It has to be,' he shouted.

'Has to be what?' Callum asked.

'It's Robyn's teacher, Miss Ward, and Wardy! There has to be a link, a connection. They must be related, father and daughter? Wardy saw me this morning with his dog. And he said he would get help from his daughter, and then she turns up at my house with a Stem soldier. They're in on this together. You see Robyn told Miss Ward her secret, that she's a Non-dreamer, like me, and then the next thing, these Stem soldiers break into our home and start shooting at us. And then Wardy must have known who I was. He must have followed me to the Plaza.'

'Look, Jenson, I promise you we'll do our best to help you,' Chloe said reassuringly, 'but, for now, you need to calm down until we piece it all together.'

'I am piecing it together,' Jenson replied. But he knew he was getting a little carried away, so he took a seat. 'I can't believe this is all happening,' he remarked, picking up the water bottle again. His fingers massaging the tension in his forehead. 'Everything is just so crazy now. First Davrin, and then all of this!'

A confusion installed itself inside of Callum and Chloe,

'Who is Davrin?' Callum questioned.

'A classmate. Well, he's not really a friend. But something strange happened with him in school yesterday. And I think he was asleep.'

'What happened?' Chloe asked. She was just as intrigued as Callum now, both eager to latch onto anything that could possibly help them.

'It doesn't matter. It has nothing to do with what's going on with me and my family. Forget I said anything.'

'No, Jenson!' Chloe remarked. 'Anything you say, no matter how small you might think it is, it could help us. What happened?'

Jenson gave her a reluctant gaze—he felt silly continuing his story. But he understood her scrutiny. And the fact that she had mentioned 'us' in her statement, it had given him some encouragement that maybe, just maybe, he now had a chance at getting his family back.

'He's just a big bully if you ask me. He deserved every bit of it. He just throws his weight around, always with his gang.'

'Who Davrin?' Callum interrupted.

'No, Joey, another classmate. He woke up with blood pouring from his nose and he blamed Davrin for it. He was screaming and shouting about Davrin throwing his I-pad at him. At first, I was thinking he must have lost his mind. Davrin was at the other end of the classroom. He couldn't have thrown his I-pad, I was there. I didn't see it. But then he kept saying it was in his dream. I dunno. Maybe he made it all up just to get Davrin into trouble. I know it sounds stupid, but he never touched him. Joey was asleep at his desk and then BANG! He fell and his nose was bleeding. He must have hit his nose and was blaming Davrin. But then there was this light.'

Callum and Chloe were staring at each other, as if, each knowing what the other one was thinking. Their reaction provoked Jenson,

'What is it?'

Then Callum began to speak, recapping what Jenson had just described.

'Okay, so you're telling us that this guy, whatever his name is, he was asleep and then Davrin popped into his dream and hurt him? Was Davrin asleep as well?'

Jenson realised how ridiculous it sounded, but something in Callum's questioning hit home.

'Yeah, I think he was asleep, well It looked like he was asleep. I know it sounds stupid, but his eyes,' he said, remembering how bright Davrin's eyes were, 'they were glowing. It was as if he was in a trance or something.'

'He's a Dream-drifter!' Callum declared.

'A Drifter?'

'Yes, a Dream Drifter. Have you ever heard of them?' Callum questioned.

'Yes, they're like Searchers, aren't they?'

'Yes, but you know the way we have an ability to look for each other in our dreams?'

'Yes'

'We have a bond, a blood bond, like any siblings. Myself and Chloe we search for each other in our dreams to help each other. But then there's a more advanced form, and that's 'Drifters'. They have the ability to drift in and out of nearly anybody's dream. They even have the ability to bring people into their dreams or manipulate dreams. So maybe this Davrin guy did hit him with the I-pad in his dream?'

'What about the light, the green light?' Jenson asked.

'I've never heard of a light.' Callum answered. 'Can't help you there. Maybe those headaches are affecting your eyes, like migraines with the light? Anyway, I remember reading an article on this. The first known person to have this ability was a woman. It was about fifteen years ago, just after we were born. She went completely mad. She kept saying she could hear a voice in her head...... 'Lilith' I think she called her, or him, the voice in her head. She killed this young family saying they were 'Non-Dreamers', and that they had to die, she even killed their new-born baby. And while she was locked up for it, these Dream-deaths began to increase. People continued to die. She was blamed for starting the whole thing. I think her name was Stephanie.'

'But how could she?' Jenson questioned. 'She was locked up.'

'I know it sounds crazy, but two brothers, 'Searchers' just like us, well one of them died one night and the other one, he recognised her from the T.V. and he started to blame her for it. He said she was in their dream even though she was locked up. As far as I remember she was only a little older than us at the time. Poor girl didn't know how to control it. She was that unstable. Nobody knew how to control her, so they drugged her and sent her off to Stem Industries for testing. She was never heard of again.'

They all sat there, allowing Callum's words to sink in. Callum then spoke again.

'I don't know how close you are to this Davrin guy,' he said, 'but if Stem Industries find out about him, he's in danger. I think ever since this woman killed those people; Dream drifters are just as scarce as Non-dreamers. Let's just say there are not many of either anymore. And those that do exist, you can bet your life they are as far away from Stem as possible.'

'What about you two?' Jenson asked. 'You two are Searchers?'

'Yes, but they don't think we are as important as these 'Drifters' and 'Non-dreamers.' We are only blood tied.'

'But how can this help us?'

A silence loomed, and then Chloe spoke,

'I know your sister doesn't dream but your parents, do they dream?'

'Yes.'

'So it must have skipped a generation. Maybe this Davrin guy can help us? Maybe he can find your parents? He can communicate with them?'

Jenson realised how bizarre this suggestion was, but it seemed like the only option he had.

'You think it will work?'

Chloe looked enthusiastically at Callum, feeling this was a big leap.

'Well, it's worth a try,' She answered. 'Plus, you could look at it as helping Davrin out. Just in case Stem industries have found out about him. You did say that your sister, Robyn, her teacher was a spy. So maybe other teachers are spies?'

'But I don't know where he lives,' Jenson muttered.

'He goes to your school, doesn't he?' Chloe replied.

Jenson nodded, but he didn't know what she was getting at.

'Well, they have to have a file on him there.'

Jenson didn't like where this conversation was heading.

'You don't mean?'

He looked up at Chloe, his eyes now wide with regret.

'Yep,' Chloe interrupted. 'His address has to be in the school files.'

Callum was already ahead of her. His rummaging again found a small bolt-cutters.

'So what are we waiting for?' He asked, holding the bolt-cutters in the air.

'Not now, Callum,' Chloe said, trying not to dampen his excitement too much. 'It should be dark soon. How about we get something to eat first and then we'll go when it's dark? That way I can finish my story, seen as I was interrupted.'

She sneered, now smiling at Jenson.

'Sorry Chloe,' Jenson apologised, only now realising he had cut her off earlier.

He felt awful, especially considering how brave she had been to go and get the tablets for him.

'I'm really sorry, I feel terrible, especially after all you did for me.'

'It's okay, I forgive you but don't let it happen again.'

Chloe smirked.

Callum dropped the bolt cutters and placed it against a broken bench.

'You're right, we'll leave at dusk. I'm actually starving—what's for dinner?'

Chapter 16

'Over there!' Jenson pointed. His finger directing towards his school.

He could just about make out the shadowy outline of the two-storey, stone-faced building as the night sky had fallen.

'How are we gonna get in?' He added, pulling up beside the school perimeter.

'Leave that with me,' Callum suggested as he retrieved the small bolt-cutters he had brought with him. 'We'll park our bikes up over there.'

He continued around to the side of the school as Chloe followed with Jenson on the back.

Abandoning the bikes behind the ruffled bushes, the three of them hopped over the mesh railing and dropped down to the other side, landing inside the school grounds.

Hiding behind the bike shelter, they scoped their surroundings.

Earlier, Jenson had given them a rough layout of the school, a simplistic sketch of what they may encounter. But now, it was too difficult to see any opening with only a distant gleam from the streetlamp, a shallow light providing a pathway to the darkened school.

'We need to get closer to find a way in,' Chloe suggested. 'Where is the alarm system?'

Jenson wasn't sure. He had never searched for the security system before, not having ever thought that he would be attempting to break into his school.

'There are electricity boxes and things like that over the other side.'

'Right so,' Callum replied, 'I'll go over and find the main fuse box and dismantle the alarm. You two go round the back and find a way in.'

Callum ran, hunched down, across the front of the school towards the other side, bolt cutters in hand.

'Come on,' Chloe muttered, counting on Jenson to show her around the back to find a way in.

Standing at the back entrance to the school, the very same doorway Jenson had slept in the night before, Chloe got her miniature torch out and shone it in through the window beside the door. Jenson stood behind her, his back to the building, looking out into the darkness and keeping watch. His pulse was racing. He was freaking out.

A few minutes later Callum turned the corner, startling him.

'Very jumpy, I see!' He commented. His approach was so sudden.

'Stop messing, Callum,' Chloe instructed, trying to implement a seriousness. 'Did you do it?'

'Did you do it?' Callum reiterated with a sneer. 'You're not the only one who can get things done. Of course I did it.'

Chloe rolled her eyes as she moved over to the door. Without hesitation, she stuck the pin into the keyhole and began to screw.

After a few moments, and with a little bit of hand choreography, a click sounded. The door unlocked. Chloe turned round and smirked at Callum.

'After you,' she suggested, pushing the door open.

Just then, a loud ringing sounded; it was the school alarm system going off. The noise was deafening, like drums pounding their eardrums.

'I THOUGHT YOU CUT THE ALARM?' Jenson yelled. His shouts applying pressure over the resonating alarm.

Jenson was furious at Callum. And Callum was speechless. He just stood there, stunned.

'I THOUGHT I DID,' he eventually replied. The embarrassment showing on his face.

'COME ON—QUICK! WE DON'T HAVE MUCH TIME,' Chloe suggested.

'WE CAN'T GO IN NOW! WHAT IF SOMEBODY CATCHES US?'

'WE HAVE TO JENSON, IT'S NOW OR NEVER! YOU COME WITH ME. TAKE ME TO THE PRINCIPALS OFFICE, AND CALLUM, YOU STAY HERE AND KEEP WATCH, THAT'S IF YOU CAN EVEN DO THAT RIGHT!'

She grabbed Jenson's arm and pushed him ahead of her into the school.

Jenson knew he had to move quickly. He used his initiative, taking the torch and sprinting up the corridor with Chloe close on his trail.

Whizzing down two dark corridors, Jenson came to a third. He stopped abruptly. Chloe ran straight into his back, forcing them both to the ground.

'WHAT HAPPENED?' Chloe yelled.

Jenson got up quickly and helped her to her feet.

'SORRY,' he muttered uncomfortably. 'THIS WAY IS QUICKER.'

Jenson pushed open two wooden doors and the pair ran through what looked like a canteen. It was a big room, large enough to cater for the entire school. It had huge floor to wall windows lined up all along one side, all parallel to each other and overlooking the unlit backyard.

Running past the empty food counters, Jenson caught a glimmer of a figure outside,

'Get down,' he instructed, scurrying behind a table, and turning off the torch.

'What is it?' Chloe asked. Her voice subtle against the deafening alarm.

Jenson, able to hear her whisper, took hold of her and crouched down closely.

The moon allowing enough light to see the shadows outside. But just as Jenson nudged her in the direction, the shadow was gone. Chloe saw nothing.

'I can't see anything, Jenson. Nobody could be here that quick anyway, come on, we've no time to stop,' she added, getting to her feet, and suggesting him to continue.

~~~

'Come on! Come on!' Callum rasped. His brain was pounding from the overhead alarm bell. He stood there in the doorway, restless, and tapping the bolt cutters against his leg.

His rattle abruptly ceased. He thought he heard something. His eyes wandering all over the backyard, his gaze lurking beyond the shadows. Then he heard it again. He wasn't sure which direction the noise was coming from, but suddenly the beating alarm perished, supressing itself into a lingering pulse. The dumbing vibrations allowing Callum to think more clearly. He knew somebody had made this happen. He knew somebody had already made their way here.

'Shit,' he said in a low whisper, stepping back into the door frame and closing the door behind him.

Chapter 17

Outside the principal's office, Jenson turned the doorknob; it was locked. He looked at Chloe, hoping she would use her secret weapon and open the door with her pin. But she didn't. Instead, she snatched the torch from Jenson, and with one quick swipe, she smashed it against the top half of the glass in the door, shattering it.

'What the…'

But before Jenson could say another word, Chloe reached her arm in and opened the door from the inside.

'We've no time,' she explained, stepping into the office.

Jenson brushed past her and ran towards the school filing cabinet.

'It's locked!' He declared, attempting to pull the top drawer open. And with that, an overhead vibration replaced the howling alarm bells. Jenson turned to face Chloe.

'Let me try.' Chloe acknowledged as she stepped in.

'But the alarm has stopped. What does that mean?'

'It means we have to hurry, quick, you look for a key just in case.'

Jenson immediately ran over to the principal's desk and started rooting through some papers. Then, he heard a sound from outside the room; it was Callum,

'Chloe? Jenson?' He called out softly.

Chloe and Jenson hesitated for a moment. Jenson glanced over at Chloe, and knowing she had the better chance at getting what they came here for, he instinctively stopped searching and ran out past the smashed door, stepping over the shards of glass.

'Callum?' He called out, running down the corridor.

Turning the corner, he saw Callum approaching with a worried expression on his face.

'What is it Callum?' He asked, reaching him in at the corridor.

'We have company. Where's Chloe?'

'Shit!' Jenson declared, realising his brain wave had just been intercepted with bad cells, now confirming this to be a terrible idea.

He turned sharply and led Callum back to his sister.

'Chloe! We have to get out of here,' Callum informed her.

But Chloe didn't turn around. She was still concentrating on opening the cabinet with her pin.

'Just one more second, I nearly have it.'

'NOW Chloe! We've no time. Someone is here. COME ON, WE'VE GOT TO GO!'

'I've nearly got it Callum,'

But before Chloe could manoeuvre her pin any further, Callum grabbed her by the shoulders and dragged her away from the filing cabinet.

'We can get out over here,' Jenson suggested.

Callum and Chloe stepped out of the office and saw Jenson standing in the doorway of some classroom.

Jenson ran over to the window and opened it. He leaned out, headfirst, and threw his leg out over the ledge.

'Not much of a drop,' he suggested, looking out of the first-floor window. 'Quick! The coast is clear!' And with that he jumped, disappearing out into the darkness.

The sudden sound of a dog barking could be heard over the reduced alarm system. It was coming from inside the school and was getting closer.

Callum pushed Chloe ahead of him.

Chloe hopped onto the ledge, backside first, and then slid her two legs over while holding onto the top of the window.

The classroom light immediately came on just as she hurled herself out the window. This distraction caused her to fall out uncomfortably onto the ground.

Jenson stepped over to help her up.

Callum, who had managed to lift one leg out over the ledge, had somehow retreated.

'Callum, come on!' Chloe instructed.

But Callum looked as if he was being held back; he was trying to shove something away from him.

'GET OFF ME!' He shouted, desperately trying to break free.

Jenson dashed over to the window after hearing a low growl. He then recognised what was holding Callum back. It was 'Meatloaf', the dog he had encountered earlier that day. Meatloaf seemed to be chewing aggressively at Callum's foot. He had taken hold of his trouser end and wouldn't let go, sending Callum's legs into a spiralling spin.

'What is it boy?' A voice called out from within the classroom.

Jenson looked up and saw 'Wardy', the Viking like figure, meandering towards the window, his gut not allowing him to come at a steady pace.

Jenson looked around to see if there was anything he could throw at Meatloaf, something to distract him from Callum's ankle. He looked around and spotted the torch he had dropped. He leaned down and grabbed hold. He climbed back up onto the window ledge, and in the same movement, struck the torch downwards, smacking Meatloaf on the nose.

Meatloaf let out a loud squeal and released his grip.

Callum immediately fell backwards out of the window, crashing down on top of Chloe who was eagerly trying to pull him away.

Jenson, still hanging over the ledge, spotted Wardy, only a few feet away now. Wardy reached out to grab him, but Jenson flung the torch right at him, smacking him in the face.

Jenson then instantly dropped away from the window and helped his two friends up from the ground.

It all happened in seconds. And just as they were about to run off, Wardy reached out the window.

'Hey kid, don't run away,' he shouted. 'We wanna help you.'

Jenson froze and turned. He could see the sincerity on Wardy's face, along with the blood trickling down from the gash on his forehead.

'COME ON JENSON!' Chloe screamed, grabbing his arm, and trying to snap him out of his trance. 'We need to move.'

Sirens sounded in the distance as Callum hobbled off in front with Chloe and Jenson following.

They were just about to hop over the railing when Jenson turned around again. He could see Wardy staring out from the lighted classroom. He was holding what seemed like a phone up to his ear.

'JENSON, come on, we need to go, NOW!' Chloe said again, this time with a distress in her voice.

Finally listening to her, Jenson jumped over the school railing.

'Did you see him? That was Wardy and his dog—the ones I was telling you about.'

'Okay Jenson,' Chloe replied, hopping onto her bike. 'We really do need to get out of here now! Quick, get on.'

Jenson jumped on the back of her bike. He realised it had to be Wardy, and Robyn's teacher all along.

'Can we go somewhere first before we go back to the church?' He asked. 'It won't take long on the bikes.'

'What for?' Chloe questioned.

'Plan B!'

'You never mentioned anything about a Plan B?' Callum barked.

'I didn't know Plan A would fail, did I?' A hint of blame in his response.

'Okay, let's go then.' Chloe interjected. 'You okay to drive Callum?'

'Yeah, I'll be fine,' Callum replied, as if trying to carry off a light graze. But Chloe knew by his reaction that he was in pain. 'It's just a scratch.' He added. 'Now let's get out of here!'

Chapter 18

Just as Jenson had said, after a short drive, they had pulled up outside a big lavish house, iron gates in front, indicating the importance inside. And a concealment of cement, a six-foot wall, caging its perimeter and safely securing the property from any intruder.

Callum and Chloe watched on as Jenson retrieved his phone from his pocket to reactivate it. This was the first time they had seen him with a phone.

'Rich friends I see?' Callum suggested, examining the outside of this impressive house. 'Why didn't you come here sooner?'

'I did!' Jenson answered. His phone now up to his ear and listening to the ringing tone.

Callum's attention turned back to his ankle. He ruffled up the leg of his black combat trouser to see how bad his wound was. It had stopped bleeding and wasn't as deep as he'd expected. But the pain proving powerful as he winced whilst rolling the trouser leg back down.

'Should heal up nicely,' he said. 'Another scar to add to my collection.'

'Not everything is a joke Callum.' His sister declared. 'You could have been caught back there.'

'But I wasn't.'

'This is my friend Ethan's house,' Jenson cut in, still waiting on the other end to pick up.

'Didn't you say he might have something to do with all of this?' Chloe asked. Her words arousing suspicion.

106

'I don't know what I was thinking. My head was all over the place. I now know he had nothing to do with any of it. His dad works for Stem, but he hates Stem. It was Wardy and his daughter.'

'Hello?' Jenson said. His attention now returning to the cell phone. 'Yeah, yeah, I'm fine. I'll explain everything— are you home?'

There was a brief pause for a few seconds and then Jenson began to speak again,

'Cool, meet me at the back door. Is anyone else home?'

More hesitation,

'Okay, but don't say anything to her. I'll be there in a minute.'

Jenson hung up the phone. He turned toward Callum and Chloe. But his focus was distracted as the beeping of incoming messages rang out. His attention alerted back towards his phone. He began to read the messages out:

[Are u ok?]
[I take it ur not comin?]
[I'm worried pal???]

'How could I have been so stupid to think he had something to do with this?' Jenson blurted out loud after reading Ethan's messages. 'He's my friend. He was worried about me all this time. And you even heard Wardy, calling me back as if he wanted to help me.'

Callum and Chloe never said a word. They watched Jenson, allowing him to evaluate everything. And with that, he hurried over to the secured perimeter, climbing the wall, and eventually disappearing out of sight.

'Did he say his friend's father works for Stem?' Chloe asked.

'I think so,' Callum answered.

'Something doesn't feel right Callum.'

'There he is,' Callum called out, acknowledging Jenson as he came into view a few minutes later.

'Great news, guys. Ethan knows where Davrin lives.'

Chloe looked at Callum. Her suspicion returning, but Callum didn't notice her stare.

'I hope it's okay if he comes with us to show us where he lives?'

'Yeah, of course it is, isn't it, Chloe?' Callum asked, not really expecting her to disagree.

Chloe held back her interest. Her silence provoked concern, but in that moment, an electronic clicking sound emitted as the iron gates began to pull back. The front door opened, and a curly-haired stout boy stepped out eating a bar of chocolate.

'Callum and Chloe, this is Ethan. Ethan, this is Callum and Chloe. And you're sure you know where Davrin lives?' He asked.

Ethan nodded confidently while chewing the remains of his chocolate bar.

'Yeah, my Mum was doing some church charity thing and she collected me from my cousin's house with this old lady in the back. We dropped her home and I think it was Davrin's grandmother. She kept talking about him, you'd swear he was her son or something, and before you say it, I didn't tell my mum anything, just said I had to get something off him for a school project on Monday.'

'Right, Ethan, you can come with me,' Callum offered, wanting to get on the road.

'Okay, let's go.'

~~~

After whizzing in and out of the Saturday night traffic on the main carriageway, Callum and Ethan eventually crossed over to get off at exit five towards the Falls-way. Ethan gave Callum the directions, Chloe and Jenson followed.

The Falls-way wasn't a bad area, just somewhat deprived. It was a settled estate where most of its residents were either pensioners or near retirement age. Not many new house hunters moved here as most residents were the last remaining believers in God. The majority elsewhere stopped believing in God since the Dream-death disease had come about—they just couldn't accept that a kind God would allow innocent people to die in their sleep. A dwindling community confined to these catchment areas.

The area was darker than most, a result from the strain of Stem's power. A lot of houses had only one or two lights on. They looked old and silent with many of the streetlamps broken.

The group eventually reached their destination, pulling up outside a house with a flickering bedroom light. Downstairs seemed to be consumed in total darkness.

They retreated from the bikes and then hesitated, each waiting on their next move.

Jenson spoke up.

'I think myself and Chloe should go and talk to him, it's less intimidating. Nobody wants four strangers knocking at their door at night. What do you guys think?'

Nobody really minded and the more they thought about it, the more it made sense.

The garden path was dark with a dim light from the bedroom allowing them to avoid the weeded cracks in the pavement.

Stepping over the moss filled stonework, they approached the porch door.

Jenson reached in and pressed the doorbell. A swift jerk to retrieve his hand caused Chloe to respond,

'What is it?'

'I think it was a web or something. Don't know, I can't see, but I'm not pressing that again.'

Jenson tried to pull the porch door ajar so he could use the knocker inside. He was unsure he had pressed the bell properly, but the porch didn't budge. It was locked from the inside.

He and Chloe stood there in anticipation.

A few seconds later Jenson raised his arm to press the doorbell again. But Chloe shifted her arm to meet his.

'Wait, I think somebody's coming,' she said.

They saw the curtain twitch as a soft light began to shimmer, announcing somebody's arrival.

A small figure revealed itself from beyond the curtain. An added layer of protection distorted the shape as the stain glass window scrambled their outline.

Jenson and Chloe looked at each other.

A moment later the curtain dropped.

The front door creaked open. And the rickety porch vibrated as the door pulled back, revealing an elderly woman.

She looked to be in her seventies. She had a full head of grey hair tied back in a bun. She wore a long navy skirt and had a big woollen blanket hanging over her shoulders. She stepped into the porch and stared cautiously at Jenson and Chloe.

'Can I help you?' She asked. Her frail voice probing, an expression of confidence from within her locked confinement.

A sudden spurn of guilt washed over Jenson as he realised, he could be putting them in danger. Asking for her grandson's help, could mean involving them in something they could never turn back from. But he knew he had to. This was his only hope in getting his family back.

'Sorry for calling so late. We are friends of Davrins. We were wondering if we could speak to him, please?'

The lady's eyes were squinting, wrinkles defining even further with every judgemental glare. Her frail wrist pulled back the loose strand of grey hair that had fallen onto her face. She then wriggled her wrist to spin her watch around. She spoke,

'It's very late. And Davrin does not have any friends. What are your names?'

'My name is Jenson, Jenson Rose, and this is Chloe,' he answered, attempting to be completely honest with the old lady. 'I'm sorry,' he continued. 'We're not really good friends of his. I am in his class though, and I was wondering if he was okay after yesterday in school? Don't know if he told you what happened and I know it's late, but we only found out where he lives.'

Jenson wasn't being completely honest, but he thought that maybe Davrin had told his grandmother about yesterday's event in school, so perhaps she would see some truth behind his explanation.

The old woman paused. She seemed to be considering his request, sizing each of them up.

A few moments passed. She turned round and stepped back into the house, closing the door behind her.

'Please, wait?' Jenson asked.

But there was no hesitation from this woman. She was gone.

'Do you think she's gonna get him?' Chloe asked, feeling unsure.

'I don't know.'

The old lady must have known there was some truth in what Jenson had said, because less than two minutes later, Davrin appeared. He stepped out into the porch jar, staring out from beyond the glass.

He was taken aback to see people at his front door, looking to talk to him. He just stood there, speechless.

111

'Hey,' he uttered shyly, running his hand in one sweeping motion through his black hair, brushing it from his face, the same sweeping motion his grandmother had just done.

Jenson noticed how uncomfortable he looked, even though he was standing on his own turf. He knew Davrin was probably sceptical of them being here, so he began to speak, aiming to ease any concern.

'Hey Davrin, we're sorry to knock so late. I'm sorry I've never really spoken to you in class. This is my friend, Chloe. I was wondering if you'd be able to help me. I saw what you did to Joey in class yesterday. Personally, I think he deserved it, but I was wondering if you can...I don't know...use that gift you have to find my parents, and my sister, to talk to my parents in their dream?'

Davrin didn't know how to react to this appeal. He could tell that Jenson seemed sincere. He understood the purity in his plea, but this was all so sudden. Everything was new to him. It was too soon to help somebody else, for he had only come to understand these powers himself. He was still unsure how to control them.

'I know you're a Drifter.' Jenson continued, a lump forming in his throat. 'I am begging you, please, I don't know what else to do.'

Davrin hesitated for a moment. He then responded. A discomfort proving too real with his reply.

'I'm sorry Jenson, I don't think I can help you. I don't know what you think you saw, but it wasn't me.'

He began to fidget. His hands overlapping and his eyeline dropping, losing all eye contact.

'But you're a Dream-drifter!' Jenson declared. A force in his statement. He was desperate. 'Please, Davrin, I'm begging you. I wouldn't ask if I didn't have to. I've no other option. My family were taken by Stem. I'm sorry, I know I never helped you out all those times you got bullied, but I'll do anything. I know its cheeky of me to come here now expecting you to do this for me, especially when I never helped you, but, please, I've lost my family. I might never get them back.'

Chloe could see everything piling up on Jenson like a heavy weight, now finally reducing him to nothing. She raised her arm and began to rub his back.

'I'm sorry, I just can't,' Davrin said. A tearful look in his despondent eyes. And with that, he turned and stepped back into the house.

'Davrin, please! You could be in danger yourself,' Jenson called out.

But Davrin didn't listen. He continued his retreat and closed the door.

Jenson was trying to understand what had just happened when the curtain lifted again. The small figure returned. But within seconds, the curtain dropped back down, and the porch light distinguished. Their conversation had finally ended. Both Jenson and Chloe stood there in total darkness.

'What are we gonna do Chloe?'

'We'll find another way Jenson. There's always Plan C.'

'And what's that?'

'I'm not sure yet. We need to go back to the church and get some rest. We can look into other options then.'

Chapter 19

Well?' Callum asked. He spotted Jenson and Chloe returning. 'Where is he?'

Jenson's expression showed deep pessimism.

'Where's Ethan?' Chloe responded, noticing he was missing.

'Hey, sorry, nature called,' Ethan said, as he approached them from the darkness.

His phone beeped.

'Must be my mum. She's unbelievable, always worrying about me,' he said. A smile appearing on his face as he rolled his eyes. 'It's not even ten o'clock,' he added with a light chuckle. 'How did you get on? What did you want from him anyway?'

'Don't know why we even thought he'd help us,' Jenson answered.

'Maybe I can help.' Ethan offered. 'What did you need?'

'Right, let's go. I think we could all do with some rest,' Chloe said. Her timing, instinctively cued to cut Ethan off. But Ethan didn't back down.

'Where are we going?' He asked curiously.

'You're full of questions, aren't you?' Chloe replied quickly before anybody else could answer.

'Wow, relax Chloe,' Callum instructed. He began to scrutinize this sudden confrontation. 'He was only asking a question. No need to take his head off.'

Chloe didn't acknowledge Callum; she kept looking straight at Ethan.

'Sure, didn't you say your mother wanted you? We'll drop you off on the way. Can't have her worrying.'

'Chloe, that's enough,' Callum ordered, not knowing why she had taken a sudden dislike to Ethan.

Chloe turned towards her brother as he scolded her. She didn't know what to say because she really had no reason to dislike Ethan; there was just something about him.

'Are you sure there's nothing I can help you with?' Ethan asked as he approached Jenson.

Jenson had zoned out of this whole conversation. He was oblivious to the atmosphere between Chloe and Ethan. His disappointment still looming after Davrin's rejection.

'Thanks Nathan,' Chloe maliciously interrupted. She deliberately got his name wrong, seeing how far she could push him before he snapped. 'But I think we need to get out of here.'

'It's Ethan.'

'What?' Chloe rasped.

'My name. It's Ethan!'

'Well whatever it is. You ready Jenson?'

Jenson didn't have time to think. He followed Chloe's call and moved over to her bike.

'Don't mind her Ethan,' Callum said. 'I don't know what's gotten into her. Thanks for your help, let's go.'

'Yeah, let's go.' Chloe uttered. 'We'll drop you off at home. Wouldn't want your mother worrying all night.'

She started up her engine.

Ethan walked over to Callum. He checked his phone and typed something in before getting onto the bike.

'Sorry about that,' Callum said. 'She's not normally like this. I don't know what's gotten into her.'

Ethan remained silent, trying to understand Chloe's dislike towards him. He hopped on behind Callum and they drove off after Chloe and Jenson.

~~~

The journey back to Ethan's house was a quiet one. Jenson felt miserable and Chloe's mind was in overdrive. She just felt something wasn't right with Ethan. First, his disappearance for a toilet break when he had only left his house thirty minutes prior to their trip. And then all the questioning when he returned. And not to mention the last-minute text before getting onto Callum's bike.

Chloe slowed down, knowing Callum would overtake her. And like clockwork, he did. He flew past with easing acceleration.

Drifting off the carriageway, she slowed even further, generating enough distance behind Callum to pull in and stop without him noticing. She didn't want him thinking anything was wrong.

'What is it?' Jenson asked her, not knowing why they had suddenly stopped.

'I'm sorry Jenson, but something smells funny. How long have you known Ethan?'

'Most of my life,' Jenson replied. He was surprised by her question. He stepped off the bike and took off his helmet. 'Why are you asking this?'

'Well back when we talked in the church, you said you thought he had something to do with this, yeah?'

'Yes. I thought maybe because his dad works for Stem, but then we found out it was Wardy and his daughter.'

Jenson looked puzzled.

'What if they're all involved?' Chloe asked. 'I don't know, Jenson, but don't you think he's been acting strange? Asking questions and then disappearing and randomly getting texts. He only left his house not so long ago. Why would his mother be checking up on him so soon? And I think I saw him sending a quick text just before he got on Callum's bike.'

'Why are you saying this to me?' Jenson snapped. 'You heard Wardy back at the school shouting at me, telling me to practically hand myself over. These people at Stem Industries, they are the people who took my parents and my sister—can't you see that? You don't even know Ethan.'

~~~

Callum looked in his side view mirror and noticed that Chloe was not on his tail. But, by now, he had reached the top of the street, Ethan's house just down a little further.

'Something's wrong,' Callum suggested to Ethan as he swerved the bike round. 'Are you okay to get off here while I go back for them?'

Ethan never got a chance to answer.

A sudden movement caught Callum's eye from his wing mirror. He noticed two bikes outside Ethan's home. They were all too familiar to him. They were Stem bikes!

'What's wrong?' Ethan asked, holding onto the back of him.

'Don't know Ethan, but I don't think it's safe for us to go any further.'

'Why?'

'There are two Stem bikes outside your home. I'll let you off here. We have to go.'

'No,' Ethan replied. 'I'll come with you.'

'Shit!' Callum rasped.

He didn't hesitate. He hit his foot hard on the accelerator.

'What is it?' Ethan asked.

The bike spun around fast.

'It's Stem. I think they know we're here!'

117

Callum didn't think. His actions caused him to leave immediately. Suspicion had already corrupted his mind. He sped off again with Ethan still on the bike.

'It's okay, you don't have to go,' Ethan advised. 'I'll tell them you're my friend. They won't suspect a thing.'

Looking back through his wing mirror, Callum could see two Stem soldiers mount their bikes and quickly fire their engines. They instantly manoeuvred out onto the street and followed in their direction.

'Shit, Shit, Shit!' He shrieked. His suspicion confirmed. He held down the throttle and accelerated harder. 'It's too late. They've spotted us!'

Chapter 20

'Chloe, there's no reason at all my best friend would have something to do with this, I'm telling you. You don't know him like I do. I'm sorry Chloe, but I think you need to let this drop.'

Chloe's stare blew straight past Jenson.

'Are you even listening to me Chloe?'

'Jenson! Get back on the bike. We need to go.'

'What?'

'Jenson, we need to go now.'

'I don't understand?'

'JENSON, we have to go, NOW!' She demanded, swinging the bike around.

And just as she did, a car spun round in the middle of the road, making a sharp U-turn. It proceeded to speed back towards them.

'Who's that?' Jenson rasped, throwing on his helmet, and jumping back on the bike.

They quickly shot out towards the carriageway again.

Jenson kept looking behind him, but he couldn't make out who it was tailing them. The wind was blowing hard against his visor, and even though Chloe didn't turn her head, he could still make out what she was shouting.

'I THINK IT'S THE RED-HAIRED WOMAN I SAW AT YOUR HOUSE, ROBYN'S TEACHER. SHE'S IN THE CAR WITH SOMEONE—THEY'RE AFTER US!'

Chloe moved to the inside lane, nearly ploughing into a truck. The car shot out too as it attempted to gain momentum.

Callum and Ethan could see a red car veering into the middle of the road, causing other cars to skid aside. The loud honking of horns indicated caution up ahead, but Callum knew it was something to do with his sister.

Driving a small motorbike was useful for whipping in and out of traffic, so before Callum knew it, he had caught up with the red car that had caused the disturbance up ahead. He was tailgating and trying to disguise his motions to get a better look.

Now approaching the car side by side, he noticed a red-haired woman driving with a male passenger. He didn't recognise the flame-haired female, but he remembered Chloe talking about her. He tilted his head to investigate further and instinctively recognised the passenger. It was the man who had set his dog on him. The man from the school. It was Wardy.

Callum sped up and managed to manoeuvre past the red car. And as he overtook it, he realised why it was going so fast. He saw Chloe and Jenson about fifty yards ahead of him. He knew he could catch up with them, Chloe's driving skills were of no match to his. A game he would have relished if it were under different circumstances. But he needed to catch up on Chloe and perhaps distract the red car. For he knew they were after Jenson.

Callum increased his speed to the max, but was so distracted himself by the car, he momentarily forgot about the two Stem soldiers on bikes.

He glanced back into his wing mirror. The two bikes following him had just swerved out, overtaking the red car. These bikes looked fast, faster than the car, and faster than their bikes—it was only a matter of time before they would catch up with them.

Jenson gripped Chloe's waist and kept checking on the red car. He saw Callum and Ethan overtaking it.

'CALLUM AND ETHAN ARE RIGHT BEHIND US!' He shouted.

Chloe checked her mirror and saw her brother and Ethan.

'Why didn't he get rid of him?' She whispered, her mind focusing on Ethan. She then spotted the two bikes right behind them. She knew they were Stem soldiers.

'THERE'S MORE!' She screamed.

'WHAT DO YOU MEAN?' Jenson questioned.

'THE BIKES, THEY'RE STEM SOLDIERS!'

Chloe revved the bike even further.

Jenson turned to see the two Stem soldiers on bikes. He watched on as one of them raised his arm. And with this action, a tranquiliser gun came into view.

'THEY HAVE GUNS!' He shouted.

Callum, who had caught up with Chloe and Jenson, was now driving right beside them,

'I'LL DISTRACT THEM,' he called out.

But this effort was short lived. A sharp thud pressed against his back causing his steering to shake. He lost control. His bike wobbled as he drifted out into the middle of the carriageway.

An oncoming car nearly ploughed into him, but he managed to recover. He realigned his bike back towards Chloe's. No numbness or pain, but he realised what it was. He could feel the full weight of Ethan's unconscious body pressing in against his back.

'HE'S BEEN SHOT!' He screamed. 'I CAN FEEL HIM SLIPPING.'

Chloe and Jenson watched on helplessly. Jenson panicked. Both bikes travelling in unison, he tried to lean over and help his friend. He wanted to keep him upright, but Chloe could feel him overstretching. She could feel the bike pulling to one side. She immediately moved away from Callum's bike.

'WHAT ARE YOU DOING?' Jenson screamed. He appeared angry.

Chloe knew he could fall off while trying to help his friend. She ignored his cries and instructed Callum to follow her.

'LET HIM GO!' She ordered, taking the next exit.

'HE COULD DIE?' Jenson roared.

But Chloe ignored him again. She took the slip road and Callum followed behind her.

They both came speeding up towards the lights which were about to turn red.

'WE'RE GONNA MAKE IT!' Chloe screamed as she zoomed through the red lights, making a sharp left turn onto another road.

Callum bolted through the red lights, just a fraction of a second behind her.

'HE'S GONNA FALL!' He shouted.

Ethan was thrown from the bike. His body heavily landing in a side ditch.

'ETHAAAAAAN!' Jenson roared as he watched his friend plunge to the ground.

The offloaded weight caused Callum to regain his position. Now beside Chloe again he shouted,

'I'M SORRY JENSON,' he said. 'I HAD NO OTHER CHOICE.'

But before he could say another word, he fell forward on his bike.

Chloe Shrieked.

Panic set in as she noticed a dart sticking out of his back.

'CALLUUUMMMMMM!' She cried, watching the bike tip over and skid sideways along the ground, and Callum's body ricocheting after it.

'WE CAN'T LEAVE HIM!' Chloe declared, now a distance away and turning the bike around.

Jenson didn't answer. He knew he would do the same if it was his sister.

Only one of the Stem soldiers arrived on the scene, slowing down his bike as he reached Callum, who was lying on the ground. *The other one must have stopped to get Ethan, Chloe thought.* But she didn't care. She ferociously revved the engine and accelerated hard, motioning back towards the Stem soldier. And as they got close, she screamed back at Jenson,

'JUUUUUUMP!'

The Stem soldier had no time to dodge this advancement. Chloe, at full speed now, rammed her bike head-first into his, just as she and Jenson jumped off.

The two bikes, producing a huge explosion, created a fireball that veered off down the road, with the unfortunate soldier tangled up inside.

Jenson and Chloe soared into the air before plummeting to the ground.

Chloe was dazed and confused with a ringing in her ears. She managed to lift her head and look up. She tried to get up, but she was too weak. The stinging throbs causing her to remain motionless. She noticed Jenson's unconscious body. He was now lying just metres away from her, the impact proving too tough on his body.

Suddenly, the forgotten red car came into view. Chloe could see it swerve past the burning crash site. Her body arched and aching, but she couldn't move. She needed to get up. She needed to help Jenson.

The red car pulled in, and both occupants got out.

Chloe could hear them just as her body began to recapture its senses. Her hands began to twitch as her body began to lift slowly.

'That's him!' The red-haired woman acknowledged. 'Quick, get him into the car,' she demanded, pointing over at Jenson.

Wardy dipped onto his hunkers and picked up Jenson's unconscious body. He walked back over to the car as the woman opened the back door. They bundled him inside.

Chloe had succeeded in getting onto her feet, but it was too late. She watched on as the red car rippled away like a taunting wave, the current too strong to chase. There was nothing she could do.

Then, searching through the remnants of debris, she could see her brother, his body lying flat out on the ground, the tranquiliser still in his back.

She staggered over and yanked it out before throwing it away. She gently began shaking his face.

'Callum! Callum! Please wake up,' she cried.

Callum was slowly coming round, his groaning becoming louder.

Chloe eventually helped him to his feet, allowing her weight to support him.

'Come on, we've got to get out of here,' she said, guiding him over towards the scratched-up bike he had fallen off.

'Where's Jenson?' Callum asked. His unsteadied balance struggling to get onto the bike.

Chloe started up the engine.

'They took him,' she replied. 'Stem have him now.'

Chapter 21

Jenson gradually opened his eyes. His blurred vision trying to focus on something certain. The smell of embers burning close by ignited a calmness. But a moist vapour clung to his hand. He was in, what looked like a living room, and managed to finally open his eyes wide enough to identify his surroundings.

The room lacked modernism, but what it lacked, it gained in warmth. The toasty fire gave some relief as Jenson tried to piece together what had happened. The last thing he could remember was the motorbike accident. *Maybe the dampness by his hand was blood, an injury from his fall? He thought.*

His eyes sluggishly began to examine his arm, tracing down towards his hand. A gobbling noise resonated. Jenson felt the touch and quickly retracted his arm. He looked up. It was Meatloaf, Wardy's brown and white boxer dog.

Jenson automatically seized his arm tighter and shifted it into his chest, his other arm holding on, as if shielding it. Sinking into the corner of the couch, he watched on. But Meatloaf didn't move. He just stared back. His lips circling around his snout, creating all the moisture that had been lost by the heat in the room.

Jenson's eye-contact remained. He couldn't abandon his gaze, a response from his reaction of smacking him with the torch back in the school. He was unsure of Meatloaf's intentions. He didn't want to aggravate him, but at the same time, he knew that this staring contest could not last forever. Meatloaf just sat there in an upright position looking back at him.

'Ellie, he's awake,' a voice called out. An interruption to this stare-off.

Jenson twisted his body round, taking his eyes off Meatloaf for the first time. He saw Wardy approaching from the room next door.

A red-haired woman wearing black jeans and a frilly green blouse appeared also. She made her way over to Jenson. And Jenson immediately knew who it was. It was Miss Ward, Robyn's teacher.

'What do you want from me and where's my family?' He asked.

Jenson didn't shout. He was angry, but he knew they had the upper hand, for he was still hurt. But he was determined to get some answers.

Before anybody could say a word, Meatloaf's sharp cry broke the awkwardness from within the room. His loud bark commanding attention as all faces turned to watch him.

'Stop it boy!' Wardy instructed. His authority overruling Meatloaf's yelp.

'Please calm down, Jenson. Don't be afraid,' Ellie affirmed.

'I don't understand. What is going on?'

'Please, Jenson,' Ellie said again, holding out her arms and pleading with him. Her body shifting into the armchair opposite.

She paused for a few seconds, giving him a chance to settle down and take it all in. She then began to explain,

'I don't know if you know who I am, but I'm Robyn's teacher, Elizabeth Ward, but please call me Ellie. I believe you've already met my father, Jim. You probably know he likes to be called Wardy—he likes to think he's still young.'

'Well I'm not too old to give you a smack on the backside,' Wardy threatened. His joking manner was followed by a hand gesture as he walked over and sat on the arm of his daughter's chair. Meatloaf sauntered after him, wagging his tail.

Jenson was completely taken aback. The picture enfolding right in front of him, a picture of a placid scene, a family home, a father and daughter, something he did not imagine he would ever have woken up to. He wondered who these people really were and what they wanted.

'I'm sorry, I still don't understand,' he muttered.

'You've no need to apologise Jenson,' Ellie assured him. 'We know Stem have taken Robyn and your parents. We just want to help. I do have one question though. Why did you run from us?'

Jenson didn't know what to say. He believed that these people, his rescuers, had an involvement into his family's abduction. He had convinced himself that they were after him. But now, sitting in front of him, these two seemingly sincere people who appeared to be just as much in the dark as he was.

'I'm not too sure,' he replied. His thoughts focusing on a reassessment. The whole situation cluttered his brain. 'Well, Robyn told us that she opened up to you about her secret. The next thing we know is, Stem soldiers are breaking into our home. I thought you two were part of it.'

Jenson sat back and watched as Wardy and Ellie looked at each other. They were both mesmerised at what he had just said. Ellie's grimacing face alerted confusion.

'I'm sorry you thought that Jenson. You must have been so scared.' She said, turning to her father and placing her hand on top of his. 'We are so sorry we gave you that impression. My father came looking for me, saying there was a boy who had slept at the school doorway. He thought you were in some sort of bother, with head pains. When he mentioned your name and described you, I knew exactly who you were. I couldn't believe it! Robyn's big brother, she talks about you all the time. You were gone when we got to the school. I then felt I had to call round to your home to see if everything was okay. I was a little concerned, so I went over yesterday afternoon. I was planning

127

to drop by anyway, because of what Robyn had told me. I wanted to let your parents know that her secret was safe with me. But when I knocked at your door there was no answer. I came back down the path and a man called me over to his car. He was a Stem soldier. I didn't notice him when I got there. He must have been watching the house, watching me. He asked me a lot of questions. I said I was a close friend. But that was a mistake because he brought me into the house, I don't really know why. I think he was perhaps trying to get some information out of me. He showed me around, and when he gave me his card, I knew exactly what was going on.'

Ellie paused for a moment. She got to her feet and scurried out to the kitchen. Retrieving her handbag, she returned with a small business card in her hand.

'This is what he gave me,' she said, handing it to Jenson.

It was identical to the one Chloe had shown him.

'My best friend was taken by Stem a few years ago, and I haven't seen her or her family since. They all just vanished without a trace.'

'I'm sorry,' Jenson said. 'But why were you at the school last night?' He added, turning his attention to Wardy.

'I'm the caretaker.' Wardy answered. 'When the alarm triggers, I'm the first person notified.'

Jenson paused. He noticed the mark on Wardy's forehead.

'I'm sorry I threw that torch at you. And I'm sorry for hitting your dog.'

The guilt began to cling to his chest.

'It's okay kid, you've been through a lot. We forgive you, don't we, boy?'

With that, Meatloaf barked.

'Tell me this kid, why did you break into the school?'

'We wanted to find somebody.' Jenson then hesitated. 'You don't know what happened to my friends, do you?'

'Who?' Ellie questioned.

'Callum and Chloe?'

'I'm afraid we don't Jenson, I'm sorry,' Ellie responded. 'We just took you because we didn't know who the others were. But I do remember the girl getting to her feet as we drove off. I don't know what happened then, I'm sorry.'

'So they could have gotten away?'

Jenson struggled to get to his feet.

'What are you doing?' Ellie questioned.

'I have to go now—I have to make sure they're okay.'

'Wait Jenson! Ellie cautioned. 'You're still weak. I have a car. I can drive you if you want?'

Jenson didn't want to get any more people involved, but he knew he needed their help.

'Okay, please,' he acknowledged.

'Right, hang on and I'll grab my keys. You can tell me where we're going on the way. You'll have to keep your head down, there's a lot more Stem soldiers out patrolling the streets this morning.'

Chapter 22

Chloe stood up from the sink behind the altar. Her attention was alerted by the sound of a vehicle approaching. But it was an unfamiliar sound, not the usual rumblings of Callum's bike.

Frantically grabbing a towel, she wiped her face and ran straight over to the side aisle.

Peering out through the half-broken window, she knew it was too early for Callum to be returning with breakfast. She saw the red car pull up with Jenson stepping out of it.

An enormous feeling of happiness overwhelmed her. But it was cut short when she noticed the other passengers getting out of the vehicle with him.

'He betrayed us!' She rasped.

Had Jenson been so disloyal, leading these Stem people to their hideaway? Had he abused their trust? She thought.

A wave of panic came over her. She immediately turned and sprinted towards the altar to retrieve the tranquiliser gun Callum had picked up.

'CALLUM? CHLOE?' Jenson yelled as he burst in through the church doors.

There was no response.

'They're not here,' he said, disappointedly. 'And there's no bike outside. Are you sure you saw them get away?'

Meatloaf sauntered past him, sniffing the ground towards the altar.

'What is it, boy?' Wardy asked.

Meatloaf stepped onto the altar, his sniffing urging him closer to Chloe who was hiding behind the consecrated table.

'Stop now or I'll shoot!' Chloe demanded, her voice stern.

She stood up pointing the tranquiliser gun directly at them, hovering it back and forth from Meatloaf to the others.

Meatloaf started to growl.

'Chloe, please put the gun down, it's not what you think,' Jenson retaliated. 'Please Chloe, these people want to help.'

Before Jenson could say another word, a big white shopping bag was flung into the air from behind the partition wall. The bag, which was full of food, smashed onto the ground right in front of Jenson.

Callum raced out like a wild bear, swinging a broken church leg he had picked up.

Meatloaf was startled, just like the rest of them, but he stood his ground. He began barking and growling at Callum.

'Meatloaf! Get over here now!' Wardy called from the bottom of the steps.

Meatloaf quietened down and slowly backed away from the altar.

Callum's swiping also eased. His sudden spurt coming to a halt as the dog retreated.

'Callum! Chloe! Please...' Jenson negotiated. 'I know what this looks like. But these people are on our side. I was wrong, please, just put the gun down and I'll explain everything.'

Chloe lowered the gun.

After a while, all questions were answered. Ideas bouncing back and forth like a shared exercise, each suggestion reviving the discontinued idea beforehand. And even though some of it felt like a lost cause, Jenson felt at ease. He quickly realised these new friends of his were all helping to get his family back.

'We have to try Davrin again,' Chloe concluded. 'If he can get in touch with your parents while they sleep then maybe we have a chance of getting them out of Stem. Maybe they can tell us what's going on?'

'So what are we waiting for? Let's just go and make him help us,' Callum said, standing up from the altar step, and swiping the dust from his trousers.

'We can't make him change his mind,' Jenson replied. 'He refused us last night. Why would this time be any different? Plus, there are more Stem soldiers out on patrol.'

'I can drive,' Ellie said. 'Nobody knows about us. Stem won't see us coming.'

'But your car was there last night?' Jenson replied.

'Yes, but I'm sure those Stem soldiers didn't even notice it while they were after you lot. They flew right past us, and I think one of them probably won't remember anything.'

Ellie was referring to the soldier that got smashed up in the bike crash.

'How do we know that Stem haven't found out about Davrin already?' Jenson questioned. 'Maybe word got out about what happened in class on Friday. Maybe they have him now?'

'We have to try,' Chloe interjected.

'You do want your family back, don't you?' Callum asked, knowing well what Jenson's answer would be, but just making sure he was motivated enough.

'Of course I do!'

'Right, that settles it. I'll drive,' Ellie answered. 'Myself and Jenson will go. The rest of you can wait here. We won't be long.'

'Do we have any other choice?' Callum asked. His enthusiasm dipping. His lack of involvement caused him to begrudge the whole idea. He loved getting his hands dirty, but this plan triggered a cleanliness he was never used to.

And Chloe realised this.

132

'Come on Callum,' she said. 'Let's see what you got for breakfast.'

'I'm not hungry anymore!' Callum stated. His pout showing signs of a sulk.

'Don't take it personally Callum. They'll need us again. This is far from over.'

Chapter 23

'Jenson?' Ellie called out, glancing at him as he hunched down in the passenger seat. 'We're nearly here. You can get up now, there are no more Stem soldiers.'

Jenson sat up properly in the seat. He directed Ellie towards Davrin's house. No sign of anyone suspicious, they pulled up outside.

The house looked as if it had not seen a lick of paint since it was built, a decrepit sight in need of some encouragement. Jenson was unaware just how run down it was as the darkness of last night had managed to shield some of the tiredness. And by the look on Ellie's face, he could see that she too, was taken aback by the state of the property, though never voicing it.

Jenson pressed the doorbell, his hand reaching in through the hole he had already made in the cobweb. A few seconds later, the front door opened. His mind went into overdrive. Were they expecting him? Could this be an ambush of Stem soldiers? But just like the night before, the older lady he had spoken to appeared.

She stepped back out into the glass protection of her porch. Her appearance displaying a presentable attire this time, all kitted out in her Sunday best. A long black skirt, crème blouse and a matching black jacket. And a black head scarf camouflaging most of her grey hairline.

'Davrin?' She called, tilting her head back and looking up the stairs.

It was a frail call, but she seemed different this time, somehow friendlier. She pressed forward, and unlike last night, she lifted the latch. She slowly slid the door across, the same door she previously refused to unlock last night. A slight difficulty in her movement, but neither Jenson nor Ellie felt the urge to intrude. A determination written across her face, detailing a vulnerability but requesting to be left alone.

'Hello,' she said, 'I don't mean to be rude, but you must excuse me, I'm late for Mass. Not that you youngsters believe in God anymore. But somebody has to pray for what is left in this world.'

She stepped out past Jenson and Ellie, nodding at them both. She then paused and turned round,

'Well, don't be shy, what are you waiting for? Go straight in through to the kitchen. He'll be right down.'

Jenson was surprised with the display of hospitality. It was a far cry from last night. This woman who refused to unlock her porch door, had now openly invited them into her home without question. Something wasn't right, but if he wanted Davrin's help, he needed to enter.

The old woman continued down the mossy pathway leaving her presence felt.

Jenson and Ellie looked at each other before stepping into the neglected house and shutting the door, closing it off from the outside world.

Everything inside was outdated, just as stale as the exterior, from the carpets to the wallpaper. But a sentimental yearning came flooding back. Jenson recognised the vinyl floor in the kitchen. It reminded him of his late grandparent's house. The room was rustic but homely with the aroma of home baking in the air.

Jenson and Ellie sat down at the small dining table, alone, and waiting to be addressed further.

And just as they familiarised themselves with their settings, the kitchen door creaked open. Davrin entered.

'Hey,' he said, taking a quick look at them both before dropping his head and walking past them towards the counter.

He picked up an old kettle, filling it with water and dropping it back on the coil. He then pulled out a chair and sat down.

'Look, Davrin,' Jenson started. The ice finally breaking. 'Thank you for listening to us today. I don't know what has changed your mind, but I am so grateful that you are giving us a second chance. As I said last night, I really need your help. I'm not too sure if you know who this is? This is Ellie. She's a friend. She's here helping me.'

Davrin lifted his head up. He took one glance at Ellie and nodded. He then lowered his head again and began to create a disorder amongst the kitchen table, laboriously sifting through the arranged photographs. His eyes focusing and eventually picking one up. He handed it to Jenson.

'That's me and my mother,' he said, staring at the back of the photo as Jenson began to examine it.

It was a picture of a woman with long straight black hair. She was holding a baby.

Jenson guessed the woman could not have been much older than him in the picture. She looked so young, holding a tiny baby all wrapped up in a blue knitted blanket. He was unsure as to why he was presented with this.

'This was the last photo taken of her before she got sick,' Davrin clarified. His eyeline now attaching to theirs for the first time.

Jenson could see the inflammation around his green eyes. Piercing as they were, the redness somehow muted their existence. He looked as if he had been crying.

'I'm so sorry Davrin,' Jenson said. 'What happened to her?'

The whistling from the kettle startled Jenson and Ellie.

'Tea anyone?' Davrin offered.

'Please, let me make it,' Ellie suggested, placing her hand on top of his.

136

She felt so sorry for this boy. She also felt uncomfortable. It was as if she had just walked in on something, a situation she knew absolutely nothing about. She needed a distraction—anything—something to occupy herself and leave these two boys to talk.

She stood up from the kitchen table and set about making the tea.

Jenson passed the photo back. Davrin looked at it once more. His eyes staring beyond the picture.

'After my Mum had me, I dunno...something happened to her. She became really sick. I never knew any of this until this morning. My Nan had told me she died when I was born. She only told me the truth today because she said it was time, time I needed to know. When my mother had me, she changed. She couldn't sleep. She kept saying people were in her dreams and demons who wanted to do bad things. She went crazy.'

Davrin paused. A tear dropped from his eye. He quickly mopped it away, trying to conceal the hurt and sorrow from it all. But it was too late. He continued,

'It was me, my Mum and my Nan. My Nan said my mother had some sort of involvement into the deaths of a young couple and their child. She was so crazy, the police came and locked her up. Nan said, when she went to visit her, she was hysterical, voices talking to her in her head. After a while of taking the medication, she forgot about me. My Nan said it was easier this way. She was never going to get better. Stem couldn't even help her. So it was best I didn't know. She lied to me all these years.'

Davrin looked past Jenson as the teardrop had now multiplied. A stream fell down his cheek. But he made no attempt to hide it this time. He just sat there.

Jenson didn't know what to say. He remembered Callum telling him a story not so different from this one.

Could this person be Stephanie? Could his mother be the one who started this whole Dream-death disease? He thought.

Ellie returned to the table with two cups of tea, placing them both out in front of each teenager. She didn't know what to say either, so she just blurted out what came to mind first,

'I'm so sorry Davrin,' she said. 'Is she still alive, your mother?'

'Yes. She's been in that mental place all this time, the one up near the summit, St. Anita's. My Nan said she hasn't been up there in months. She doesn't visit as much anymore. She says her mind isn't right. Stem did tests on her in the early days. And with all the medication she's on now, she barely recognises anyone. It's like she's a different person. How could she leave her there to rot? How could she stop visiting?'

Davrin took a sip of tea.

'Why is your Nan only telling you this now?' Jenson asked.

Davrin stared back at him.

Jenson felt unnerved.

'I dunno.' Davrin answered. 'It's strange. I heard the phone ringing late last night. My Nan was talking to someone. I thought one of her church friends had died but when I asked her this morning, she said no one had died. She said it was an old friend. And then she told me all about my Mum, telling me it was the right time. We rarely get phone calls, especially so late at night. Somebody must have said something. Someone must know what's going on. And then my Nan brought your name up. She said I should help you.'

Jenson was dumbstruck, as was Ellie.

'Did she say why you should help us—help me?'

'Nope,' Davrin answered.

He lifted his cup again and drank some more. 'Thank you. This is a nice cup of tea.'

138

Chapter 24

Ethan was nervous. He could feel his whole-body tremble. It was either anxiety setting in, or else the aftermath of being thrown from a moving vehicle last night. Perhaps a bit of both. He curled his fingers around the banister and proceeded to descend.

Reaching the bottom of the stairs, he could see his father's legs jutting out from the room. Each folded with a soft kicking motion of his foot. His face masked by the angle of the room. Ethan knew his father wanted him and he knew he could be in serious trouble. He would have preferred a scolding, but that wasn't his father's style. The waited silence was much worse.

Ethan stood in the doorway feeling somewhat underdressed. His father was sitting there in his committed black suit and tie, a chosen attire to command presence in any room.

'Good morning son, how are you feeling today?' He asked.

To any spectator, this greeting would have been of genuine concern. But his father's tone insinuated scepticism. His father's leg now reducing the swing to a rest. His eyes homing in on his son. The questioning was about to begin.

'A bit sore but okay,' Ethan replied. His hesitancy showing.

'Well, don't worry son, I've gotten rid of the soldier who shot you with the tranquiliser dart. Come in. Sit down and tell me everything,' he ordered.

Ethan's mother was gesturing him over to the chaise lounge, her tapping on the cushion beside her provoking his direction. An artificial smile on her face, claiming encouragement, but

Ethan knew this was an act. It was a cued response she had rehearsed down to a T.

'The last bit of it is hazy,' Ethan answered, sitting down beside his mother. A supportive hand reaching out to take hold of his.

Ethan had always felt sorry for his mother. Growing up, he watched his parent's relationship evolve into a lobsided one. Comrades harnessed with different strings. An equal understanding committed, but his mother always obeying her superior. For just like himself, his mother was in two minds about her husband's work. Yes, it seemed to be for the benefit of mankind, but at what cost?

For Ethan and his mother both lived in fear of the man they shared a home with, the leader of this dominant organisation. Who knew what the consequences disobedience would bring?

Ethan continued.

'Jenson picked me up with two others and we went to the Falls-way, to a house. It's where Davrin lives. I don't know why they wanted to go there. When I asked Jenson, his friend— the girl—she kept butting in. Then we got chased and I don't remember much after that.'

Ethan shrugged his shoulders.

'Why did Jenson want to go see this Davrin boy in the Falls-way?' His father asked.

'I don't know. I couldn't get a proper answer.'

'And are you sure you're me telling the truth?'

'Yes, I swear.'

'The last time you told me he was at the Plaza, he never showed?'

'I don't know what happened. Something must have spooked him. But this time was different. He trusts me, I know he does. But his friend, the girl, she wouldn't leave me alone

140

with him. I'm not sure why she disliked me, but she never gave me a chance to find out.'

'Okay,' his father replied. 'You remember where this boy lives?'

'Yes.'

'Good. You can show me. I want to have a word with him.'

Ethan walked past his father and out the front door to the waiting black car outside.

His father's right-hand man was leaning against the back passenger door. 'George' had a strong presence to match his physique. He was dressed in a similar black suit and tie, but with shaded glasses, refusing to reveal any assurances.

'Hey George,' Ethan greeted quietly as the large bald man opened the door.

'Ethan,' George acknowledged in a deep tone, nodding his head as Ethan hopped into the back seat. The tinted windows cloaking his involvement as George sealed him in. The door mechanically locking and securing his contribution.

Ethan felt he was going on a secret mission, a mission he knew would not end well.

Another suited man Ethan had never seen before was sitting in the driver's seat.

'The Falls-way,' his father instructed as he hunched down into the back seat, beside his son.

'Okay Mr White,' the driver said, turning on the ignition.

The journey lacked conversation as they drove towards the Falls-way. Ethan sat there, as quiet as a mouse. His eyes never leaving the back of the headrest.

His father exhibiting his disengagement, proving his phone to be of greater importance than his son.

Only moments away, George retrieved a handgun from the inside of his suit jacket. He checked the ammunition and then slid it back into the holster.

'We're coming up to the Falls-way, Sir,' the driver said.

Ethan's father looked at his son without saying a word, expecting him to give the direction from here on in, which he did.

They pulled up outside Davrin's home. A questionable silence loomed as Ethan was unsure of what would happen next.

George got out of the car and stepped round to open the back door.

'Stay here son,' his father ordered as he got out of the car.

Both he and George walked up the mossy pathway towards the front door.

Ethan looked out through the tinted window of the car, watching on in secrecy as his father began fixing his jacket while George stood there poised, both waiting outside the front porch.

'Can I help you?' A voice sounded from the garden behind the two men.

It was Davrin's Nan. She began to stroll cautiously up the garden path towards them. Her judgement questioning their motives.

'Hello, my name is Payton White. I am the CEO of Stem Industries. I would like to speak to Davrin. Is he home?'

Davrin's Nan became increasingly suspicious. Her thoughts provoked a sudden threat. These two men were blocking her entrance. Both dressed in professional suits, standing at her door, looking for her grandson. And not even a 'please' in his sentence.

142

'And what do you need to speak to him about?' She questioned. Her tone becoming nervous now.

Payton White smirked. He could sense this.

'And you are?' He asked. His refusal to answer her question added substance to his arrival. He held out his hand.

'Margaret,' she answered, extending hers, and gently shaking his. She could feel the strong hold on her delicate hand.

'I'm just home from church so let me see if he's in. You can wait out here,' she insisted.

Margaret dissected the men. Her arms ruffling each suit as she pushed them out of the way,

'Some manners please,' she suggested, stepping into the porch.

Fixing the key in place, she twisted her wrist. The front door opened.

She retreated inside, now losing the feeling of protection, a place that once provided sanctuary.

Unable to seal the door behind her, she turned around.

George's foot had followed her. It was now perched against the small step, preventing the gap from closing.

'Do you mind?' She cautioned, powerless to this force.

'No, not at all, do you?' George retaliated.

His hand pressing up against the stain glass window for additional support.

And without any further response, he pushed forward with great strength, sending Margaret flying towards the stairs.

Stumbling forward, she smashed her temple into the bottom spindle. Her head scarf slipping from her head as the blood began to reveal itself from underneath.

'DAVRIN!' She roared. A panic in her scream, hoping to tip off her grandson.

143

George overruled any further warning. He took out his gun and delivered a hard blow to the back of her head.

She fell to the floor.

'Stop!' Payton instructed, just as George was about to administer another blow.

He then motioned with a head gesture for George to search the house.

'We don't want to hurt you,' he cautioned. 'I'll ask you again, where is Davrin?'

Margaret looked up at him; she was terrified. Her vision began to blur. She could feel the blood seeping down her neck. But she knew she had to say something before it was too late.

'You'll never take him,' she said.

'I think that's where you're wrong Margaret. I can do what I like.'

'Over my dead body!'

'That can always be arranged.' Payton replied.

Chapter 25

'We're hoping you can do what you did to Joey? If you can somehow get into someone's head or access their dreams, to talk to them, contact them?'

Davrin was a little unsure of what Jenson was asking him to do. He had been brought up to speed now. The journey back to the abandoned church had been somewhat interesting and revealing. Jenson refused to leave any stone unturned.

'I'm not sure?' Davrin answered. 'It was the first time anything like that has happened to me. I've been having these strange dreams lately. I was so angry at him for cracking the screen on my I-pad. I wasn't sleeping well, so I think I drifted off in class. I fell asleep. And then, I just remember waking up, but I was still dreaming. And Joey was there.'

'So what you're saying is you just pictured him and then he ended up in your dream, or you ended up in his?' Jenson asked, trying to piece it all together.

'I think so. I'm not sure.'

'Then you just need to know the person, or see them before you fall asleep?' Chloe interrupted.

'Yes, I suppose, but I don't think it's that simple.'

'Would a picture of Jenson's family be enough?' Chloe suggested.

Before Davrin could reply, Callum spoke,

'So, we get a picture of Jenson's family and then wait for Davrin to fall asleep? He'll contact your parents, presuming they are asleep. We come up with a plan to get them out of Stem, and then we go into hiding? Why don't we use my tranquiliser gun to put you to sleep?'

'Brilliant idea!' Chloe agreed. 'Now all we need is a photo of your family Jenson.'

Callum began to laugh. His sarcastic summary had just been overlooked. And his reaction ignored as Jenson retrieved his phone.

'The screen is cracked from the bike crash, but it still works,' he said.

Callum was amazed that these people, even his sister, had convinced themselves there was a chance that this ridiculous plan could work. He let out a deep sigh.

Chloe gave him a cross look which nobody else identified. But Callum knew this look too well.

'Here,' Jenson said, selecting a photo of his family and passing his phone to Davrin.

Davrin looked down to see the picture of Jenson's family on the cracked phone screen. He, like Callum, believed this plan was slightly outlandish, but as he studied the picture, he noticed that the people in it looked happy. It reminded him of a photo, the picture of his mother holding him as a baby. She, too, looked happy back then.

'I know it's a stab in the dark,' Jenson said, 'but maybe, just maybe, something could happen. Maybe you can communicate with them?'

'I can try, but I can't promise anything,' Davrin said. The pressure now corrupting his mind.

Chloe grabbed the gun.

'So where will we do this?'

'WE?' Callum asked. His unwillingness to accept Chloe's participation had proved great in his remark.

'Yeah, well, I was thinking I could do it with him. Maybe he could find me in a dream, and I could help him, just like we do?'

Callum sniggered,

'You can't be serious Chloe?'

Another silence took over the room.

'You are serious?' He acknowledged. 'You're just as mad as the rest of them. And even if you meet up in this perfect dream? Who's to say Jenson's parents are even asleep? It's a ridiculous plan.'

Callum stood up and began to walk down the aisle.

'Don't mind him, he'll come back once he's cooled off,' Chloe said. 'Now let's get this done.'

The midday light was beaming into the church. Chloe and Davrin lay on top of the sleeping bags, each one placed side by side on the altar floor.

'Do you need to be holding hands or touching?' Ellie suggested. Her gaze startling as she watched on from the bench a few feet away. 'I don't know, but you see those types of things in movies.'

Chloe smiled. She glanced over at the uncomfortable looking Davrin, 'It might help?' She agreed, moving closer and grabbing hold of his hand.

'So you've done this before?' Davrin asked nervously.

'Yep. But only with my brother. Sure, how hard can it be to find each other? I've met you twice now, and if we both just concentrate, you should be able to do it. Just fix your mind on me and this church. We can meet here, and then I'll go with you to find Jenson's family. Hopefully one of them is drugged and asleep in Stem.'

Jenson handed his phone to Chloe. They both took one last glance at his family photo.

'You ready?' He asked.

They both nodded.

Jenson picked up one of the tranquiliser darts he had taken out of the gun. He moved towards Chloe.

'Sorry,' he muttered, sticking the dart into her arm.

Chloe just nodded her head and closed her eyes.

Jenson did the same to Davrin, but Davrin didn't even nod. His eyes were already tightly shut before Jenson could do anything.

The others watched on as the two drifted off into a dreamful sleep.

'We're just going to take Meatloaf outside for a walk and let him do his business,' Ellie explained as she and her father got up from the benches.

They sauntered down towards the main doors, closing them behind and leaving Jenson, Chloe, and Davrin, all alone inside the crumbling church.

~~~

Chloe's eye's opened; she was back in the church.

'HELLO?' She called out, slowly getting to her feet, and glancing round the empty candlelit church. Nightfall had approached causing her to wonder how long she had been out for. Had she even dreamt at all?

'Hello? Anybody?' She repeated, stepping down from the altar steps.

Suddenly, a noise startled her as the church doors squeaked. Her body angled away from the source, but then she remembered why she was here.

'Davrin?' She said. 'Is that you?'

Her voice clamouring with uncertainty as she investigated down the aisle.

No response, she called out again. This time louder as she approached the church doors.

'Anybody there?' She called. Her tone more vigilant now.

She noticed one of the doors flapping from the wind. It was slightly ajar and creaking from side to side.

She pushed the door open but saw nothing. It was all darkness outside.

'CALLUM?' She called out. A black abyss staring back at her.

The church grounds were unanswerable.

Suddenly, a gust of wind blew across her face like a sharp cold sting. Only then did she realise she was, in fact, still dreaming.

A chill went through her body. This was the first time she had dreamt without Callum.

For some strange reason, she began to feel unsafe. It was as if something was watching her from the shadows of the abyss, waiting for her to step outside.

Reluctant to proceed, she stepped back into the church.

Fear stimulated her insides, and she closed the doors behind. She began to panic. Something was different. Something just didn't feel right. Where was Davrin?

She began to scurry towards the altar, the fiery candles leading the way.

But before she had the chance to reach the top, every single candle inside the church blew out. The extinguishing smoke created an even darker cloud from within.

A loud bang sounded.

The two church doors burst open.

A coldness advanced from the outside, and a true darkness drifted in. A darkness Chloe hadn't felt in a long time.

Chapter 26

A soft groan caused Jenson to react. He turned his body round to face the pair lying on the ground. It was Chloe; she was twitching. Jenson didn't know what to think. Was this a normal feature amongst these 'Soul-Searchers' and 'Dream-Drifters' as they tracked each other down?

He just sat there observing.

Chloe jerked a little more and began to mumble something under her breath.

Jenson glanced over at Davrin, but he was lying there motionless.

He stood up from the nearby bench and walked over to where the two of them lay.

Chloe's mumbling was becoming louder but he couldn't make any sense of what she was trying to say. He knelt beside her and leaned in closer, listening carefully.

'Callum?' She said in a soft whisper. 'Callum?' She said again. Her body began to move more rigorously.

Jenson became worried—he felt as if something was wrong.

'Chloe?' He responded.

He began to shake her gently. But her body trembled even more. So he shook her more firmly.

He started to shout her name, hoping she would hear him and waken. Suddenly she screamed and this time Jenson could hear her as clear as day,

'CALLUM! HELP!' She shouted.

The next thing Jenson felt was a sharp shove in the back. He was thrown along the altar floor.

He gathered himself and turned around.

He saw Callum dropping to his knees beside his sister.

'WHAT HAPPENED?' Callum shouted, trying to get his sister to sit up.

He saw the tranquiliser dart sticking out of her arm.

'FOOLS!' He barked, yanking the dart out of her arm, and flinging it across the floor to where Jenson was sprawled.

The phial broke, causing whatever liquid was left in it to seep out onto the floor.

'CHLOE?' He shouted. He had immediately taken hold of her shoulders and began to shake her sleeping body. 'CHLOE—WAKE UP!'

His violent shaking caused Jenson to panic even further.

'QUICK! GIVE ME THE GUN—YOU DON'T KNOW WHAT YOU'VE DONE!' Callum roared.

Jenson could hardly believe what was enfolding right before his eyes. He stood up,

'There are no more bullets left,' he said, not knowing what else to do.

'WHAT?' Callum yelled.

'We used the last of them.' Jenson answered.

Callum let go of Chloe, dropping her hard on the altar floor. He then ran over to where he had thrown the dart.

'SHIT!' He snapped.

He saw the broken pieces from where the phial had smashed.

He turned around to face Jenson. But just as he did, he unexpectedly saw Jenson charge at him.

Jenson leapt on top of him before he could do anything. A loud thud sounded as both boys wrestled to the ground.

Callum felt a sharp sting in his gut. His vision blurred as Jenson got to his feet. He couldn't move. His body drooped and began to sink deeper into the ground.

Jenson watched on as he stood over his body, a tranquiliser dart jutting out from Callum's abdomen.

Jenson wasn't sure if he had done the right thing. But he knew he had to do something.

The church doors swung open as Ellie, Wardy and Meatloaf came bursting in. They had returned from their walk and had heard the commotion from outside.

'WHAT'S WRONG?' Ellie shouted, as they ran up the aisle. 'We heard screams…'

They froze in complete shock. They could see the three bodies on the altar, and Chloe now in the throes of a seizure.

'I don't know what happened?' Jenson answered. 'She just started to freak out in her sleep. I couldn't wake her. She called out for Callum and when he came in, I stuck a dart in him. I took it from Davrin's arm. I thought he could…I don't know…help her or something?'

Chloe's body suddenly rolled over onto her front, face down. Her hands were moving uncontrollably. Then her body slid across the altar floor, as if some invisible force had been dragging her.

'What do we do?' Ellie squealed.

Unexpectedly, the swoosh of fabric took hold of Chloe and ripped a seem down her back. An incision pierced her flesh. As if by magic, an obscure object, invisible to the naked eye, had sliced down her shoulder blade, blood oozing out.

Ellie gasped for air as Meatloaf began to bark.

'How is this even happening?' Ellie responded.

'It's all my fault!' Jenson bellowed.

His hands placed either side of his temple as he stood over Chloe's body.

Callum's body began to twitch now, just as Chloe's had done earlier.

Jenson knelt beside Chloe and cupped her head, trying to secure it from any further damage.

'Please Chloe! I need you to wake up. I'm sorry, please wake up!'

He sat there, rocking her twitching body as Ellie removed her cardigan and applied pressure to the wound.

Davrin woke up. His sleepy eyes shifting around the room, struggling to understand what was happening.

'What's going on?' He asked, moving away in a backwards crawl, the commotion becoming too much for him. He didn't know what was going on, or whether he was awake, or even if he was still dreaming. But nobody took notice of him. They were all too busy with the event unfolding.

Davrin collided with the altar table and just sat there, watching on, terrified to move.

Jenson felt the trembling in Chloe's body ease. He realised how tight he had been holding her. He released his grip, extending her body out from his chest and holding her upright.

'I think she's coming round,' he declared, watching her, and waiting to see if she was alright. The effects of the sedation wearing off, but there was nothing else he could do. He had to remain patient.

Chloe's eyes opened gradually.

'Callum?' She whispered in a low resonating voice.

Jenson looked at Callum's twitching body.

'Quick, someone take the bullet out of his stomach. Wake him up!'

Wardy hobbled over to Callum while Jenson brushed away a strand of hair from Chloe's face. He accidently smeared some blood from the wound on her shoulder blade, staining it onto her forehead.

'I'll get my first-aid kit from the boot,' Ellie declared as she went sprinting down the aisle.

'Chloe, are you alright?' Jenson asked, still nervous and not knowing if she was, in fact, okay.

'Yeah, I think so,' she replied. Her voice was still drowsy. 'Where is Callum?'

Jenson looked at the motionless body of her brother.

Just then, Wardy gave him a thumbs-up, confirming that Callum was alright.

Jenson smiled at Chloe.

'He's gonna be okay,' he said.

Callum woke, and as soon as he realised where he was, he got to his feet and sluggishly moved over to his sister.

'I knew this was a bad idea,' he scolded, grabbing Chloe from Jenson and giving him an angry look. 'I told you, but you wouldn't listen,' he said to Chloe, 'I told you this was stupid.'

He noticed the blood on her forehead,

'Are you okay?'

'My back is sore,' she said, wincing with the pain.

Callum sat her up straight. He saw the gash on her shoulder blade and the blood seeping from the pore. He pulled her into him and began to plead.

'I'm so sorry Chloe. I should have been there for you.'

'You were there for me Callum, you were there just in time,' she replied. 'Did you see it?'

'Yes,' Callum answered, referring to the demon. 'I saw it.'

'This one was different from the one that took Carly,' Chloe said.

'I know. You should never go to sleep without me.'

Callum was annoyed at himself for letting her do this alone.

'It's all my fault,' Jenson said. 'I'm sorry. I shouldn't have asked you to do this for me.'

'Yes, it is your fault—if it wasn't for you, this would never have happened!'

'Callum, please stop,' Chloe requested. 'It was my decision, so don't be blaming Jenson.'

They all turned towards the two main church doors when they heard them smash open.

Ellie burst in, holding a first-aid box under her arm,

'Are you alright?' She asked. 'Let me have a look at the damage. What happened?'

'It's those demons, they're back,' Callum explained.

'I don't think they ever left Callum. I think they were waiting for one of us, to get us on our own. This felt like no other dream.'

Davrin got to his feet and moved closer.

'I'm sorry I couldn't find you,' he said. The guilt striking him in the chest as if it was his fault.

'It's okay, Davrin, you're new to this, you'll get better at it,' Chloe replied.

'What do you mean when you say demons?' He asked.

'Sorry Davrin,' Chloe uttered, realising that nobody had asked if he was alright; after all, he was trying to help as well.

'A demon hunted us in our dreams when we were younger. It killed our sister. It has something to do with those Dream-deaths, but we don't know why? And ever since that night, myself and Callum, we never leave each other's side, even when we're dreaming. But this was a different demon. It felt as if it was ready to strike, as if it knew I was alone. They're a lot stronger than I remembered.'

Jenson picked up his grey hoodie and put it on.

'Thank you, all of you, thank you for your help, but I'm just gonna go straight into Stem Industries and take my chances. I just can't let any of you get hurt again. Maybe if I hand myself

155

over, they'll let my family go? Chloe, I'm so sorry again for what happened to you today.'

'Wait, Jenson!' Ellie called as she gestured for Callum to hold the bandaging up to Chloe's back.

She ran down the aisle after Jenson.

'Let's get one thing straight here,' she added, now catching up on him.

For the first time, Jenson could see the teacher in her. He now felt like a schoolboy about to be told off.

'Do you think they will just hand your family back? What about Robyn? She is a Non-dreamer. They want you both. They'll make you all disappear, just like my friend and her family! No matter how many people see you walk into that building, they will cover it up. They have the power. You'll never be seen again.'

With her bloodstained surgical gloves, Ellie pointed to the church doors and raised her voice.

'There's the door and if anybody wants to leave, they can go straight ahead. Nobody is stopping anyone from leaving. My friend was taken. I'm sure everyone else has their own reason for being here, but I for one am sick of Stem Industries. They are picking us all off, one by one, looking for some stupid cure, a drug that might never exist. People are too scared to stand up to them.'

Meatloaf barked at them.

'That's it boy, you tell him,' Wardy mouthed.

This lecture had given Jenson a boost of encouragement. It had given him a reason to stay.

They both returned to the altar.

'Don't worry, we'll find another way Jenson,' Ellie said, positioning herself behind Chloe and continuing to mend her wound.

'I'm so sorry,' Jenson repeated, looking at Chloe and then at Callum.

'Well, at least you put me to sleep so I got the chance to distract that demon,' Callum said.

Chloe smiled. She could sense her brother's forgiveness for Jenson, looming inside.

'My mother?' A voice called out.

Davrin had got to his feet, his back leaning in against the altar table. The guilt of not being able to help weighing heavily on his mind.

'What about your mother?' Callum questioned.

'My Nan said that she got so deep into her dreams, it was like a reality. Maybe she can help?'

'But Davrin, she's in that place, St Anita's,' Jenson replied. 'How would you know if she'd recognise you? She has never seen you, the way you are now. You were only a baby when she left. She's been in there all this time, and who knows what kind of drugs she's been given?'

'I know Jenson. I've thought about it all. But ever since I heard about her this morning, I…I don't know, I just can't think of anything else but meeting her. I want to know what she looks like, what she sounds like? And if I can't help you, maybe she can somehow?'

Davrin was beginning to get emotional.

Jenson thought hard about another plan, but he came up short; there was no other plan. Maybe this was his only choice.

'Are you sure you want to do this?' He asked, giving Davrin every chance to back out.

'I'm sure.'

'Okay then, let's go meet your Mum.'

Chapter 27

St Anita's looked more like a prison than a psychiatric hospital. And even though the sun was shining, the whole place looked dull and unwelcoming.

Ellie rolled down the window as the car pulled up towards the main gates. Jenson and Davrin both sat patiently.

They were greeted by a waving guard who lifted the barrier and gestured them to keep moving.

Jenson looked out the window and saw that surrounding the main structure of this eerie site, there were other sections which looked newly built. There seemed to be additional one and two-storey buildings adjoining the main one, with even more structures scattered throughout the grounds. Perhaps an addition to the highlighted centrepiece, a result of the dreaming phenomenon and people losing their minds within their dreams.

Jenson felt a little spooked. It was his first time passing the gates of the "hell-hole", as it was otherwise known,

'I've heard so much about this place,' he declared.

'Ever since dreams became people's reality, there is a huge demand for these places and they've had to expand,' Ellie answered. 'I feel sorry for the people in here. It's like when your head gets so messed up from your dreams, they just lock you up in here and throw away the key.'

A panic poured across her face. She had not meant to be so brutal, especially considering Davrin was here to see his mother. She had her words, and they were already out there, something she could not take back. She just hoped Davrin had not been listening so attentively.

They pulled into a car space right outside the dreary looking main building. They then got out and walked into the reception area with an unfamiliar plan.

An uninteresting black and white marble floor met them inside the entrance. And an even more uninteresting waiting room led on from that, with a reception desk slumped in the middle, a doorway either side. The room looked vacant until an aging nurse stretched her neck up over the partition,

'Hello, can I help you?' She asked, her tone flat. Her gaze returning to the paperwork out in front.

The place was quiet, oddly quiet, not that any of them knew what to expect, neither one acquainted with such predicament.

'Hello, yes please,' Ellie replied, while Jenson and Davrin stood back. 'We are doing a student study on a patient here,' she added, handing over her teacher's I.D.

This was the best plan she had come up with in such short notice. Davrin had never visited his mother before and had no identification on him, so the truth would surely question disbelief.

'We are here to see a specific patient of yours—Miss Belshaw,' Ellie continued.

'I'm sorry I don't see any authorisation here Miss Ward,' the nurse muttered, searching through some papers, and handing back her I.D.

'There must be some mistake. Can you please check again?'

Ellie knew there had been no request made. She hoped some sort of a mix up would present a lucky break.

'It has to be there, maybe he got the day wrong? I was told this morning that the phone call was made, and the papers were sent over.'

'What papers?' The nurse asked. 'And what sort of school send their student's out on a Sunday?'

159

Ellie could feel her throat tighten. These lies were digging her deeper into a hole, soon unable to ever climb out. Her component seemingly too strong for any deception.

'Extra curriculum.' She replied. Her face producing a friendly smile. 'I assumed papers were filed for this visit?'

'Filed by whom?'

Another great retaliation.

'Franklin......Professor William Franklin,' Ellie answered. A lecturer from her old college faculty, a reputative person she had hoped would impress this stranger.

'I'm afraid I've never heard of a Professor William Franklin,' the nurse muttered.

She flicked over a page in her logbook, glancing at the script. She then looked up at Ellie again, her vague response waiting for a plausible answer.

Ellie could feel the hairs on the back of her neck stand up. She had just been outplayed. And with one last attempt to gain access, she turned round and waved for Davrin to approach.

'Look, I apologise for lying, you've caught me out. Let me start over. This is Davrin Belshaw, Miss Belshaw's son,' she confessed, presenting Davrin as he approached the desk. 'I'll leave my bag here. You can hold onto all my valuables.'

Ellie dropped her bag gently down on top of the desk, hoping it would place nicely as a bargaining chip.

'Davrin is the real reason we are here. He would just like to see his mother, if only for a few minutes. We can wait here. It can be a supervised visit of course? I apologise I lied, but he has no I.D. on him, so I figured you wouldn't believe us even if we told you the truth.'

The nurse's eyes squinting, curious of the oncoming boy. She spoke,

'You can start all over and as many times as you like, but why would I believe you now after you've just admitted to being an untrustworthy person?'

160

'I assure you I am not untrustworthy. I have apologised. This was a bad move on my behalf, to lie, but I am owning up to that now. Please do not take it out on this young boy. He just wants to see his mother.'

'How do I know you're not lying to me again?'

'You have my word.'

Ellie put her hand up against her chest, gesturing a solum promise. But the nurse didn't seem to care.

'I've worked here at St. Anita's from the day we opened. I even remember Miss Belshaw being admitted, God love her soul. And throughout all these years, there has never been any mention of her having a son. So, do you want to tell me again why you are really here before I call security?'

'My grandmother,' Davrin muttered. His shy frame standing tall against the reception desk.

'You'll have to speak up son,' the nurse demanded, not quite hearing him.

'He said his grandmother.' Ellie interrupted. 'She frequently came to visit her daughter, Miss Belshaw.'

'I wasn't talking to you.' The nurse continued. 'I don't trust you, so if you have any hope in seeing anyone, then I'd advise you to keep quiet. What sort of example is this to show to young boys?'

Ellie got the message. She inched away from the counter, leaving Davrin to fend for himself.

'My grandmother, Margaret Belshaw,' Davrin declared.

'Margaret?' The nurse duplicated, a hint of recognition in her voice.

'Ah yes, that's her,' Ellie answered. 'You know Margaret?'

The nurse shifted her head, giving Ellie a scolding look.

Ellie pressed her lips firmly together. And with one hand signal raising again, she backed away even further from the desk, slowly lowering her apologetic signal yet again.

'You know my grandmother?' Davrin questioned.

161

'I do, and quite well,' the nurse said, 'but she's never mentioned you, not a single word of having a grandson in all these years of visiting.'

'But she is my grandmother, I assure you of that.'

'Then why isn't she here with you? Are you lying to me as well?'

Davrin went silent. He was lost for words.

'Well, you see......Gail,' Ellie interrupted again, stepping forward and noticing the nurses name tag. Her protective teacher instinct kicking in once more. She knew she was warned off, but she felt she needed to intervene again. This nurse seemed too durable, with enough evidence to distrust them all.

'I'm sure you're a mother yourself who is fortunate not to be in Margaret's position. But if you were, I'm sure you can see why she never mentioned Davrin, well with how his mother was and all that. She just wanted to protect her grandson from the truth.'

'And I have to protect my patients in here,' the nurse instructed. 'Now how many times do I have to tell you to keep quiet? This conversation is over. I am not, and will not, allow any of you entry without authorisation. Am I clear?'

'Can you not find it in your heart to let him in, please?' Ellie begged. 'If only for a moment.'

'Get the hell out of this reception area now. I have just pressed the security button.'

'Right, well, thanks for nothing Gail,' Ellie barked, snatching up her I.D. and handbag. 'Come on guys, this woman is heartless.'

~~~

The outside air brought with it a taste of defeat.

162

'I'm sorry guys,' Ellie began. 'I opened my big mouth too many times. I was trying my best to convince her. Perhaps if I had of just stayed quiet like she asked.'

'I don't think there was anything you could have done to persuade her,' Jenson answered. 'She was a tough nut to crack.'

'So what now?' Ellie asked.

She turned to Davrin who looked more deflated than any of them.

'Alrigh?' A male voice called out.

A uniformed man came walking towards them. His chiselled face was framed with stylishly brown hair flopped to one side. He must have been in his late twenties, not much older than Ellie.

'I'm sorry, we don't want to cause any trouble,' Ellie confirmed. 'We were just leaving.'

'Why so soon?' The man asked.

'I'm sorry?' Ellie questioned. She figured this man was part of the security team, called in to escort them off the premises.

'I couldn't help but overhear some of your conversation in der abou Miss Belshaw,' he said in his broad Irish accent.

'Yes, but that nurse wouldn't let us in,' Ellie explained.

'Ah Gail is alrigh, but she's a stickler for da rules. I'm Henry, what are your names?'

'My name is Ellie. And this is Jenson and Davrin.'

'Ya do look like your mudder,' Henry acknowledged as he finished shaking Jenson's hand and turned to shake Davrin's.

'So you believe us then?' Ellie asked.

'Well I believe sometin strange is goin on wit dis place an Stem industries. I certainly don't tink two young lads an a good lookin woman like yourself have anytin to do wit it.'

Ellie blushed.

'But that nurse back in there,' Jenson said. 'She won't let us in.'

'Well lucky for you's, Miss Belshaw isn't in der. She's stayin in one of da outhouse buildins.'

'Why are you telling us this?' Ellie asked.

'Well for one, I know der is no such ting as your school exercise. So call me curious, but I'll bring ya ta see Miss Belshaw if you's tell me exactly why ya's are here?'

'I'm not sure you'd believe us,' Ellie declared.

'I've been a nurse here for five years now. Ya don't tink I've seen some weird shit in dat time? Why don't ya try me! Come on, let's go. Ya can tell me on da way. We need ta move before de firin squad come.'

Chapter 28

Henry brought them on what felt like a hiking trail. The barren landscape dotted with wild pampas, revealing just how forgotten this place was. The leisurely walk led them to the outskirts of the border, enabling Ellie to have another stab at her convincing methods, although she had an advantage this time, she didn't need to lie.

They approached a single-story shelter, an outhouse building with barred windows and branded stripes, painted in almost identical colour to the window frames. It looked more like a secure bungalow rather than a hospital unit.

'Here we go,' Henry informed them.

He unclipped a swipe card from his belt and scanned it to a device on the wall. An unlocking sound clicked, and the front door opened.

'Deez are de longest patients here in St Anita's—well, ever since da Dream-death disease started,' he said, gesturing for the others to quickly move inside.

He took one last look beyond the grassland vegetation and joined them inside the entrance hall, locking the door behind.

They continued down through a narrow hallway with doors aligned on either side, each door rendering a different serial number.

'Der are six patients in dis unit. We're not allowed to put der names up on da doors,' Henry explained, his fingers outstretching like inverted commas hanging over his head. "Security reasons", he added. 'But as ya can see der are identity numbers to help us distinguish whose room is whose. Stephanie's room is just down here on da righ.'

Henry had just passed a room on his left when suddenly the door unlocked.

Ellie was startled. She launched herself diagonally out of the way, pressing in against the wall opposite.

Both Jenson and Davrin stood still, neither one eager to pass the door.

A frizzy haired man in a white gown stood in the doorway as a nurse followed him.

'Blaine, wait up,' she said, slipping out of the doorway and grabbing hold of his hand.

'Hey Stella, hey Blaine,' Henry saluted, circling back towards the sudden disturbance.

'Hey Henry.' The female nurse greeted.

'Henry…..I…..I……I saw her again last night,' the patient denounced. His stammering affecting his flow of speech. 'I'll only t…..t….tell you. She came for my tooth.'

Blaine stood there, his mouth stretched open, his jaw prolonged as he tried to show Henry the gap in his gum from where his tooth had been plucked.

'Come on Blaine, we've to go for your daily exercise,' the nurse instructed, leading him away towards the entrance.

'I'll come find ya later Blaine. Ya can tell me all abou it,' Henry replied, waving back to the patient.

'Dat fella has insomnia,' he whispered to Ellie. 'Says he won't sleep in case da demons get him. He says he see's fairies in his dreams. He pulls out his own teeth so he can give it to dem, like some sort of ritual. But we always find them hidden somewhere in his room. Shouldn't last much longer as he doesn't have many teet left. Don't know what he's gonna do den? We'll probably have to double up on his care for our own safety. He better not tink he can take ours.'

166

Henry smirked, his facial expression implying just how crazy this patient was.

'Dat's what happens when Stem Industries gets a hold of ya, an den dumps ya in here. He'll only talk to me abou it because he says I'm Irish, an fairy's originated in Ireland. He loves fairies, but da man's crazy, crazy but harmless. Anyway, follow me,' he said, continuing down the narrow corridor towards Davrin's mother's room.

Jenson hung back as the others followed Henry down the corridor. His attention was drawn to the opened door. He stepped forward and nudged the door in a little further, his curiosity hijacking any concern.

The room resembled the innermost part of an art studio. Pictures hanging from every panel. A chaotic disorder of artwork powered by a creative mind, and all scattered around the walls. The drawings, depicting fairies, a whiter shade of pale, and each charcoal creation just as imaginative as the next. Jenson was fascinated. The imagery, each picture, reigniting a fire from within. His mind, provoking his thoughts, taunting him to dig deeper into his childhood. He felt as if he had seen these characters before, the big eyes, the ears, the long hair. But whatever the memory was, it had been suppressed for far too long, suppressed beyond any recognition.

Jenson stepped closer, allowing his mind the freedom to intercept. But the more he concentrated, the more frustrated he became. Then suddenly his forehead pulsated. A wave of nausea toppled his balance. He felt dizzy.

'Jenson, you alrigh?' Henry called back.

'Yeah, yeah, I'm fine,' he replied.

His hand resting firmly against the door. The framework enabling his weight to distribute evenly. He closed his eyes. He stood there motionless, his hand still gripping onto the door. He shook his head. And with one deep breath, he managed to dislodge the oncoming migraine and extract himself from the doorway. He hurried forward to join up with the others, leaving the uncertain canvasses behind.

'I'm sorry but it's only one visitor at a time. An I'm tinkin it's only Davrin here who wants to go in?' Henry questioned, not waiting on a reply. 'You two can wait over der,' he said, pointing his swipe card at the two chairs sitting in the hallway opposite.'

'Thank you,' Ellie replied, as she and Jenson made their way over.

'Ya ready?' Henry said, swiping his card against the door panel and taking one last glance at Davrin.

The door opened.

'I'll just come in ta introduce ya, den I'll leave ya. But I'll be righ outside, so if ya need anytin, just call.'

Henry examined his watch.

'Your ma hasn't had her midday tablets yet, we're runnin a bit behind schedule. I'm just lettin ya know. Ders notin ta worry abou, but she could be a little off, I suppose. Doze meds she's on are strong, so she's dependent on dem and is probably a little cuckoo da longer she goes witout dem. Don't get too upset if she's not very responsive. Okay?'

Davrin understood. He nodded, and they walked in.

Chapter 29

'Stephanie, ya have a visitor,' Henry said. His friendly tone bringing a calmness to the room.

An overhang of dark hair draped the back of the rocking chair, with speckles of grey trying to smoother the raven colour. Davrin hesitated. He closed the door behind him and watched Henry approach his mother, a 'stranger' who was seated and facing the window.

Her friction suddenly reduced, bringing the rocking chair to a halt.

Henry crouched down on his hunkers beside Stephanie and rested his hand on top of hers.

'Stephanie, ya have a visitor.'

He repeated himself just as she slowly turned her head around the wooden backrest. Her stare was intense. Her eyes edging themselves deep into her brow. Her forehead wrinkled with curiosity. She did not recognise him at all. But Davrin could see himself in her. She had the same eyes as him, only hers were notably faded. She looked like the woman in the photograph holding her baby—holding him. But just as he had grown older, so too, had she. She must have only been a few years older than Ellie, but she looked a hell of a lot older. The grey strands neatly combed within her black hair but trying to overtake the even distribution. And the creased lines on her face giving her an aged character of a hard-working older person. Perhaps it was the paved destruction taking its toll, or the amount of medication that affected her deterioration, but either way, Davrin knew this was his mother sitting there in front of him.

Stephanie shook her head. Her mind unable to recognise the origins of this visit. She spun back around and began to rock the chair once more. Her stare now returning to the window.

Davrin was unsure what would happen inside this room. He didn't know what sort of reaction to expect; he didn't even know what way to react himself. He just stood there nervously.

'Come on over, Davrin, don't be shy,' Henry said, beckoning him.

Davrin stepped forward. His approach had been marked with caution.

His mother remained seated. Her eyeline never leaving the windowpane. She sat there as the chair continued to rock. A pink knitted blanket cocooned her body. It looked like an old blanket, ragged, and stained, but wilted with memory. It looked warm and comfortable all the same.

Henry moved his fingers along Stephanie's arm until he reached her hand. Gently stroking it, he spoke to her once more,

'Stephanie, are ya not gonna say hello?'

'Hello,' she repeated, just like a child would have done if prompted by a parent. Her eyeline still gazing out the window.

'Hi,' Davrin replied hesitantly. His eyes filling with fluids.

Henry could see how distressed he was, statically standing there with his arms down by his side. And an uncomfortable twitching of his fingers.

'Take a seat, Davrin, make yourself at home,' he said, nodding towards the bed as it was the only place to sit other than the floor.

The moment Davrin sat on her bed, Stephanie immediately turned around and looked at him. Her head tilted forward as the tops of her eyes edged towards her eyelids again.

Davrin flinched and immediately stood back up, inching himself off the bed. He could see her mouth tense up. She seemed annoyed.

'Stay seated,' Henry said affably. 'Stephanie, it's okay. He just wants ta sit down. His legs are tired. It's okay for him ta sit on your bed, isn't it? Don't worry Davrin, she won't bite.'

'I won't bite, I won't bite,' Stephanie repeated, an intent expression on her face. She smiled, revealing her stained teeth. She turned back, accidently dropping her blanket and quickly scurrying to lift it back up.

Davrin noticed the food marks on her gown, presumably from the morning feed. He couldn't believe how childlike she was. By the looks of things, she couldn't even feed herself, let alone choose a word to say.

Is this the reason his Nan had stopped coming to visit, he wondered? He also wondered if him coming here was a mistake.

'Righ, Stephanie,' Henry said, as he got to his feet. 'I'm goin ta leave ya's alone. It'll only be for a few minutes. Davrin wants ta get ta know ya, but don't worry, I'll be righ outside if ya need me. It's okay Stephanie.'

He lifted his hand again, reprising the role of stroking her arm.

'Okay, it's okay Stephanie,' she repeated.

Henry slowly walked towards the door, turning back to see the two of them sitting nervously across from each other.

He then left the room.

Davrin looked into his mother's green eyes. She looked like an innocent child, terrified of being left alone with this stranger.

'Mum, it's me, Davrin,' he said.

~~~

Henry walked over to where Jenson and Ellie were sitting, 'Any of ya's smoke?'

'No,' they answered in unison.

'I know it's a bad habit, but I am tryin ta give dem up.'

Henry turned round and started to walk up the corridor,

'I'll be back in a sec,' he said.

'Wait!' Ellie blurted as she got to her feet. 'Can you mind my bag?' She whispered to Jenson.

'Yeah, of course,' Jenson replied, intrigued by her sudden interest. 'Where are you going?'

'I just want to ask Henry some questions.'

Jenson watched her saunter off. He turned back towards the door. He couldn't help but wonder what it would be like to be a fly on the wall, to be able to see this unbelievable reunion, especially under these incredible circumstances.

~~~

Davrin noticed a jug of water positioned at the furthest end away from his mother.

'Would you like some water?' He asked, reaching across the feeding table.

Stephanie looked at the water and then back at Davrin. She didn't say a word. She just kept staring at him and then back to the water.

Davrin was confused. *Was she thirsty or unable to answer the question? He thought.*

He reached over and picked up the empty glass beside the jug. He then picked up the jug and started to pour.

As Davrin had just filled the glass of water, he noticed her lips roll together with pure anticipation.

'Here you go,' he said, handing his mother the glass of water.

She snatched it from him and started to gulp it down, not even taking a breath, like a very thirsty baby that had been waiting for her bottle. She drank it so fast it began to spill down her chin and onto her gown.

172

'Here, let me help,' Davrin suggested, taking the glass of water from her.

He suddenly remembered the photo of his mother holding him as a baby. He had shoved it into his pocket before leaving his house earlier. And sticking his hand into his jeans, he retrieved it.

'I found this photo, well, Nan gave it to me. It's you when you were younger and that's me in your arms. Nan said she had to knit me another one.'

Davrin had no realisation as to what happened to the first blue blanket, a secret Margaret would never share with him.

He gifted the photo to his mother, with full intentions of getting it back.

Her initial reaction was refusal. She didn't know what to do with this object. She simply stared at it for a few moments. But then, releasing her grip from the pink blanket, she snatched it off him. She looked lost, as if trying to understand what this picture meant.

'Yeah, Mum, that's you and me when I was a baby.' Davrin said.

Her eyes widened as she looked from Davrin to the photo. Davrin could see his mother's eyes filling up, just as his were. She seemed to be remembering something from her past, even if it was a small memory. Something from within her was trying to provoke a feeling, but she couldn't say anything.

She stood up now, for the first time. And sluggishly stepping over to her wardrobe, she opened it.

Within moments, she had retrieved what she was looking for. She knew exactly where it was. And then, removing her arm from the wardrobe, there it was, clinging to her grasp, the blue knitted blanket in the photo. The very same blanket that held Davrin in as a baby.

All this emotion finally did a number on Davrin. He began to weep.

At first Stephanie was taken aback by this. She hesitated. But then she stepped over to her chair again and sat down. She didn't know what to do. Her arms pressing tightly in against her body as she held onto the blue blanket.

But Davrin reached out his hands and slipped off the bed. He held onto her knee.

Stephanie released her clasp, opening her arms, and gently placing them around his shoulders.

Davrin reached in further and hugged her.

'I'm so sorry Mum, if I'd have known I would have come to visit you sooner,' he cried. 'I promise I'll get you out of here—you hear me, I promise!'

Davrin felt an overwhelming surge of adrenaline throughout his body, a surge of calming adrenaline. But a desire to do nothing took hold. There was no need to fill the silence anymore. He wanted to live in this precise moment, allowing time to stop, granting a lack of tension or stress to equate a feeling of nothingness.

Unbeknownst to himself, a ripple of light glimmered hope. His eyes shun a bright green. He hugged his mother tightly. And for the first time in a long time, her eyes stimulated. She let go of the blanket and took hold of him. And just like her son, a luminescent green glow ignited.

The room suddenly filled with a signal, but it was short lived. Both Davrin and his mother closed their eyes tightly, just before each could comprehend the light, both distinguishing their glow and allowing a blanket of darkness to elevate their embrace.

Chapter 30

Walking back down the corridor, Ellie noticed that Jenson was slouched forward with his head in his lap, and his elbows resting on top of his knees. Her brow creasing as her concern caused her pace to quicken. And as she got closer, she realised he was having another migraine attack.

'Is he alrigh?' Henry asked. He too noticing something was up.

'You okay, Jenson?' Ellie asked.

'Yeah, I'll be okay, I just need a minute.'

'Are ya on any medication?' Henry asked. 'I can get ya sometin ta ease da pain. We've plenty of dat around here.'

'I lost them,' Jenson replied, realising his tablets must have fallen out of his pocket from the motorbike crash. 'I'll be fine though. It'll go away in a minute or two. I don't even know the name of the tablets I'm on.'

'Well, I tell ya what,' Henry said, taking a pen and paper out from his pocket and writing something down.

He tore out the page and handed it to Ellie.

'Here's me number, ya can phone me wit da name of da tablets when ya find out, an I'll hook ya's up.'

'Are you sure?' Ellie asked. 'Are you even allowed to do that?'

'Well, I won't tell if you don't,' he replied. 'On one condition,' he added, his index finger saluting the air, revealing a hidden agenda.

Ellie nodded,

'Yes, sure, anything.'

'Ya have ta meet me for a drink—a coffee perhaps? Or an alcoholic one if ya prefer? So I can give ya de tablets of course?'

Ellie smiled. But Jenson's groan destroyed any further dalliance. This trade off was poorly timed, and Henry knew it.

'Righ, well let me know. I have ta go back inside ta check on dem. I'll be out in a minute.'

Henry walked over to the door and swiped his card.

He disappeared inside.

'Did you get the answers you were looking for?' Jenson asked, now coming round.

'Not too sure.' Ellie replied. 'I was wondering what Stem's connection is with this place. He told me that most of these patients in here came from Stem. He thinks they must still be of some importance to Stem. He believes they still need them for something, like lab rats, stored here and used when they like. Maybe your parents and Robyn will be moved here? I've given him their description and asked him to keep an eye out.'

Jenson could see the hope in her eyes,

'Thank you, Ellie,' he said. 'I appreciate that.'

'No need to thank me Jenson. We'll get them back. I just know it.'

'Everytin okay?' Henry asked, stepping into the room, and noticing Davrin and Stephanie's embrace.

The light had distinguished as Davrin began wiping the tears from his eyes. He nodded and untangled himself from his mother.

'Yes, everything's great,' he said.

Henry could hear the sheer joy in his response and realised they were happy tears. He then looked at Stephanie, who had lifted the pink blanket up over her head. She seemed to be hiding behind it, shielding her emotion.

'Stephanie, are ya okay? What's wrong?' He asked.

He dashed over to her, feeling somewhat anxious. He took the cover from her face. But what surprised him the most was that he could see the tears in her eyes too. And there, clutching to her chest was the blue baby blanket.

'Stephanie are ya okay?' He repeated.

Stephanie looked at him and then turned to face her son.

'That's my baby, my baby boy,' she answered.

'Yes, Stephanie, dat's very good. Well done! But I tink you've had enough excitement for one day, so Davrin has ta go now, but he'll be back very soon. Won't ya Davrin?'

'Yes Mum, I'll be back real soon,' he answered, hugging her one last time, and whispering in her ear,

'I'll get you out of here Mum, just hang on.'

Jenson and Ellie got to their feet as Davrin walked out with a big smile on his face.

Henry followed, holding the arm of a female who was wrapped in a pink blanket, whilst holding onto a smaller blue one.

'Righ, say goodbye Stephanie.'

Henry positioned Stephanie in the doorway to say her goodbyes. She looked calm. But then her eyeline shot directly over towards Ellie and Jenson. Her expression froze in sheer turmoil. Her eyes bulged and her body began to tremble.

Opening her mouth, she tried to say something, but nothing would come out. She began screeching and it was evident she was becoming hysterical. Her eyes illuminated—not the bright green like before, but the darkest of black. Her face became distorted for a moment, attempting to reveal another identity. She then pointed over at Jenson.

177

'Okay, it's okay Stephanie, you're okay,' Henry bellowed. His voice, trying to sooth this sudden rage.

The others didn't know what to do. They stood back watching Henry attempt to control the distraught woman.

'Come on Stephanie, we'll get ya back into your comfy chair. You've had enough excitement for one day. Can you all please wait outside while I get Stephanie settled,' he ordered, nudging her around and bringing her back inside her room.

Ellie, Jenson, and Davrin proceeded down the corridor as instructed. The silence allowing each of them time to think, but neither one fully comprehending what had just happened.

'She was fine a minute ago?' Davrin questioned. 'She even remembered who I was. I don't know what happened.'

'She remembered you?' Ellie asked, a surprised look on her face.

'Yeah, kinda. She didn't say much but I could just feel it. She remembered my blanket. I don't know why she reacted like that. She was fine.'

'I'm sure there's a simple explanation.' Ellie suggested. 'Maybe she gets frightened when she leaves her room? Or maybe it was too much, seeing myself and Jenson as well. Too many people perhaps? Anyway, Henry will help her now.'

'My photo?' Davrin exclaimed.

'What?'

'My photo! She has my photo, the one when I was a baby.'

'Well, you can't go back now,' Ellie insisted. 'Maybe it will be good for her to have it. It could bring back some memories perhaps?'

'Yeah, I suppose.'

'Right, well anybody need to use the toilet before we go?'

Ellie had just realised her parental tone had been used again. She smiled.

'Sorry guys, I'm just so used to doing this with my students.'

'I could do with it,' Davrin replied.

'Okay, we'll see you outside.' Jenson interrupted. A certainty in his voice to leave quickly. And just like that, he marched off towards the front door.

'Is everything okay Jenson?' Ellie asked, following him. She could sense something was up.

Jenson had already reached the front door. He motioned for her to follow,

'I'll explain when we're outside.'

The barren grounds greeted them just as the female nurse returned with the patient on her arm. It was the man who had depicted all the fairy drawings. He had suddenly tried to stop, but the nurse tugged on his sleeve,

'Come on Blaine, leave these people alone.'

And with that she smiled, ushering him back into the house.

'I'll see yu, yu, you again.' He called out towards Jenson and Ellie, scratching his white frizzy hair, and disappearing inside.

Jenson had forgotten all about the fairies, his mind now preoccupied with what had just happened,

'Did you see her eyes?' He asked.

'What eyes?' Ellie queried. 'Are you sure you're alright Jenson?'

'Stephanie's eyes, they changed colour, and her face?'

'I'm not quite following you Jenson?'

This made Jenson uneasy. Ellie seemed to have no notion as to what he was going on about.

'Her eyes—they went black, and her face, it changed. It looked like one of those Spackle's from 'The Chaos Walking', have you ever seen the movie? But it was different, like some sort of a dark creature. She was morphing into something. And before that, I saw a green light coming from the room. I know it sounds strange but....'

'I'm sorry Jenson, I didn't see any of that. Are you sure you're okay? Maybe you were hallucinating from that migraine? Migraines can be caused by the sensitivity of light. Henry said he can help you. Do you want me to ask him?'

'Ask me wha?' Henry questioned, stepping out of the front door.

'Does that happen a lot?' Jenson intervened. He didn't want Henry knowing the truth about his visions.

'Yes, but never dat bad. I'm sorry ya had ta see dat. It sometimes happens when dey don't get der medication, but I've never seen it dat bad. Is Davrin okay?'

'I think so. He just needed to use the toilet,' Ellie answered.

She looked over at Jenson. A puzzlement in her eyes, wondering why he didn't want to ask Henry for his help.

'Oh righ. Well please tell him his ma gets de attacks quite often, not as bad as dat doh, but it's quite normal. Tell him not ta worry. We're not too sure what causes dem, but when dey happen, we just need ta increase her dosage. Ya don't mind seein yourselves out? I just have ta get her medication. Oh, an just call me when ya want da tablets. Nice to meet ya's.'

And with that, Henry vanished back inside the building.

'Are you sure you're alright Jenson? I can see if he has anything for your migraines now if you want?' Ellie asked. 'I'm sure it'll be no problem at all.'

'No, it's okay.'

Jenson knew what he saw, just like in class with Davrin and his glowing eyes. But nobody else seems to be noticing these things. It was pointless trying to make them understand. This was something he would have to try and figure out on his own.

Davrin stepped out, and without any further chat, they all made their way to the car, allowing the previous situation to sink in.

'It's probably a bad time,' Jenson suggested, just as they had reached the car park outside the main building. 'But I don't suppose your mum said anything about helping you find people in your dreams?'

'I'm sorry, Jenson. I didn't ask,' Davrin replied. 'But I'll come straight back tomorrow after school. I'll ask her then.'

'What about your Nan?' Ellie asked. 'Will you tell her?'

'I don't know.'

'Well, you don't have to decide straight away. You two must be hungry', and there it was again, Ellie's teacher mode kicking in. 'We can stop off on the way back to your Nan's and get some food. Plus, we need to get you back into hiding before you get recognised Jenson.'

Ellie began to rummage through her handbag.

Retrieving her keys, she unlocked the car.

'You two go ahead. I'll just ring my Dad and tell him we're stopping off for some food. And then we'll drop you off Davrin. I'm sure your Nan is beginning to worry.'

Chapter 31

The sun was slowly fading behind the thickening clouds. This cast a shadow over Davrin's house, intensifying the compromising conversation he would soon have with his grandmother.

'Do you want us to go in with you?' Ellie asked. The car suddenly pulling up outside his house.

'No thanks,' Davrin replied. His hesitancy in opening the back door displayed caution in his next step.

'Are you sure Davrin?' Jenson confirmed. 'After all you've done for us, we don't mind coming in with you?'

'Yes, we're here to support you as well,' Ellie added.

'It's okay. I'll be fine.'

Davrin stepped out of the car and gently closed the rear door.

He stood outside his driveway, reluctant to go in. He then opened the gate and began to ascend the mossy pathway.

Sliding the porch door open, he stepped in.

Putting his key into the front door, and with a slight nudge, he opened the door and disappeared inside, without even the slightest of waves back to Jenson or Ellie.

'Poor Davrin.' Ellie suggested. She had noticed his fragile approach.

'I do feel sorry for him.' Jenson agreed. 'His mind must be all over the place. Can you imagine finding out you have a mother after believing she was dead for so long?'

Ellie nodded. She realised the irony in this situation, for Jenson had also lost his mother and could possibly never see her again.

'What time is it anyway?' Jenson added, trying to deflect the subject.

This sudden talk of mothers had made him think of his own mother. He was missing her. He was missing them all.

'It's nearly four o'clock,' Ellie replied. 'How are you Jenson? How are you holding up?'

Jenson looked straight into her eyes. Feeling a bit awkward and not wanting to open-up, he simply smiled. It was a fake smile, hiding the uncertainty of everything.

'Are you sure you're okay?' Ellie asked. She was once his age and she knew how heavy certain situations could weigh in on a teenager's mind, not to mention the fact that his whole family had been ripped away from him.

Jenson's eyes began to fill, but before he could speak again, a loud bang resonated throughout the car. They both jumped in sheer fright. The bang came from behind Ellie, outside the car.

Ellie swivelled back round, and in complete horror, she screamed.

Jenson tilted his head to look past hers. He could see the blood smeared across the window.

Davrin was standing there, tears in his eyes and panic written all over his face. His hands were pressing up against the car causing the blood to stain the window.

Ellie immediately rolled down her window.

'What happened?'

'It's my Nan!'

Davrin could barely catch his breath. His hands clung to the top of the glass as it lowered. And blood streaks smudging the glass, disappearing with every lowering inch.

'Davrin, what's wrong?' Ellie asked again.

'It…it's my Nan…I don't know what happened?'

Davrin stepped away from the car so Ellie could open her door.

Jenson and Ellie both got out and followed Davrin back towards the house, neither one acknowledging or even contemplating Stem's involvement.

Jenson managed to get to the front door before Ellie. He pushed the door wide open, not knowing what to expect on the other side. A terror took over, and once inside, he just froze. He stood there, watching.

'Please help!' Davrin begged. His position, now kneeling beside his Nan in the hallway.

Ellie nudged her way past Jenson. She could see Davrin, slouched on the ground in the hallway with his grandmother in his arms. Her grey hair, darker in colour now, and sweaty with red stains. There was blood all over her face.

Ellie knelt beside them. She could see the extent of the wound as the blood seeped out of his Nan's head.

'She's lost a lot of blood,' she said, pressing her forefingers against Margaret's neck.

Davrin's uncontrolled emotions had wilted. He was calmer now, watching, and waiting for Ellie to tell him if his Nan would live.

'There's a pulse, a low pulse, but I can feel one. There is too much blood coming from her head. Quick, Jenson, go into the kitchen and grab me some towels or even a cloth. What is your Nan's name again—Margaret?' She asked. Her first-aid mode kicking in again.

Davrin saw his Nan's favourite head scarf. It was sitting beside her and drenched in a pool of her own blood.

'Hello Margaret?' Ellie called out. 'My name is Ellie. I am here with your grandson Davrin. Can you hear me? If you can hear me, let us know—just squeeze my hand.'

Ellie placed Margaret's hand inside hers.

Margaret responded by lightly squeezing her hand just as Jenson came back with some dishtowels.

'Okay, that's good Margaret,' Ellie said, wrapping one tightly around her head and pressing the others against the blood stains to locate any other wound.

'I can hear her—she's trying to say something. What is it Nan?' Davrin cried.

He leaned in and put his ear up to her mouth.

An uneasy silence broke as Davrin listened.

Moments later he raised his head and spoke,

'She said it was Stem, two men from Stem. They were looking for me. They want me to hand myself over or they'll be back.'

At that moment, Margaret squeezed her grandson's hand and closed her eyes. She took her last breath. She was gone.

'NO! NAN! WAKE UP!' Davrin screamed.

'I'm sorry Davrin.' Ellie said, reaching across and placing her bloodstained hand gently against his shoulder.

But suddenly an anger inside of Davrin caused him to shrug her hand away. He turned to face Jenson. A rage forming across his face,

'THIS IS ALL YOUR FAULT!' He yelled, raising his arm, and pointing it up at Jenson. 'Stem must have followed you here.'

Jenson stood there, stunned. He was lost for words.

Was this all his fault? He thought. Did this happen because of him?

Ellie stood up, placing herself between the two boys.

'I am sorry Davrin. But this is not Jenson's fault. It was Stem Industries.'

'But if he hadn't of come here. If he had of just left us alone?'

185

'I know you're hurting right now, and I'm so sorry this has happened, but you cannot blame Jenson. Your Nan urged you to help him.'

'I'm so sorry Davrin,' Jenson said. His gaze lowering with guilt. 'I didn't mean for any of this.'

Davrin had no response. He just stared at Jenson. His mind was desperately trying to deal with the situation.

'Is there anything we can do?' Ellie asked.

'Get out!'

'Davrin please. We're not leaving you, not like this. We're all in this together.'

Davrin turned to face his grandmother. This heartbreak was so sudden. He didn't know what to do. But then the rage returned,

'Who is Payton?' He demanded. His anger visible again.

'Who?' Ellie questioned.

'Payton White?'

'Where did you hear that name?' Jenson asked.

'My Nan said that was the name of one of the men from Stem.'

Jenson responded with a startling gaze. His eyes moved towards Margaret's dead body on the floor.

'Payton White is Ethan's dad. I haven't seen him in a long time, but that's him. He must have been here.'

Jenson paused for a moment. His shrouded doubt evaporating.

'Chloe was right all along,' he said. 'Ethan must have been behind this. He must have led them here. His father is the one who is doing all of this. He took my parents...my little sister, and now this!'

'Ethan White?' Ellie responded. 'Ethan's mother, Claire White, she's the principal at my school. I saw her outside the toilets when I was speaking to Robyn on Friday. She must have been listening in on our conversation. It had to be her who informed Stem about Robyn. She must be in cahoots with her husband. They both are.'

'Ethan's mother?' Jenson suggested. 'But I've met her loads of times, she's lovely. And she knows my family. She wouldn't have done that?'

'You'd be surprised where your loyalties lie if you're afraid of how powerful your husband is.' Ellie explained.

They had both forgotten about Davrin. And turning round, they watched on as he held onto his grandmother, cradling her dead body on the ground, just as she had cradled his when he was a child. His fingers carefully stroking her cheek. A despondent look on his face as he stared into her lifeless eyes. He raised his fingers and closed each eyelid, crushed at the thought of never seeing them open ever again.

Chapter 32

Payton White stood over Robyn's unconscious body. His gaze lacked any remorse.

'How are the tests coming on?' He asked. 'Is she compatible?'

His stare never leaving Robyn, but his questions travelling over to Tom who was working on the lab's computer.

'It's looking good Mr White,' Tom answered, swivelling round in his chair.

Getting to his feet, he scooped up some sheets of paper and waved them enthusiastically at Payton.

'The general activation of the brain is at its highest when first awake and this is almost the same in a dream-state sleep. We know this from the first Dream-death phenomenon which was noted fifteen years ago. But, in Robyn's case, her neuromodulators are non-existent when she sleeps, and her ratio of cholinergic to aminergic-neuromodulator release is off the charts. She has something else. She is certainly a Non-dreamer, but I believe she is the strongest one yet. I figure if we use the formula we have, and inject it into Robyn, we could potentially break the REM barrier....'

'Okay Tom,' Payton interrupted, not really listening. This was a science lesson he could do without. 'Is she compatible? Will it work? Will you be able to add this to what we have and stop these Dream-deaths from happening?'

'I think Robyn has the component we need. But I have more tests to run. In my opinion, I believe it should work, in theory.'

'Excellent Tom, keep up the good work.'

Payton headed for the door,

'I'm going home now for an early night. George will dispose of the bodies when you've finished. I'm sure you will stay back to get it all done. Goodnight Tom.'

Payton didn't wait for a response. He swiped his card and left the lab.

Tom looked down at Robyn's unconscious body. The word "dispose" kept circling around in his brain.

'I'm so sorry Robyn,' he said, 'but you won't die in vain. You are going to save millions of lives.'

~~~

'Should we go in and get him?' Jenson asked.

'Yes, I think we should.' Ellie agreed. 'We need to get out of here just in case Stem come back.'

It had been over thirty minutes since they moved Margaret's body into the living room and placed her on the couch. Davrin had asked if he could spend some time alone with her to say his goodbyes properly.

'I'll get him,' Jenson insisted, leaving the kitchen.

Moments later, suddenly the sound of the kitchen door bursting open made Ellie jump. It was Jenson rushing back in,

'HE'S GONE!' he shouted.

'What?'

'Davrin is gone!'

'Are you sure?' Ellie asked.

'Yes, he's not here.'

'Is he upstairs?'

'No. I've checked. He's gone!'

Ellie grabbed her handbag and keys.

'I'll go look for him. I'll drop you off at the church.'

'No, I'll go with you.'

'No Jenson, it's too dangerous for you, they're looking for you.'

'But you can't go searching for Davrin on your own.'

'I'll get Chloe. They're not on the lookout for two females, come on, we need to go. The longer we leave it, the further he'll get.'

'What will we do with Margaret's body?' Jenson asked.

Ellie hesitated for a moment.

'I feel terrible for saying this Jenson, but we just have to leave her here.'

'What?' Jenson asked. He was completely taken aback by the lack of empathy Ellie had for Davrin's dead grandmother.

'I know it sounds harsh Jenson, but we cannot risk even making a phone call. We could get the blame for it. Our fingerprints are all over the house. They're all over her body. And if we do try and explain ourselves, well then Stem could get involved, and who knows what could happen? Come on, we need to go. We need to find Davrin, and quick, before he does something stupid.'

Chapter 33

The clammy soil provoking no obstacle for Davrin as he sat hidden behind the bushes. Ethan's family home was presenting itself through the spacing of shrubbery. Across the road and nestled inconspicuously behind the coverage, Davrin watched on. His fretting now replaced by an angered stare. His teeth grinding in anticipation, waiting for somebody to appear. He was waiting for Ethan.

Time slowly lapsing, when suddenly he noticed the electronic gates breaking to allow passage. A revving engine caused his stare to flicker. A flashy sports car came into view, the windows tinted, empowering any passenger with anonymity.

It continued straight into the driveway, veering off to the side and out of sight behind the protected wall.

Davrin wondered if this was Mr White, the man his Nan had told him about. Was this Ethan's father, the man who had murdered his grandmother?

Davrin wasn't sure, and he knew he couldn't just run over there and do something stupid. He wanted all of them to pay, starting with Ethan for his betrayal. But before he could see who it was, the iron gates automatically shut, blocking any intruder from the outside world.

He sat there for what seemed like an eternity, going over it all in his head, the different scenarios he could think of. Different ways of getting into their home, ways of punishing Ethan and his family. He wondered what he would say and do, questioning every move. Hiding and waiting for nightfall in the hope that Ethan would reveal himself.

Dusk was settling. Davrin could no longer contain his anger. And Ethan was yet to show his face.

Davrin retrieved a tablet from his pocket. It was one of his Nan's sleeping tablets.

He pressed it in against his tongue and poked it as far back as he could. The dryness in his mouth causing the tablet to struggle, a refusal to let go. His body telling him this was a mistake. Davrin didn't listen. The tablet gripping onto his tongue, desperately trying to reject its intent. But Davrin poked his finger even further. And eventually a gaging reflex caused it to slip down his throat and fall into the pit of destruction.

Minutes went by and Davrin's anger began to diminish. His eyes became heavy, like hefty weights dragging his eyelids down. Even though he had planned this, his body battled with the endurance to stay awake. But his efforts were in vain. His eyes shut for the last time. And they remained closed as he fell back into the damp shrubbery.

~~~

Davrin opened his eyes again. But instead of the thick shrubbery, he was now situated outside Ethan's home. He was standing by the front door. It was dark outside, and a grey mist surrounded him. He felt confused and couldn't remember how he'd gotten here. He couldn't even remember crossing the street. He raised his arm towards the front door but before he touched the handle, the door creaked open, revealing a glimmer of light in the plush hallway.

For the first time in Davrin's young life, he realised he was in a lucid dream. He knew straight away that this was his own dream, unlike before, in class, when he hadn't realised it until he'd woken up. He felt different. This was unlike any other dream he had ever experienced. He felt more in control. This was something he wanted.

He felt a surge of adrenaline, the same adrenaline he felt when he hugged his mother earlier. He wondered if she had helped him with his ability, if she was the reason, the guidance behind his dream, allowing him to be inside the home of the boy he was looking for, to be inside his dream.

He moved further into the house. It was dark but he could see a staircase. He stood there watching. The wait was over.

Ethan was fast asleep in his bed. He was still weak from the fall and had decided to have an early night.

He tossed and turned as the bedcovers began to draw back slowly. The dipping temperature caused him to stir. His body now unprotected from the cold. His eyes gradually opening now. Confused and still only half awake, he watched the covers moving down the bed.

He leaned forward to grab the top of the quilt but as he reached down, the covers flew off the end of the bed and onto the floor.

'Ethan?' A voice spoke.

Ethan could hear his name being called from downstairs. He did not recognise the voice. Fear increased from within. His body began to tremble and then he heard the voice again.

'Ethan, show your face!'

Ethan was afraid. He didn't want to get out of bed. But as the covers were dragged off, he felt cold. He felt helpless. He knew he had to follow the instructions.

He slowly stepped off the bed and onto the cold flooring.

He crept out onto the landing.

Reaching the top of the stairs, he peered down and saw somebody standing at the bottom. His eyes squinting, an attempt to see into the grey mist, but he couldn't identify who it was.

Davrin took a step forward, his shadow revealing itself from the mist.

'Davrin? Is that you?' Ethan whispered.

He couldn't understand why Davrin was in his home. He didn't realise he was in a dream.

The front door suddenly slammed.

Ethan jumped back. He didn't know what was going on, the fog cloaking any movement.

Davrin didn't budge.

'What do you want?' Ethan called out.

Davrin began to speak, his voice deep and enraged now.

'You know why I am here. Your father killed my grandmother. He also took Jenson's family.'

'I didn't mean it,' Ethan confessed. He knew this was a consequence of his betrayal.

He attempted to call out for help, but he was speechless. His body began to raise up off the ground. His eyes circling to try and understand this levitation. And suddenly a charge of suffocation took hold, as if somebody was holding him up by the throat and was choking him.

He clutched his throat, an attempt to loosen the grip, but he couldn't see what was holding him up. He tried to yell but his airways were restricted. He gasped for air.

Looking to Davrin for help, he noticed his outstretched arm pointing at him. It looked as if Davrin had him by the throat, but a confusion clenched his breath as Davrin was nowhere near him.

Unexpectedly, Ethan dropped onto the top of the stairs and came crashing down. His body hitting hard against the sharp edges.

He landed right in front of Davrin.

He lay there, looking up at him. His body aching. A fear in his eyes.

Davrin raised his arm again and Ethan's body lifted once more into the air.

'You're going to pay for what you did! You betrayed us! You betrayed us all!'

Ethan's body slowly elevated back up the stairs. His struggle proving worthless.

As soon as he reached the top, Davrin didn't hesitate. He threw his body back down once more.

Davrin was in the grip of a total rage. He lifted Ethan's body up again. But Ethan's body remained limp. He had no struggle left in him this time as his defenceless body was dragged back up the stairs.

But suddenly, Davrin heard a voice, a familiar tone.

'Davrin, please stop this. This isn't you,' the voice said.

Davrin felt a hand gently press against his arm, lowering it, resulting in Ethan being lowered smoothly onto the landing.

Davrin turned his head. A faint vision of his Nan flourished in front of him, a white glow radiating around her.

The mist around him suddenly vanished. His rage, subsiding as he felt her touch. He stood there watching her as tears streamed down his face.

'Nan?' He cried. 'They did this to you. They need to pay for it!'

'I know, my dear,' his Nan answered, 'but not like this. You are not like them. Remember who you are.'

Davrin didn't respond, but his Nan knew he was listening.

'I often heard you crying yourself to sleep in your room at night,' she said. 'I knew you couldn't tell me. You didn't want my help. I knew one day you would grow into a strong, brave young man, but by doing this, you are only turning into those people, those bullies. You are stronger than this, you are better than this. Keep making me proud, my dear grandson. I love you. I will always love you.'

Davrin closed his eyes. He could still feel his Nan's aura. A calmness took over.

'But Nan?' He questioned, opening his eyes again. 'They took you away from me.'

But Margaret was gone. The image had disappeared. Her matter and energy had vanished, but the calmness remained. Davrin dropped to the ground. His hands were clasping his face. He began to cry.

A wavering groan bellowed upstairs.

Davrin immediately looked up to see Ethan's body hanging over the staircase. His groans conveying the pain he had just endured. And Davrin, suddenly realised the damage he had done.

He stood up. The black mist returned and surrounded him. And just like before, the fog encircled him and absorbed his entire body.

Davrin opened his eyes. He was no longer in the hallway. He was back where he had started; back across the road, huddled within the bushes, facing Ethan's family home. He was now awake.

'What did I do?' He whispered to himself, wiping the tears from his face.

He noticed a light flicker on in the upstairs of Ethan's family home. Ethan's cries resonating in his mind. He could hear him but could no longer see him. He had woken from this dream. He had woken from the nightmare he had set upon Ethan. He was scared. He felt alone. He didn't know who to turn to. He had nothing left.

He got up and ran, leaving the bushes rattling in his wake.

~~~

Payton could hear his son's screams.

Running across the landing, with his wife in tow, he ran into Ethan's bedroom.

'Ethan, what is it?' He asked, shaking his son by the shoulders.

Ethan's eyes were open wide as he looked at his father. Despite his screams, he didn't look as if he was in pain. He looked petrified.

'Ethan, talk to me?' His father demanded.

'It was Davrin, Dad, he was here.'

'Nobody was here son,' his father explained. 'It's only myself and your mother. It was probably just a nightmare.'

'But I saw him. It was Davrin, Davrin Belshaw. He said we will all pay for what happened, for what you did to his grandmother and to Jenson's family.'

Both Ethan's father and mother watched on in dismay.

'It's okay son, you're safe here. Nobody will hurt you. I'll find this Davrin boy.'

At that very moment, Payton knew Davrin was more special than he had expected. He knew Davrin had to be a 'Dream-Drifter'. But suddenly a panic washed over him as he could feel a stiffness in his son's posture.

'What's wrong Ethan?'

'I don't know Dad.'

'You can tell me. What is it?'

'I can't feel my legs.'

Chapter 34

'Do you think we'll find him?' Chloe asked Ellie. Her eyes in search of Davrin walking the streets.

'I don't know Chloe. It's late and I really hope he hasn't done anything stupid.'

'I just can't help but feel sorry for his Nan. Is there nothing we can do for her?'

'I'm afraid not Chloe,' Ellie answered. 'If we get Davrin and everybody's safe, maybe we can do something, make an anonymous phone call perhaps, but for now, we'll just have to depend on a neighbour or a friend finding her body.'

'It's just so sad.'

'I know Chloe.'

Suddenly, turning the corner onto Hedgemore Road, they could see a security checkpoint up ahead. It was too dark to see much, but the flashing lights alerted them to some sort of disturbance.

'What's that up there?' Chloe asked.

Two Stem jeeps were barricading the road. And a Stem soldier came into view, gesturing them to stop.

'Hello,' Ellie said calmly as she rolled down the window. 'Is everything okay?'

'Sorry Miss, you can't come through here,' he informed her.

'What happened?' Chloe muttered, sitting upright, and repositioning her body to see what was going on beyond the two vehicles. And with further shuffling, she noticed an ambulance parked up ahead.

'An unfortunate incident has occurred. I'm not authorised to give any information,' the soldier said. 'So you and your daughter will have to take a different route.'

Chloe looked at Ellie, a smirk growing on her face.

'Okay thanks,' she said, 'let's go mum.'

She could see the disgust on Ellie's face.

'The cheek of him!' Ellie said, driving off, not even waiting to roll up her window. 'Do I look that old? Like what the fu....'

'WAIT! STOP! STOP THE CAR!' Chloe interrupted.

She suddenly realised where they were. She had remembered this place from the night before.

'What is it?' Ellie muttered. A panic set in as she pressed down hard on the brakes.

Chloe looked back. She tried to focus in on the ambulance, attempting to retrieve some sort of a clue, but it looked too far out of reach. It was too dark up ahead.

Then suddenly, luck struck when the paramedics came into view, their high-visibility clothing reflecting their fluorescent material like beacons. They were approaching the ambulance. And It looked like they were holding onto a stretcher.

'What is it?' Ellie asked, her angle proving too difficult to get a clear view.

'I think it's Davrin?'

'Can you see him?'

'No, but that's Ethan's house. We were here last night.'

'What makes you think it's Davrin?'

'I don't know. But I think they're putting a body into the back of that ambulance. And you heard that soldier, something bad has happened. Maybe Davrin came for revenge?'

Ellie didn't know what to make of this situation. She manoeuvred her head to look out her window, but suddenly a Stem soldier had emerged from the shadows. She didn't see him creep up. She let out a squeal.

Chloe turned and saw the soldier. It was the same soldier who had spoken to them seconds earlier.

'Everything okay Miss?'

Ellie was trying to collect herself.

'Yes, she's fine.' Chloe answered. 'You just frightened her. She worries a lot. She was only saying how she hoped it wasn't a young girl like me who has been hurt. Can you imagine if it was, oh my god!'

'Don't worry Miss. It wasn't.' The soldier replied.

Chloe's rambling had paid off. Her trickery had worked again, proving favourable in their search. And the soldier's failure to fulfil his duties grew evident on his face. He instantly realised he had said too much.

'So it was a boy then?' Chloe asked. 'Is he okay? I hope he's okay. Can you imagine what his mother must be going through?'

Her rambling had again thrown the soldier off course,

'Yes, it was a boy…' He stammered, trying to compensate for his sudden disclosure. He had somehow given more crucial information. '…but there were no fatalities,' he added.

'Okay, and do you know….'

But the soldier was ready this time,

'So where are you ladies off to?' He interrupted.

This threw Chloe off as she didn't know the area that well. She also felt her time was up. The solider refused to fall for anymore deceit. She looked at Ellie, who had regained her composure.

'We're going to visit my father in Oakwood,' Ellie replied without hesitation.

The soldier nodded.

'You know another route to take?'

'Yes, thank you.'

'Okay, well, I'm going to have to ask you to move on so,' he confirmed.

'Yes, thank you, Goodnight.'

Ellie rolled her window back up and drove off.

'Will you get my phone out of my bag and ring the boys please?' She asked. 'Tell them we're going to the hospital to find out if Davrin was in that ambulance.'

~~~

Ethan was half conscious on the stretcher. The paramedics were leading him out to the ambulance as the oxygen mask clung to his face.

'Dad?' He said, clutching at the mask and trying to remove it.

One of the medics gently took Ethan's hand away.

'You're okay, son,' his father replied, 'don't say anything.'

To the medic this was a concerned father who wanted his son to rest and not worry, but Ethan knew what this meant. His father's facial expression spoke volumes, and it was one Ethan had seen too many times before. This was a warning to say nothing about what had just taken place.

'Your mother is going to go with you to the hospital,' he continued. 'You'll be fine.'

Payton turned to his wife who held onto a worried expression.

'You go with him, and I'll follow,' he said, guiding her gently but sternly into the back of the ambulance. 'I'll sort this out,' he added as his wife looked out to see police, medics, Stem soldiers, and neighbours scattered in the street, just as the back doors of the ambulance closed.

Payton turned towards the house. He took his phone out of his pocket and began dialling.

'Hello Tom,' he said, walking towards his front door. 'We have a problem. Have you got all you need for the formula?' He asked, pausing, and waiting on a reply. 'Good,' he added, 'well, you know that Davrin kid who's been linked to Jenson? Turns out he is a more valuable than I imagined. There is gonna be a slight change of plan. You carry on there and I'll drop in after I tidy a few things up here.'

Payton stepped into his house where he made the acquaintance of some Stem soldiers in his hallway.

'I need you to send out a search party,' he confirmed. 'Forget about Jenson Rose. I want somebody else. I need another boy, and I want him captured alive. His name is Davrin Belshaw. I'll get you a description.'

Chapter 35

'Mr White?' Tom called out, surprised to see him so soon. He glanced up from stitching a small incision on the top of Robyn's temple.

'Tom.' Payton acknowledged, stepping in through the automated doors and shoving his swipe card into his suit jacket. 'How is it coming along?'

'Well, in theory the formula should work but there's no way I can be certain the treatment actually works unless we test it out.'

'Have you got enough material to do more tests?' Payton asked hastily, as if he were under pressure.

Tom looked at him, his body still leaning over Robyn's. He wondered why Payton seemed so anxious,

'Are you okay, Mr White?' He asked.

Payton turned around abruptly to face Tom.

'As I said on the phone, there has been a change of plan.'

Tom grew edgy.

'What happened?' He asked.

'Regrettably, my son Ethan has been taken into hospital.'

'Oh, I'm sorry. What happened? Is he okay?'

'I will find out more when I get there,' Payton answered, without any real concern. It seemed as if he had more important things to worry about.

'Ethan has no movement from the waist down. He says this Davrin boy was in our home and did something to him in his sleep.'

'A Dream-Drifter?' Tom questioned. A rasp in his reply.

'It's the only explanation. As you know, these individuals don't come around often, so I can't afford to let this one get away.'

'How did Ethan get hurt? Was it an accident?'

'No Tom,' Payton replied harshly. 'This was no accident. I need to find this boy. I cannot let this happen again. Davrin is dangerous. I know he is involved with Jenson, so I need her brother to help me. I need you to do something for me,' he said, pointing towards Robyn on the reclining chair.

'Yes of course, what is it?'

'Instead of disposing of these bodies, we're going to put them back safely. I want you to ensure their safety, Robyn's safety.'

'Yes, yes of course.'

'Good! And when Jenson is reunited with his family, he will eventually lead us to his friend Davrin. But don't worry, we will get them all back as soon as we catch this Davrin kid. And you can have as much time to do whatever testing you like on them all.'

'So you're not killing her?' Tom asked. His questioning seemed full of relief.

'I don't know why you seem to care about this one.'

'I don't.' Tom answered. His lack of affection for Robyn was not convincing.

'Just get what you need and finish up here. I have to get them back home. I cannot risk my family's safety. I believe Davrin has some sort of an alliance with Jenson, I have to show a sign of goodwill. And hopefully Davrin sees it and doesn't come back to hurt anyone else.'

'How are you going to put them back?' Tom asked. 'She's seen my face.'

'She's only a child. She won't remember. Anyway, that is not your concern. When we send them back to their home, and Jenson is reunited with his missing family, he should lead us straight to Davrin. We'll have them all captured again in no time.'

'When do you plan on putting them back?'

'Tonight. My family come first. I don't want any more casualties.'

Tom's face dropped.

'But that doesn't give me enough time to make sure Robyn is stable. All the tests are bound to have a reaction. I'm only stitching her up now. What about the treatment?'

Payton picked up a small test tube containing blue liquid.

'How many can you make up before morning?' He asked, gazing into the vessel.

'I'm not too sure,' Tom replied. This request was unexpected and seemed too sudden to complete.

'Five? Ten?' Payton asked.

'I don't know. The results are not conclusive. I don't know if we're ready to test it out.'

'I can't wait any longer. I need this so Davrin cannot get inside any of our heads. I'll get George to drop by. We can send the samples out to St Anita's. Let them test it out on those freaks first. George is going out there anyway.'

'Yeah but, as I said...' Tom muttered.

He discontinued his sentence, cutting himself short because Payton was already walking towards the lab doors.

'I'm sure the samples will be fine. Don't worry. You'll have a test subject from St Anita's to keep you occupied in the meantime. George is bringing you back a surprise.'

Tom turned to look at the innocent little girl in the chair. He was worried this new cure would not work. He was unsure of its results. He was unsure of the consequences his experiments had on Robyn. But he was relieved she was not being disposed of like the others. A silver lining glazing over the uncertainty.

Twenty minutes later, the lab doors in Stem Industries opened again.

'Mr White sent me down to collect the body. Is she ready?' George asked as he walked in through the doors, dressed in a different suit to the one he was wearing at Margaret's house. The blood stains seemingly too difficult to wipe off.

'I didn't think it would be this soon,' Tom replied, standing over Robyn's body, and taking the syringe out of her arm. 'She will be okay, won't she?'

'My orders are to put her and her parents back as soon as possible,' George answered. 'Why do you care anyway?'

'I don't,' Tom answered. 'I was just wondering. This should keep her knocked out until she gets home.'

Two Stem soldiers walked in through the automated doors to assist George with the body.

'We'll bring her out now,' George instructed. He no longer wanted Tom near the body. 'She is ready to go, yes?'

Tom looked uncertain about handing Robyn over.

'TOM?' George called out, his hand sweeping the fibres of his bald head. 'Don't have me to ask again!'

'Yes, sorry. Yes, she's ready,' Tom answered, pressing his foot down on the chair break to unlock it.

He repeated the same step, scurrying around the body to open the other locks. He looked restless.

The two Stem soldiers then intercepted, taking each end of the chair and wheeling Robyn's body out towards the lift.

Tom followed them out to the lift. An awkward silence loomed as they continued down towards the jeep. And when they got there, Tom noticed two other bodies tied up and already on the floor in the back. He knew they were Robyn's mother and father.

'Careful,' he advised as the two soldiers roughly hauled Robyn up from the chair.

'What is your interest in this one?' George asked. 'She's unconscious. She won't feel a thing until she wakes up. They're all the same. Lab rats!'

'Not this one.' Tom retaliated. 'She's not like the others. She's special.'

George began to snigger.

And within seconds, the two soldiers joined in as all three of them continued to laugh at Tom's statement.

George gestured for them to bundle the body into the back of the jeep by any means necessary.

He then took out his gun from the inside of his jacket pocket and waved it in Tom's face as the back doors shut.

'You sure they won't wake before we get them home?' He asked. An indication of what would happen if things were to go wrong.

'No, definitely not, I've just given her a heavy dose.'

'Good. Cause we wouldn't want anything bad to happen now, would we?'

Tom didn't acknowledge this comment. He knew better.

'And I'll be back to collect those samples for St Anita's. Make sure you have them ready.'

Chapter 36

'What do you think will happen if it is Davrin here in the hospital?' Chloe asked.

Ellie was focused on the road ahead. The long day was beginning to take its toll on her. She rolled down the window again, allowing the cool breeze to inject some awareness into her.

'I don't know. That all depends on how bad he is and how many Stem soldiers are guarding him,' she replied.

Stopping at the traffic lights, Chloe noticed the sign for the hospital.

'How do we find out if Davrin is here?' She asked.

'I presume we'll just go in and ask at reception. I'm sure someone will know if he was admitted or not.'

They approached the hospital, noticing an empty ambulance outside, however, they didn't realise it was the same one that Ethan had been transported in. Ellie followed the signs for the car park.

'Just drop me off here and you can wait outside.' Chloe suggested. 'I won't be long. I'll just find out and be straight back.'

'Are you sure?'

'Yeah, of course, I'll be back in a few minutes.'

'Okay then.' Ellie muttered. 'I'll be right here if you need me.'

Chloe removed her seatbelt and opened the passenger door,

'Sure, what's the worst that can happen?'

Chloe shut the door and started to walk towards the hospital. Ellie watched her every step until she turned into the entrance and disappeared out of sight.

Walking in through the revolving doors of the hospital, the first thing Chloe noticed was the lavish chrome clock over the main reception desk. It read 10:15pm.

She scanned the large open room, and luckily for her it was an empty waiting area with only a few occupants.

She began to saunter up towards the reception desk. And as she approached the woman, the reception phone rang.

The receptionist held up a hand abruptly, as if to tell Chloe to wait her turn. She began to talk into the receiver. But Chloe didn't pay much attention to her. Her mind was elsewhere. She was too focused on Davrin. She waited calmly, tapping her fingers on top of the counter.

'Yes, so that's ten thirty tomorrow, bye,' the receptionist informed.

She hung up the phone and immediately tucked her head back down to record the detail.

'Do you mind?' She asked, not even looking up.

'Mind what?' Chloe questioned.

'Your tapping? It's quite rude. I'm trying to concentrate.'

'Oh I'm sooo sorry,' Chloe remarked. Her tone bubbling with sarcasm. 'I didn't know you needed peace and quiet working in a pressurised job like a hospital. Is it always this busy?'

Her sarcasm hitting new heights as she turned around to face the three other people waiting in the deserted A & E.

The receptionist's cold gaze hit Chloe as her eyelids narrowed to a fine pinprick,

'How can I help you?' She asked. A reluctance in her tone.

209

'I just have a question. My name is Chloe and I'm wondering if a friend of mine was admitted. It would have only been in the last fifteen minutes or so.'

'What's the name?' The receptionist asked. 'The name?' she repeated, not giving Chloe time to answer first time round.

'It's Davrin, Davrin Belshaw.'

Without removing her eyeline from Chloe, or even dropping her head down to check the log-in book, the receptionist replied,

'Nobody by that name has been admitted.'

Chloe didn't believe her. She figured she was playing hard ball.

'Are you sure?'

'Yes I'm sure. Are you telling me how to do my job?'

'No, not at all. Look, it's probably the end of your shift and you just want to get home.'

'I started an hour ago,' the receptionist replied, her face not amused.

'Well sorry for you, but as I said, I'm just looking for my friend, his name is Davin Belshaw.'

The receptionist dropped her pen. Her eyes rolled.

'And....I....told....you, there has been nobody admitted with that name. Are you sure you have the right hospital?'

Chloe was fuming at this stage. It was enough information for her to call it a night, but she didn't believe her, she wouldn't give up. She couldn't let this woman win. It was a competitive behaviour Callum had instilled in her.

'It must have been my other friend then,' she answered, beginning to ramble on as she usually did when she felt uncomfortable. 'You see, I wasn't actually there. I got a phone call about it.'

'I haven't got all night! What's your other friend's name?' The receptionist barked. Her patience now wearing thin.

210

'Ethan.'

'Ethan what?'

Chloe hesitated, her mind suddenly going blank.

'It's Ethan...' she said, trying to remember his second name.

'White, Ethan White,' a voice called out from behind her.

Chloe slowly turned around to thank the person. But then instant shock took over. There standing in front of her was a suited man.

'Can I ask how you know my son?' Payton questioned.

Chloe realised immediately that this man was Payton White. She hadn't heard him walk up behind her.

'Emm...I go to school with him,' she answered quickly.

'Yes, we do have an Ethan White,' the receptionist declared, looking at them both.

'How do you know what happened to my son?' Payton asked.

Chloe froze for a moment, her mind scrambling, frantically searching for something to say.

'I was here visiting my grandmother and then I saw him come in,' she replied as casually as she could.

But before Payton could react, the receptionist intervened,

'You told me you were looking for a Davrin somebody, was it Belshaw? Yes, that's it, you said you were looking for your friend, Davrin Belshaw. I don't remember you mentioning anything about your grandmother?'

The receptionist smirked. An increased sense of pride took over as she sat back watching. It was as if she had just thrown a hat into a ring, waiting to see what would happen.

'I'm sorry, I'm not feeling too good.' Chloe insisted, placing both hands on her stomach. 'A lot has happened today, and with the passing of my grandmother I'm all over the place. Where are your toilet's please, I think I need to throw up?'

Tears formed in her eyes, but she was not upset. She had just been outwitted in this immature cat fight, and these were tears of defeat.

'Over there,' the receptionist answered. Her finger pointing across the room.

'Thank you,' Chloe replied. 'And I do hope Ethan gets well soon. Tell him Jennifer sends her love.'

'Did you not say your name was Chloe?' The receptionist commented.

Chloe didn't reply. She hurried down the corridor in the direction of the toilets, an air of humiliation following her.

When she reached the toilet door, she turned back to look down the corridor. But Payton stood in front of the reception desk, staring back at her, his eyes watching her every move.

Chloe was terrified. She wasn't a stupid girl. She knew this man was dangerous. She knew he was on to her. And she knew she needed to get out of there fast.

She stepped in past the door, but immediately turned back out again, peering over at the reception desk. The receptionist now talking with Payton and flirting like mad. Her friendly manner appearing so different when talking to a man in a suit.

Payton had turned away briefly to answer her.

Chloe figured this was her chance to make a run for it. She hurried out of the toilets and began to pick up her pace. She turned the corner without even looking back.

She began to sprint down the corridor just as she heard a small commotion from the reception area. It was the receptionist shouting, and then she knew what was happening. Payton White must have left the reception area in a hurry. He must have come after her.

The previous cat fight had now turned into a cat and mouse chase. Unfortunately for Chloe, she had now been demoted to the mouse.

Chapter 37

'Are you sure you're okay Jenson?' Callum asked, crouching beside him. 'Is it those headaches again?'

'Yeah, but I'll be fine. I never knew how much I had to rely on those stupid tablets.'

He looked at Callum in the dim candlelight, noticing the scar on his left cheek.

'It could be worse,' Callum said. He had recognised Jenson's brief stare. 'You could have a horrible scar like mine. At least you only have a headache from time to time. You can cover that. I'm left with this scar for life.'

'It's not that bad,' Jenson retaliated, a guilt inside emerging.

'You don't have to lie. I'm used to people staring at the scar and wondering how I got it.'

'I'm not lying. Some girls like scars.' Jenson declared.

Callum got to his feet and walked over to the bench. He retrieved another bottle of water from a plastic bag.

'Do you know where I can find these girls?' He asked, smiling, and throwing the bottle to Jenson.

Jenson caught it and began to unscrew the cap.

'Do you think these headaches have anything to do with Stem wanting you?' Callum asked.

'I'm not sure. I don't know why I get these headaches. Maybe it's something to do with being a Non-dreamer. It's been that long since I had a bad one. And I don't really remember when I started taking the tablets. I do remember my parents saying they got worried when these Dream-deaths began. They were scared Stem would find out and take me away. I vaguely remember going to see somebody. I think he gave me the tablets. They helped a lot with my migraine. And I suppose ever since then, we've never really talked about it. I think we just felt, if we didn't speak about it, we would somehow forget about it and continue on as normal, well, until Robyn started to show the signs.'

'So she gets the headaches as well?'

'Yes, but nowhere near as bad. And who knows what Stem have done to her? I suppose we should count ourselves lucky that we don't dream. After seeing Chloe being cut open like that earlier, I don't think I would ever want to dream.'

Callum removed the wallet from his pocket. He took out a photo of himself, Chloe, and Carly.

'It's an old photo,' he said, passing it to Jenson. 'It's the last time we were all together.'

Jenson didn't quite know what to say.

'I should have saved her,' Callum said. His guilt returning.

'You were only a kid.'

'I know, but I could have done more.'

'Why are these demons after you?' Jenson asked.

'I'm not really sure. I've read up articles about demons from the Dream World. They look for souls so they can enter our world, but you hear loads of different opinions. I don't know what to believe in anymore. All I know is that I will never let anything happen to Chloe.'

Callum paused,

'Speaking of Chloe, what time is it?' His eyes glancing down at his watch. 'Did they ring yet?'

~~~

Chloe turned left and ran down another corridor without looking behind her. She began to lose her breath.

214

At the end of the corridor, she saw a sign for the stairs. Panicking, she pushed the door open to the stairwell and started to ascend.

Not more than a few seconds later, she heard the stairwell door below burst open.

Payton was after her and he was getting closer.

She reached the third floor and sprinted as fast as she could down another corridor.

Turning the corner, she immediately hit into a heavy-set Asian nurse who was carrying a bed pan, The contents spilling all over her uniform and onto the floor.

Chloe would have normally apologised for something like this. But at this point, she just needed to get away. She had no time to do anything else.

Payton was only seconds behind her, and when he too turned the same corner. He also smashed into the nurse who was bent over and cleaning up the spillage.

They both fell onto the ground.

Chloe heard the crashing sound but continued running.

'What's going on?' The nurse yelled.

Payton got to his feet.

'Oh shut up!' He said, throwing the bed pan at the nurse and continuing after Chloe.

This gave Chloe an advantage, but the added time was of no use. She came to a stop. She had come to a dead end; there was no stairwell or exit to help her escape this time.

She figured she could hide in one of the rooms, so she turned to open the nearest door, however, just as she opened it, she saw Payton racing towards her. It was too late. There was nowhere left for her to run, nowhere she could hide. The chase was over.

Chapter 38

Ellie was singing along to her favourite Abba song, sounding as if somebody had severed her vocal cords, and stitching them back upside down. Abba was a band her grandparents had liked. And she had been a fan ever since she was a little girl. They used to play songs for her all the time, and she was so bad, they had to increase the volume when she would sing. Ellie was a terrible singer, she hadn't a note in her head. But she never did care about sounding bad, just as long as nobody heard her.

As the song ended, her phone rang.

'Hey Jenson,' she said, initially hoping it would have been Chloe.

'Hey Ellie. We're just wondering if you've heard anything. Callum's getting a little worried about Chloe.'

'She's still in the hospital. It is a bit strange, I thought she would be back by now as well. I'll go check and I'll call you back.'

Ellie grabbed her handbag and got out of the car. She proceeded to walk towards the entrance of the hospital, still humming the Abba tune, and in search of Chloe.

Entering the building, she got an overwhelming feeling that something bad had happened. She stood there watching.

She then made her way over to the reception desk, over to where two Stem soldiers were standing and talking to the receptionist.

'They went that way,' she heard the receptionist say, pointing in the direction Chloe and Payton had gone.

216

Both Stem soldiers proceeded down the corridor.

Ellie looked for Chloe in the reception area, but she was nowhere to be seen. Panic set in and she turned back to step outside. She needed to call Jenson back.

~~~

Callum was pacing the church and had managed to position himself at the entrance when Jenson's phone rang. Jenson had gone into the toilet behind the altar. His phone was left on the bench and was now calling out to be answered.

'JENSON?' Callum shouted.

No response, so he began to scurry up the aisle.

Just as he got to the top, Jenson appeared out from behind the partition. The phone stopped.

'Why didn't you answer it?' Jenson asked.

'I didn't get there in time. Quick, check to see if it was the girls.'

Callum's worry was evident again.

Jenson managed to pick up his phone and was just about to dial out when it rang again.

He didn't answer it straight away. He allowed the ring to call out to him. He stood there staring at the screen as the vibrating tones echoed throughout the abandoned church, taunting him to answer it.

'What is it Jenson?' Callum asked. His eyebrows drawing together, trying to fill in the gap of concern.

Just then, Jenson answered it.

'Hello, mum?'

Callum was almost as surprised as Jenson, who appeared to collapse against the bench. He sat down.

'Where are you? Is this some sort of a trap?'

Another silence took over the room.

217

Callum waited, hoping the phone call would end soon so he would find out what was going on.

Had Jenson's parents been released? He thought. Or was this some kind of a deal, waiting to be made? What if Robyn helped find the cure?

'I'll be right there!' Jenson said, hanging up the phone and putting on his grey hoodie.

'What's happening Jenson?'

'It's my mother…they're home!'

Jenson's whole face now painted in a pale pastel.

'What do you mean they're home? Where do you think you're going?'

'Home…I'm going home.'

'What if it's a trap?' Callum asked, not sure if it was a good idea for Jenson to go.

'It's not. My mum wouldn't do that to me. Maybe they just don't need them anymore. Maybe it's something to do with Davrin?'

Jenson hurried down the aisle.

'Wait, I can drop you?' Callum offered, his voice following Jenson down the church.

Even though he figured this was a bad idea, he didn't want Jenson running aimlessly into a cage full of lions.

And with that, both boys disappeared, leaving the rattling of the doors behind them as the empty church stood still.

Chapter 39

Callum had dropped Jenson off at the edge of the park, the first place they had unintentionally met.

Jenson had begun his journey home. His approach was careful as Callum drove back to the church. If it was a trap, they both agreed they could not be captured together.

Jenson began to increase his pace. He wanted to move as fast as he could. His heart was beating furiously. He had only one thought in his head, and it was to see his parents and sister again. He was beginning to feel that this moment would never come, but somehow, miraculously, things had changed.

He was determined to see them again even if it was an ambush. But still, he remained vigilant. He cautiously walked along the darkened pathways, crossing the streets at every junction.

He had just reached the top of his road when his phone rang. He crouched behind a parked car and took it out of his pocket. It was Ellie.

'Hello?' He whispered.

'Jenson, I've been trying to call you. Is everything okay?'

'Yes, sorry Ellie, I didn't hear my phone. I was on Callum's bike. What's going on?'

'I think we have a problem. There seems to be some commotion here at the hospital. I'm not quite sure, but will you and Callum come down, we might need your help?'

Jenson paused,

'I'm sorry Ellie, I'm not at the church. My mum rang me. I'm going home.'

'WHAT?'

Ellie was completely thrown by Jenson's announcement.

'I know it seems suspicious, but I know my mother, she wouldn't lead me into a trap. They're home. Stem let them go. It's all over.'

'But what if they made your mother do this? What if they're using your sister as leverage?'

'Don't worry, I'm checking it out first. And if it is a trap, I'll meet you guys back at the church. You just stay at the hospital and wait for Chloe. I'm sure she'll be fine. From what I know of her, she can talk her way out of anything.'

'But the receptionist was talking to two Stem soldiers, and they went down the corridor after somebody. It looks serious.'

'Do you think Chloe was involved?'

'I'm not sure, I don't know.'

'I'm sure she's okay. She was only finding out if Davrin was there. Plus, nobody knows who she is?'

'Yeah, you're right I suppose,' Ellie replied, shrugging off any doubt. 'I'm probably overthinking it—don't mind me. It's been a long day. I'll go back in and check it out. I'm sure there's nothing to worry about. Maybe Chloe just went off to find more answers. Be careful Jenson. I'll ring you straight away if I find out anything.'

Jenson remained hidden in between two neighbouring cars with his hood up, concealing his full identity. He peered down the street towards his house. He could see a light on in the bottom window of his family home. His heart, pounding at the prospect of seeing his family again. Many thoughts flooding his mind and causing it to go into overdrive. *Is Davrin in the hospital? Had his ability become the number one priority? Had Stem caught him and maybe now they didn't need Jenson or his family anymore? Or was it Ethan? Had he explained to his father who Jenson was, and he let his family go?*

220

Jenson looked around the deserted street as he crept up towards his house, meticulously weaving in and out of the cars. He convinced himself that this was not a set-up. And this feeling was somehow backed up by the empty street, and no evidence of even a single Stem soldier in sight.

As he observed the area around the front of the house, he noticed a figure from the corner of his eye. It was someone lurking from a neighbouring window.

As he glanced over to see who it was, the image disappeared in a flash of light.

More questions began to plague his mind as the light distinguished. *Was it a kid with a torch? Was it somebody who had just switched their light on, and the bulb blew? Or was it a Stem soldier, their night-mode gun glimmering in the distance.* But whatever it was, it had vanished in the blink of an eye.

Jenson's attention shifted back to his house. He heard the front door creek open. The noise echoing even louder than normal. Perhaps it was his body reacting to the adrenaline, anticipating any sort of movement. He was on high alert. Everything seemed to subside except for the opening of the door.

He slipped back down behind the parked car and looked out beyond the window to get a better view.

It was his mother.

She stepped out into the garden. And taking a few cautious steps along the pathway, she stopped. She stood there looking nervous.

Jenson had never seen her so afraid. Her gaze shifting from every angle. She was waiting for somebody. She was waiting for her son.

Jenson couldn't believe it. His heart was pounding again. It was beating faster than ever before. He looked behind her in the doorway, just to be certain it wasn't a set-up.

He was half expecting a Stem soldier to be standing there with a gun pointing at his mother's back. But the doorway stood empty.

Jenson didn't care at this point. Seeing his mother had made him emotional. He just wanted to hold her, to give her a hug, even if it was for the last time. He had come too far to go back.

He swiped some beads of sweat from his forehead, as if swatting away any doubt.

He then stood up, revealing himself from behind the parked car. But before he ran across the road, a light sparked again in the neighbouring window. It was mesmerising. He stood there, his body in some sort of a trance, motionless, and waiting for the flash to return.

'Jenson?' His mother cried out.

She stood there with her arms wide open, waiting for him to run to her, the son she thought she would never see again.

Jenson shook his head, forgetting about the flashes of light.

The adrenaline kicking back in, and running across the street, he fell straight into his mother's arms.

He held onto her, closing his eyes, and cherishing every second.

His mother began to sob uncontrollably.

They stood there for a moment, wrapped in each other's embrace, neither one saying a word.

'Oh Jenson,' his mother finally said, clinging to her son, 'we thought we'd never see you again.'

She began to squeeze him even more tightly.

'Where's Dad and Robyn?' Jenson asked.

'They're okay, don't worry,' his mother answered.

She released her grip to take a good look at her son, as if examining him to see if he was okay. 'They're inside. Your sister is still unconscious, but she should be awake soon.'

'Unconscious?' Jenson questioned, pushing his mother further away and holding onto her forearms. A panic in his eyes.

'It's okay, Jenson. They drugged her. They drugged us all to bring us back here. She'll be fine. They let us go.'

'Why?'

'I don't know. Maybe we were the lucky few that survive the testing,' his mother replied. 'We're all safe now, that's all that matters. Come on, let's go inside.'

~~~

After speaking with Jenson, Ellie walked straight back into the hospital. This time there was a lot less commotion. The Stem soldiers were out of sight.

The receptionist was on the phone, talking loudly.

'I know, and he was lovely, in his posh suit, but he just ran after her.'

Could that man she's talking about be Payton White? Ellie thought to herself. And did he run after Chloe?

She walked towards the corridor, trying to look inconspicuous, but she was cut short when the receptionist stood up and called out after her.

'Excuse me, Miss? I'll need you to wait over there,' she instructed, tilting her head back towards the waiting area. 'There's something that has just happened, and I can't let anybody through until it's resolved.'

'Okay,' Ellie replied, quietly taking a seat in front of the reception area. *What is it with these strict receptionists? She thought.*

223

'Hello,' a man said as Ellie sat down.

This stranger looked dishevelled. A grey tinge to his mid-length brown hair, indicating he was older than Ellie, a lot older. And his unshaven face with grey speckles made him look tired.

'Hi,' Ellie replied politely.

'You look nervous,' the man said, 'is everything okay?'

Ellie did not want to get into a conversation, especially with a complete stranger. Now was not the time, considering what was going on, but she didn't want to be rude either.

'Yes, I hope everything is okay. I'm just waiting on somebody,' she replied, expecting to disguise her worry.

'Well, whatever it is, God is looking down on us all,' the man exclaimed as he passed a set of rosary beads from one hand to the other.

'I'm Bill,' he said.

'Ellie.'

'A good friend of mine is here, a friend from church,' Bill continued. 'There's not much they can do for him. It's his time.'

He looked away and blessed himself with the prayer beads,

'But I know when he passes, he will be in good hands.'

'I'm so sorry,' Ellie said, offering her sympathy, but she didn't really want to get into further conversation with this man.

'Thank you,' Bill said, smiling back at her. 'Maybe you could say a prayer for him?'

'I will,' Ellie answered, knowing she never would.

'You're probably wondering why I am not in with him?'

'No, I couldn't care less.'

But these words never left Ellie's mouth. She conjured them but hadn't the heart to say them out loud. She just looked back at him, waiting for him to answer. Her mind had been diverted.

She just needed him to be quiet for a moment. She needed to think.

'His daughter is in there with him.' Bill said. 'I gave him his last rites. I've said my goodbyes already. God has his reasons. I will see him in the next life.'

Ellie smiled, but her smile was weak. Something inside her snapped.

'Can you ask this God of yours how my mother is?'

Ellie didn't believe in God, and she certainly didn't have the patience to listen to a priest preaching to her, especially since her mother had died in her sleep when Ellie was only a teenager. *Where was his 'God' then? She wondered.*

'Pardon me?' Bill asked, taken aback by Ellie's comment.

'I've no time for this,' Ellie said, getting up from her chair and walking out.

This wasn't like her, but she felt herself becoming more agitated with every word this man was saying. She couldn't sit around and wait for Chloe to show up. She had to do something.

Chapter 40

The inside of the house felt just as cold as the outside. Jenson's mother only realising this now as she stepped back in. She had been so worried about her son returning, she hadn't noticed how cold the house had been.

'I'll stick on the heating. Your Dad is up with Robyn in her bedroom, go on up to them,' she said, walking towards the kitchen.

Jenson didn't need to be told twice. He scaled the stairs as if running a gauntlet, swinging round the banisters, and remembering the last time he had done this, he was dodging a bullet. He continued down the landing to Robyn's bedroom.

When the door burst open, his father turned round with a startled look on his face. He immediately jumped to his feet when he saw his son.

'Jenson!' He said. 'You're okay!'

'Yeah Dad,' Jenson answered, feeling overwhelmed at the sight of him.

Grabbing Jenson, his father squeezed even harder than his mother did.

Jenson felt his lungs drain of oxygen. He let out a deflating cough.

His father realised this and released his grip, acknowledging how rough he was. But he didn't apologise. He was so excited to see his son again. He held Jenson out just as his mother had, quickly examining him to make sure he was alright. His eyes scouring his body, his hands gripping tightly onto Jenson's shoulders, securing him into position and not allowing him to move.

Jenson appreciated this moment, especially considering his father lacked the affection sometimes.

'Where were you?' His father asked.

'I'm okay, Dad. I managed to get away. I hid out for a while. I've made some new friends. They've been helping me.'

Jenson caught a glimpse of his sister lying in the bed.

'Is she okay?' He asked.

His father shifted sideways, allowing him to see her.

'I think she's coming round,' he said, sitting down at Robyn's bedside and holding her hand.

Robyn began to toss slowly, dipping in and out of consciousness.

'Hey, sweetheart, it's me, Dad.'

Her father gently swept a few loose strands of hair from her face. Her hair, a dirty brown colour, darker than normal and in need of a wash.

Jenson felt sorry for her as she lay there with a dirty little face. He wondered what she had gone through as he watched her stir. He noticed the shaved spot on the side of her head, just along her hairline. It looked like stitches leading out onto her forehead, with the remnants of glue residue from a plaster. No doubt his parents had taken it off to investigate. His heart sank. He couldn't imagine what happened to her, the assessments, the procedures, the incisions. He then noticed bruising along her arms, with tiny puncture marks.

'Dad?' Robyn called out in a soft whimper.

'Yes, sweetheart, it's me, and your brother.'

Robyn's eyes wondered.

'Jenson?' She called out, still shy but a little louder.

'Yes Robyn?' Jenson replied, picking up her other hand and placing it in his. He could feel how cold she was.

Robyn's eyes were wide open now, her batteries still trying to recharge.

Her father propped another pillow under her neck to help her sit up further. As he lifted her into a more upright position, she threw her arms around his neck and began to weep.

'It's okay sweetheart, we're here now. It's all over.'

'My poor baby!' Their mother cried as she entered the room. John eased his grip so his wife could take hold of her.

Robyn began to cough.

'Sarah! Give her some room to breathe,' John advised.

'Sorry Robyn. I just got a little carried away. How are you feeling?'

'I'm hungry.'

'I'm sure you are,' her mother said. 'I'll be right back. I'll go and fix you something to eat. You too Jenson, I'm sure you're hungry too.'

'Where were you, Jenson?' Robyn asked. Her attention moving back to her brother.

Jenson moved closer,

'I'm so sorry Robyn. It wasn't my fault. I couldn't help you. Those soldiers, they took you all away. There was nothing I could have done to save you.'

Jenson felt guilty. He knew he had been unable to protect his sister from all of this. He knew she idolised him and always considered herself to be safe when he was around.

'I'm glad you are here now,' she said. Her body shifting in the bed to grab hold of his hand again. Her short sniffling returned. This was something that usually irritated Jenson, but now, he felt it would never annoy him ever again.

228

'I'll never let anyone hurt you again.' He claimed.

'They weren't all bad men in Stem,' Robyn said. 'There was this man in a white coat, and I was tied up in a chair and he had needles…'

'Can you describe him?' Her father asked. A stern inquisition to his tone. 'Did he have a name tag?'

'Tom,' Robyn replied. 'But he was a good guy. He said he had to do it.'

'Had to do what?'

Robyn looked down at the marks on her arms.

'Had to take my blood—but he did sneak me some jellies when I woke up. And he gave me water.'

'Did anything else happen?' Her father asked.

'He knows our secret,' Robyn answered, turning to look at Jenson. 'He knows we don't dream.'

'Anything else?' Her father probed.

'No Dad, I swear, that was all.'

Robyn looked scared. She was scared that her father might not believe her.

'It's okay Robyn,' he said, hugging her again. 'It's all over now.'

~~~

Ellie paced frantically up and down by the side of her car. She felt helpless not knowing where Chloe was. She had her phone out contemplating on ringing Jenson's number again. *But what would he be able to do? He was miles away at home, she thought.*

She threw her phone abruptly back into her handbag and walked around the side of the hospital in search of another way in. She couldn't sit around and wait.

Turning the corner, she heard some sort of a disturbance. She didn't quite know where the noise was coming from, but she knew something was happening.

Suddenly, hearing a sound from above, she looked up.

Just then, a body came hurling out of a window on the third floor. Ellie felt her heart sink. Something had just exploded from inside her chest. She recognised the body as it fell.

'CHLOEEEEE!' She screamed.

Chapter 41

Ellie immediately ran over to the unused ambulance van where the body had crashed onto. Her heart racing and trying to understand how this had happened. She couldn't see Chloe's body as it was suspended on top of the tall vehicle. And for a slight moment, she had begged that "so called" God of hers, pleaded with him for her safety.

'QUICK! GOOOOO!' Chloe ordered, jumping up and making herself visible.

Without any hesitation, she clambered down the side of the ambulance and flung herself off, even before she could reach the ground.

Only then, Ellie realised that Chloe had, in fact, jumped out of the window, strategically landing on top of the ambulance, a perfectly calculated plan to break her fall.

A loud bang resonated. Ellie's body shook with the vibrations. It sounded like gunfire. She quickly glanced back up whilst running away.

There, standing in the window Chloe had just leapt from, was a man in a black suit, pointing a gun at them. It was Payton White.

'QUICK! RUN!' Chloe screamed again.

They both turned the corner of the hospital, now shielded from any further gunfire.

'What happened?' Ellie asked, frantically racing back to her car. She noticed Chloe was limping.

'Have you been shot?' Ellie demanded. A worry in her questioning.

'No, I'm okay. It's from the fall. It's Payton White, Ethan's father. He realised who I was.'

'You're limping? Are you sure you haven't been shot?'

'No, I'm fine. Don't be worrying. We need to get out of here, quick! They'll be coming after us!'

~~~

Jenson could hear his mother rustling around in the kitchen. She was preparing food, and the sound of clatter brought back normality. *It felt good to hear some sort of normality again, he thought.*

But just as he reached the kitchen door, he let out a yelp. He lifted his hand to press firmly against his head.

'What is it?' His mother asked, rushing over to him.

Jenson was groaning with pain. He couldn't speak; it was one of his migraines again.

'JOHN! QUICK!' His mother called out.

'What's wrong? What is it Sarah?' John retaliated.

'I don't know,' his wife replied, holding onto Jenson.

'What's wrong, son?'

Jenson was still moaning.

'I'm okay, really I am...it's just these headaches. I've been getting them since I ran out of my tablets.'

'There should be some upstairs in your room,' his mother informed him as she and her husband helped Jenson onto the couch.

'I lost them. Have you anymore?'

'No, I'm sorry Jenson. They were the last of them. I was meant to get you more, but...'

'I can go first thing in the morning,' his father suggested.

'I don't know why I've to depend on those stupid tablets anyway.'

'You've been taking them since you were a child,' his mother explained. 'They help you.'

'Help me with what?' Jenson asked. 'I don't even remember why I started taking them in the first place.'

'You do remember how crazy you were before you took them?' His father explained.

Jenson looked at him. His mind, foggy now. He couldn't remember.

'Oh Jenson,' his mother stated as she sat down beside him on the couch and began to rub his back. 'You were only little. You kept saying you could see fairies with magic light. We even caught you talking to them, well...talking to yourself. We thought it was a phase, like having an imaginary friend, but this was something else. You had us nearly believing in it too. We had to get some help without anyone knowing. We were so scared that you would be taken away from us. We were scared Stem would find out. We found someone who helped us, somebody off the radar.'

'This is all my fault,' a soft voice echoed from out in the cold hallway.

It was Robyn, standing there, crying.

'Oh no honey, not at all,' her mother replied.

'But Jenson is hurt,' Robyn whimpered.

Sarah rushed over to her daughter and held her in her arms.

'This is not your fault,' she began. 'Your brother has a headache because he has no medication.'

'Come on honey,' her father said, moving towards Robyn and picking her up. 'Myself and your mother will bring you back to bed. You need to get some rest. Your brother will be up to you in a few minutes, won't you Jenson?'

The three of them turned to look at Jenson, each waiting on an answer.

'Yes of course, I'll be up to you in a few minutes. I'm okay—see,' he said, beaming a big smile at Robyn.

Jenson's parents began to walk up the stairs just as his artificial smile dipped.

Sitting there all alone, he began to contemplate what his mother had just said.

He used to see fairies when he was younger, before the tablets, and now when he stopped taking them, he was beginning to see things again; the flashes of light in a neighbouring house, Davrin's green eyes beaming, and Miss Belshaw's dark eyes and facial change.

What the hell was happening to him? He thought.

And then he remembered the portraits of the fairies in St Anita's, the pictures that had distilled a distant memory inside him, a memory he struggled to remember.

Henry had told them about 'Blaine', the patient who spoke about seeing fairies in his dreams, and how he was afraid of demons coming to take him away.

Jenson's chest began to burn. His insides churned with fear. What was happening to him?

He wasn't too sure what to think, but he knew he had to go back to St Anita's. Even though he didn't dream, he somehow had a similar story to the patient, Blaine, the frizzled white-haired man they had seen in Stephanie's unit. This man, a dreamer, who had detailed pictures of the fairies. Jenson knew he needed to speak with him. He needed some reasoning behind what was happening to him. Otherwise, he himself could one day end up in there like the rest of them. Locked up forever and never leaving that "Hell-hole".

Chapter 42

Ellie pulled into the driveway; Chloe was in the passenger seat and Callum was trailing on his motorbike. The front door of the bungalow opened, and an overexcited brown and white boxer dog came running out from the porch.

Ellie spotted Meatloaf as she turned off the car lights and hopped out.

'Hey boy!' She shouted, dropping her handbag, and rubbing him, who in turn, began to jump all over her, his tail whipping with excitement.

'He's delighted to see you all and so am I,' Wardy said, greeting them at the doorway.

'Oh Dad, what a night we've had!' Ellie declared, picking up her bag and walking towards him. 'Come on in,' she said, inviting Callum and Chloe inside. 'You'll be safe here. Just move your bike around the back out of sight.'

'What about Jenson?' Chloe asked.

'Just because you have a thing for him doesn't mean we have to go back out and risk it all again.' Callum snarled as he wheeled his bike around the side. 'It was his stupid idea to go and see his family. I tried to talk him out of it, but he didn't listen. So whatever happens, it's all on him.'

'Come on, let's just get inside.' Ellie instructed. 'We can ring his phone.'

The jeep lights were turned off as it pulled up outside the driveway of the bungalow.

'So we gonna go in, boss?' George asked Payton.

235

They both watched on as the front door closed.

'No, I think we'll leave it. There's no point in rushing into things. I can't afford to make any more mistakes that might endanger my family. We know where they live now, so we'll find out who they all are. Plus, we have other priorities.'

Payton tilted his head to disclose his next plan. And there, concealed in the back seat and hidden from view was an unconscious body.

'I guess you're right,' George replied, waiting on his boss's next instruction.

'Take me back to Stem. We have some work to do.'

'You sure you don't wanna go back to the hospital to see your son?'

Payton looked at George; his stern expression said it all.

'Just take us out of here before anyone sees us. I want to hold onto the element of surprise. I'm going to find out who each of these people are.'

~~~

Jenson went into Robyn's bedroom to say goodnight to her.

'Hey,' he said as he lay down on the bed beside her. 'You okay?'

Robyn nodded.

'Good,' he said, 'because you do know none of this is your fault. For some reason, people wanted to find out why you don't dream. Some people get really hurt when they dream, and they probably wanted to see if you could help others. That's why they needed you, and that's why they stuck those needles into you.'

Robyn hung onto Jenson's every word.

For Jenson, this gave him some comfort. He knew they would never go back to a normality. They would always be in the clutches of Stems power, waiting until the day they were

236

called upon or worse still, taken again. But for now, this was what he needed. It was something he thought he would never get again.

He leaned in and kissed her on the cheek.

'Good night,' he said, crawling back away from the bed.

He had only taken a few steps away from the bed when he heard Robyn's soft voice call out to him.

'Jenson?'

'Yeah?'

'Will you sleep in with me tonight?'

'Of course,' he said. Her fragile face looking even more innocent.

Robyn pulled back the covers while Jenson kicked off his runners and got in.

'You know when that man stuck those needles into me, I was scared,' she said.

'I'm sure you where,' Jenson replied.

'And then, after a bit, I wasn't really scared anymore. Do you know why?'

'No. Why?'

'I told him about you. And I said that you would make sure we were all okay.'

'Awh, that's so sweet Robyn,' he said, reaching his arm around and pulling her in closer. 'But do you know what?'

Robyn shook her head.

'I think you were braver!'

Robyn grinned from ear to ear. These words had meant so much to her, and Jenson could see this.

Jenson took her hand and held it in his as they both lay there in silence, both cherishing this moment. Their eyes eventually closing as they both fell into a dark dreamless sleep.

~~~

Jenson's eyes opened; it was still dark outside. It was the middle of the night.

He turned over to check on Robyn. She was deep in slumber beside him.

Just as he turned over to go back to sleep, he saw a flashing light outside the window. He sat up and looked around, but the light had vanished just as quick. It was the same light he had seen before.

He believed the trickery from his mind had manifested, a state he reckoned would fix itself once he started to take his tablets again. And with a frustrated toss, he propped his pillow with his fist and dropped his head back down against it.

Then, in fear, he jumped back in the bed. It was the flashing light once more, only this time it was clearer. This time it was inside the house. It was inside the bedroom. This time the light was lingering. It was flickering at the bottom of the bed.

Chapter 43

Jenson crawled down towards the end of the bed. He peered over the edge and kicked back. Something was hiding at the bottom of the bed, crouching down on the floor. And most of its body was sheltering along the underframe. Whatever it was it let out a sigh,

'You can see me?' A girl's voice spoke. Her body uprooting itself from her hideaway.

She seemed shocked. A life-size version of a fairy. Perhaps the same age as Robyn.

'What are you?' Jenson asked.

'You can see me?' The little voice said again.

She looked like some sort of a fairy with blue eyes that were abnormally big, doubling the size of an average human. Her face was a pale grey, and Jenson noticed her whole body balancing this anaemic shade. She had long black hair with pointed ears, small and protruding out through her locks. She looked like something from an enchanted place. Chalky brown material clung to her body with lace bodices draped all over, unsuitably matching but aesthetically pleasing. And her wings. Jenson could see wings attached to her back, jutting out over her shoulders. And even though they were small, he could see the vibrant blue of the morpho butterfly in them, the richest of blues, comparable to the waters of a coral reef, with a purple shimmer throughout.

Jenson had always been fascinated with butterflies, ever since he was a young boy. His parents never understood where this obsession had come from, an obsession he later grew out of. But now, the stories of fairies, the headaches, it had all been true!

'What's going on?' He asked. 'Am I dreaming? Is this what it's like to dream?'

'A dream?' The fairy girl questioned. She looked just as confused as he was.

'Yes, a dream!' Jenson replied. 'But we don't dream.'

The fairy began to giggle shyly. She then quickly put one of her hands up to cover her mouth, a wave of embarrassment hung over her for laughing. 'I'm sorry. But you are not dreaming,' she said.

Jenson paused. His mind was refusing to believe what was now standing in front of him.

'If I'm not dreaming, then what are you?'

'My name is Myral. I am a tooth fairy.'

Jenson's eyes widened. His breath shortened. His whole body tingled. But then, his mother's words bellowed once more,

'When you were a child, you kept saying you could see fairies with magic light.'

'Why can I see you?' He asked.

'I'm not sure,' Myral replied.

Her wings began to flutter, emitting a steady drone like hum. Her whole body elevated off the ground as she flew up onto the bed.

Jenson jerked backwards, but she didn't hesitate. She continued.

Her feet trailing the bedding as she approached, her body levitating as her hand reached out to touch him.

Jenson froze. He couldn't move. He lay there watching her sail overhead.

She gently caressed his cheek.

'So, it is true!' She declared.

'What is true?'

'The stories about you.'

'Me?' Jenson questioned. His whole body collapsing against the covers.

Myral sighed,

'I have to go.'

'Wait. Why?'

'I've said too much.'

'Wait....'

But as the flutter quickened and the hum grew louder, Myral reached into a concealed cavity, clutching a handful of colourful dust from her pouch. She pulled it out, and in one sweeping motion, she sprinkled the dust over Jenson.

Jenson fell back onto the bed, unconscious, as the dust dissipated around him, leaving a damp smudge behind.

Seconds later, Myral sprinkled the rest of the dust overhead and vanished in the same ball of light she entered with.

Chapter 44

Chloe coughed. Her dry throat caused her to waken. She glanced over and realised Callum was not in the bed beside her.

She got up quietly and stepped out of the guestroom.

Out in the hallway she could feel a slight breeze. Her body began to shiver. She could hear sounds coming from the living room. She didn't know what time it was, but it must have been the early hours of the morning. The last thing she could remember was Callum wishing her a 'safe sleep'.

Eager to investigate, she continued. The sudden sound of 'white noise' alleviated any concern. She knew Callum had not seen a T.V. in weeks. He must have gotten up early to have a look.

Chloe could see the dark sky beginning to brighten as she stepped into the kitchen. Dawn was approaching.

Over at the sink, she began to fill a glass of water.

Once done, she took a long gulp and sauntered into the living room, expecting to see Callum watching the television. But the couch was empty. She suddenly became confused, wondering where he could be.

Just then the television switched itself off. This startled Chloe, causing her to drop the glass of water.

She crouched down to pick up the pieces of glass.

Unexpectedly, she felt a sharp chill down her spine; she then realised she was not actually awake, she was dreaming. She felt scared in this lucid dream. Something wasn't right.

She suddenly began to hear a noise from out in the hallway, as if laughter, but it was barely perceptible to her senses.

She grew afraid. Something was beyond the wall, and it was coming for her.

She inched away from the couch and stood there, transfixed, waiting for the door to open. But nothing happened.

The laughter stopped. It was as if whatever it was, had gone.

She began to walk cautiously over to the kitchen, making sure she avoided the broken glass.

Just as she got to the kitchen table, she screamed.

A figure stood in the doorway. It was tall. A scrawny creature with two heads. Neither face had features—no eyes, no mouth, not even a nose. The faces had flat foreheads with horns, dispositioned towards the back of each hairless head. Even though the creature had no eyes, it seemed to know exactly where she was.

It moved towards her. Its skinny hands outstretched. A shaking anticipation took hold of its body, eager to make contact. Then the laughter returned.

'WHAT DO YOU WANT?' Chloe shouted, presenting the large shard of glass she had picked up. It was the only thing standing between them.

The demon's fingers straightened out, revealing a slit in each palm of its hand. The slits opened and a voice spoke from them.

'Silly girl, we want you,' one voice said, while the other voice laughed.

'Stay back or I'll hurt you,' Chloe instructed. A fear in her voice but she wanted to stand her ground. She desperately began to wave the piece of glass.

Both voices engulfed the room. The laugher became deafening. The creature pressed forward.

'What do you want from me?' Chloe cried. She was retreating even further.

'You are a silly girl if you don't know that,' a voice said.

'I can taste her blood from here,' the other voice added. 'Hurry up, I want to feed on her.'

Chloe felt all alone. She cautiously backed away. There was nothing else she could do, except to call for help,

'CALLUUUMM!' She yelled.

Chapter 45

Callum was lying on top of his bed. He was back in his family home. This was a bright, peaceful dream, the dream he and his sister had always shared. He lay there, enjoying the warm breeze gently cascading in from the open window. He looked over to where Chloe would sit, outstretched on the bean bag. This is where they would meet in their dreams. This was the place they would come to hide. A place they would find sanctuary. Their safe place. But Chloe had not appeared.

He figured she had not fallen asleep yet. She was perhaps still awake and talking to Ellie. Then, suddenly, a dark cloud outside cast a shadow over the whole room. Callum felt something was wrong in this dream, their dream. It was their safe place, but now, something had disturbed their protection. And then he heard it. There in the distance, a faint cry. He heard his name being called. It was Chloe,

'CALLUM!' She called out. A panic in her voice.

He immediately leapt out of the bed, distinctively knowing his sister's cry. He knew she was in trouble. It was a call for help.

He closed his eyes to concentrate, trying to pick up on where she was. This was a skill they had both learned over the years, ever since their sister Carly had died. A skill to get to where the other one was, to help them. It was an ability known to most 'Searchers'.

'Come on, come on,' he screeched, desperately wanting to get to Chloe before it was too late.

Chloe viciously swiped the glass, slashing it across the fingers of the creature's hand.

It let out a scowl while the other hand spoke.

'BITCH!' It said, as if defending its counterpart. And with that, it extended its arm, not allowing Chloe any time to run. It grabbed her by the neck.

Chloe felt a sharp bite as it latched on. Its teeth penetrating her skin. It was as if this monster was trying to eat her, using the slit in its hand.

Chloe raised her arm again and swiped down once more. The piece of glass jammed into its hand, securely imbedding itself.

The creature screamed again, pulling its hand back from her neck, revealing a bloodied tongue with razor sharp teeth.

Chloe stood there observing this creature as she too held onto her damaged neck.

Just then, she was slapped hard in the face by the other hand.

This attack, directed her across the room, and sent her crashing into the T.V.

Whilst she lay there groaning on the ground and trying to move, the creature scrambled over, swiping the couch out of the way as if it were a piece of light material.

It picked her up again by the throat, digging its sharp spikes in even further. Chloe tried to scream, but her fall had triggered a weakened state. The creatures other hand gripped onto her shoulder, firmly securing her as it too began to feed.

~~~

Callum opened his eyes. He was back in Ellie and Wardy's home, but he knew he was still dreaming. He immediately jumped out of bed.

Running into the kitchen, he saw his sister suspended in the air. It reminded him of that night in his home when he was a child, the night he recalled Carly's little body dangling in mid-air before she was taken away.

Refusing to let this happen again, he reached over and opened the kitchen drawer.

He grabbed a knife, and without any hesitation, he charged over to Chloe.

As he reached her, the monster dropped Chloe and spun around, smacking Callum in the face. This slap sent him crashing across the room and smashing into the kitchen table.

'CALLUM!' Chloe screamed.

The creature had its back to her now. She could see its eyes on the tips of the horns.

It stayed there, facing away from her while its hands, directing backwards and trying to grab her again.

Chloe hobbled over to the corner of the room. She picked up the light stand, weaving it around, trying to warn off this creature,

'LEAVE US ALONE!' She yelled.

The cackling returned as the monster began to laugh again. But before it could reach Chloe, Callum ran at it again, stabbing a sharp broken table leg into its back.

Chloe automatically charged at the creature after seeing her brother do the same. And with every ounce of strength left in her, she swung the light stand, smacking the demon and slicing off one of its heads.

Callum dropped the sharp stick. The noise was unbearable. He held his hands over his ears to shield them from the deafening shrieks coming from this creature.

Chloe duplicated this action. The crying squeals were too much. She fell to her knee's, her palms protecting her eardrums.

The screams were short-lived, but the demon spoke one last time.

'Our Master will come for you. She will come for you all!'

'What do you want from us?' Chloe cried.

'Silly girl. The souls of Dreamers keep us alive.'

With that, the demon took its last breath and dissolved into a mound of ash.

'Oh Callum,' Chloe said, holding onto him as they stood beside the demon remains. 'Your eye. It's swollen.'

'I'm okay. It was just a little slap. What's with the face. Why do they aim for the face? I'm already scarred there. Are you okay?'

'Yes, I think so.'

'Your neck Chloe, it's bleeding?'

'I know. It was trying to eat me.'

Chloe held her hand up to her throat, applying pressure to her wound.

'Your hand?' Callum said, noticing another cut.

'It was glass. I'll be fine.'

'We better wake up and get your hand seen to.'

They pressed their foreheads together and closed their eyes, concentrating on waking up.

~~~

Meatloaf stood beyond the closed door, barking in hysterics. A commotion erupted inside, but he was refused entry.

Ellie ran charging past and burst into the bedroom, slamming the door open.

As soon as she entered, she saw the blood on the bed covers. 'WHAT THE HELL IS GOING ON?'

'It's okay,' Callum replied. 'It was another demon, but we killed it.'

Ellie was dragged back from the doorway as her protective father whooshed her aside.

He hobbled out in front with a stick in his hand.

'It's okay dad,' Ellie pleaded. 'They're fine.'

'Is Chloe alright?' He questioned, now looking at her clutching onto her bloodied neck.

'I'm fine, it's just a few scratches,' she answered. 'The main thing is we're safe.'

'Yeah, but for how long?' Callum replied, holding onto his sister. 'You heard what it said. She's coming for us all!'

Chapter 46

Jenson opened his eyes. Daylight had broken the dark abysmal episode. It was like a hazy nightmare, if ever he dreamt of one. He was back in his own room and had vaguely remembered waking up in the early hours, feeling damp from presumably his own sweat, and slipping back into his own bed. This nightmare was truly over. The morning seemed somehow lighter. The sky was brighter, and he was back with his family. A feeling he would never take for granted again.

He checked his alien alarm clock; it was 8.43am. He lay there smiling to himself. This was the "cool" alarm clock Robyn had kept pestering their mother to buy him for his 15th birthday. Jenson recalled the morning when Robyn burst into his bedroom with the present wrapped in shiny paper, hidden behind her back. He remembered her excitement. It was the first time she had saved up the little pocket money she got, to buy something special.

Despite only going to bed in the early hours, Jenson could not sleep anymore. Throwing off the covers, he sat up on the edge of his bed. He realised he was so caught up in his own family affairs that he had forgotten about the others. He hadn't even bothered to find out what had happened to Chloe and Ellie at the hospital.

His contentment soon turned into guilt. These people, his new friends, who had all played a part in trying to reunite him with his family, had all been forgotten.

He reached over to his locker and grabbed his phone. There were four missed calls from Ellie. He dialled her number and waited.

'Hey Ellie,' he said. 'I'm so sorry if I woke you and I'm sorry for only ringing now. I know I should have phoned you back last night, but things just got on top of me. I completely forgot.'

Jenson listened closely as Ellie told him the full story of what had happened last night, first Payton White at the hospital, and then the demon trying to kill Chloe.

'Are they okay?' Jenson asked.

'Yes, they're fine now,' Ellie admitted. 'A few cuts and bruises, but Callum's annoying Chloe already this morning, so things are back to normal. You don't need to worry at all. How's Robyn and your parents?'

'Good. Great in fact!'

A huge smile appeared unexpectedly on Jenson's face, much to his delight.

'That's good Jenson. I'm so happy for you.'

Jenson turned down a lift from Ellie. He hung up the phone, and with the burden of everything lifting from his shoulders, he casually went in to check on Robyn. She was still fast asleep in her bed, just where he had left her.

Suddenly, a vision of the blue morpho butterfly popped into his head, flapping its wings, and flying off to another nesting place.

This confused Jenson. He couldn't understand where this imagery was coming from. He couldn't remember anything other than falling asleep with Robyn next to him. He couldn't even remember waking up and getting into his own bed.

Dislodging the butterfly picture from his mind, he shook his head and gently closed Robyn's door.

He skipped down the stairs, a spring in his step, just like most mornings before this nightmare enfolded. He felt as if a heavy weight had been lifted.

'Hey, go easy, what's the rush?' His mother whispered.

She had met him at the bottom of the stairs. 'Your father and sister are still sleeping. Anyway, what has you up so early—where are you off to?'

'Sorry,' Jenson replied, only now realising he could have woken them. 'I'm going out to meet up with the others. Remember, the people I told you about last night, the ones who were trying to help me?'

'Oh yes,' his mother replied. 'If you hang on, I'll drop you.'

'Ah no, it's fine, thanks,' Jenson said, kissing her cheek and continuing towards the front door. 'I could do with the fresh air.'

'Okay. But be careful. I'll get those tablets for you later,' his mother called after him as he shut the front door.

~~~

'That was Jenson on the phone,' Ellie stated. 'They're all safe and sound.'

'That's great.' Chloe answered. 'Is he coming round?'

'Yeah, you'd like that wouldn't you?' Callum teased.

Chloe's eyes rolled. She didn't respond. This behaviour was always something Callum would do after they got into a bit of bother. He would always deflect the undertone of a bad situation. She needed to change the subject.

'You look lovely,' she stated, admiring Ellie's clothing and the way she was fixing her long red hair into a side ponytail.

'Where are you off to all dolled up like that?' Callum asked. His attentions moving elsewhere as Chloe had predicted.

'Thank-you Chloe. I was talking to Henry on the phone, you know the Irish man, the nurse from St Anita's? He told me if I ever needed anything to ring him, so I texted him to ask if he could help you both sleep without bad dreams. And after what happened last night in your dream, I won't be able to sleep until I know you are both safe. He said a new drug came in from Stem last night. They were trialling it out on some patients. He said he would take some, for you guys. He was going to come around here after work with them.'

'Is he not coming anymore?' Callum asked.

'I gave him the address, but he texted me to say something has come up. He's been delayed, so I'm going to meet him at a coffee shop beside St Anita's, for when he finishes. I did promise him a drink after all.'

'Do you want us to go with you?' Callum asked. A sarcasm in his voice, for he knew Ellie had agreed to this.

'Shut up Callum!' Chloe said, punching him in the shoulder. 'Don't mind him. He's just trying to wind you up. Henry sounds sweet. Best of luck.'

Both Callum and Chloe knew that Ellie liked Henry, and Chloe was really rooting for her. Ellie was the first friend she had made in a long time. It was nice to have other female company.

'Thank you,' Ellie said, picking up her white cardigan and handbag. 'Oh, and as I said, Jenson is dropping by to say hello. He should be here soon. I won't be long, so tell him I'll be back shortly.'

'Yeah, sure, enjoy yourself and thanks again for doing this,' Chloe said.

'Yeah thanks, and tell Henry we can't wait to meet him,' Callum joked before getting another dig from Chloe, his immaturity weighing thin.

'No problem guys. See you in a bit.'

'You can be such a child at times,' Chloe scolded Callum. 'I'm going for a shower.'

'Are you trying to impress somebody too?' Callum shouted after her.

'You're not teasing your sister again, are ya?' Wardy asked, stepping into the kitchen, and fastening the belt on his dressing gown.

'You want some coffee?' Callum asked.

He immediately stood up and dashed over to the coffee machine without Wardy even answering.

Wardy could see a spark in him, a strange response considering they could have been killed last night. But this sudden delight and joyous feeling had somehow been a result of this new family. As a child, Callum had lost out on so much, but now, his quest to find answers, had unintentionally given him a replacement family he had longed for.

~~

Ellie was nervous as she pulled into the parking spot just yards from the coffee shop. She was so tense she could have driven back home. Even though it wasn't a proper date, she was fully aware of Henry's intentions, and she knew she wasn't solely there for the medication either.

'Come on,' she whispered to herself, 'you need to get this for Callum and Chloe.'

Ellie was not used to dating. She had always been there for her father and Meatloaf. Ever since her mother had passed away, she had simply put her love life on hold. This was the first proper date she had been on since she was a teenager.

When she reached the door of the coffee shop, she checked the time on her watch. It was 9.15am. She had arranged to meet Henry at 9.20am after his night shift had ended.

She went inside and scoured the room. No sign of Henry anywhere, so she walked up to the counter.

'Good morning, what can I get you?' The girl behind the counter asked.

'Good morning, can I have a...' Ellie glanced up at the menu overhead. '...a caramel latte, please.'

'Okay.'

'Actually, make that two please?'

'Coming up,' the waitress replied.

Ellie went in search of a free table. This was probably the best coffee shop around, so it was quite busy, even at this early hour.

She spotted a small table with two free chairs over beside the window.

When the two coffees were delivered and placed down in front of her, she checked the time again. It was 9.28am.

She wrapped her palms around the warm cup, inhaling the caramel aroma and sipping away slowly, gazing out the window to see if Henry was coming.

Suddenly, she felt a hand on her shoulder.

'Hello Miss Ward,' a man's voice said.

Excited and nervous at the same time, Ellie nearly choked. The flowing liquid had recoiled up her throat. She had not seen him approach.

She turned around. But it wasn't Henry standing over her.

255

Chapter 47

Chloe came back into the kitchen wearing some of Ellie's clothing, an instruction Ellie had left with her. Her hair was still wet from the shower.

'Was the water warm enough?' Wardy asked.

'Yes, thank you,' Chloe answered. 'I've never felt so clean.'

Meatloaf stood up from under Wardy's feet just before the doorbell rang out. He must have heard somebody approaching.

Callum and Chloe hesitated, having forgotten that Jenson was due to call. They looked nervously at each other.

'Well it's not for me,' Wardy insisted. 'Isn't Jenson supposed to be calling round? Are you gonna answer it, kid?' He asked Chloe.

Chloe looked at Wardy and then over at Callum. They both had a mischievous look on their faces, and Chloe knew why.

She rolled her eyes again, not knowing which one was more childish.

'Hey Jenson! Come on in,' she said, hugging him in the doorway. 'So, good news about getting your family back?'

'Yeah, I still can't believe it,' he answered, rubbing Meatloaf who had also come to greet him. 'I think we're the lucky few that get away from Stem. How is your neck, Ellie told me about last night?'

'It's okay thanks. Ellie patched it up for me. It's starting to become a bit of a habit for her.'

'Morning, kid,' Wardy said, greeting Jenson as he stepped into the kitchen.

'Hey Jenson, how's everything?' Callum asked, getting to his feet, and giving Jenson a hug, with a slap on his back. 'So you're off Stem's radar now?'

'I think so. They're home safe and sound. That's the main thing. I still can't believe it's all over. I hear you two had an eventful time last night?'

Jenson sat there whilst they told him their story, word for word. He was shocked. The lucky escape from Payton and then the dream which seemed a lot worse than what he had observed in the church.

'At least Stem won't find you here,' he commented. He was oblivious to Payton finding them. They all were.

'Yeah, we're so lucky Wardy and Ellie have taken us in,' Chloe remarked.

'You haven't heard from Davrin, have you?' Wardy asked.

Nobody said anything. They all paused just as the front door opened and slammed shut again.

'Is that you?' Wardy called out.

'Yes Dad, it's me,' Ellie called back, a disinterest in her voice.

She walked straight past the kitchen and into her bedroom, shutting the door behind her.

'Was she not out meeting that young man from St Anita's?' Wardy asked.

Chloe immediately realised something had happened.

'I'll go see what's wrong,' she said.

'It must be a girl thing,' Callum stated, again using his humour as a mechanism to defuse a situation.

'I never did quite understand women,' Wardy said, joining in and smiling at the two boys.

Chloe knocked gently on Ellie's bedroom door. She didn't wait for a reply. She stepped in, closing the door behind her.

'You okay Ellie?' She asked.

Ellie had just finished changing out of her more formal attire.

'I'm fine Chloe,' she answered. But Chloe knew something was off.

'What happened?'

'I was stupid, that's what happened. I can't believe I actually expected him to show up.'

'Why, what happened?'

'He never came. And I'm sorry, I never got that drug for you either.'

Chloe wasn't too sure which was upsetting Ellie the most, the fact she was stood up, or the fact she didn't get their medication.

'It's okay Ellie, I'm sure there is some sort of an explanation,' she said. 'We'll find another way. We'll just have to be more careful when we sleep tonight. Did he explain why?'

'Nope, not even a phone call or a text. I sent him a text and tried calling him but nothing—he never even answered. And the father of one of my students saw me there and came up to me. I nearly choked on my coffee. I had to lie about a personal family issue for taking the day off work. I felt so embarrassed. I don't know which was worse, that, or the fact that I have just drank two cups of coffee.'

Chloe could see her caffeine fuelled adrenaline kicking in. She reached out and gave her a big hug.

The sound of the doorbell interrupted the pair. They stood there in silence, listening to the footsteps going towards the door. And then they could hear muffled voices.

Ellie pressed over and opened her bedroom door to peer out. Wardy was at the front door talking to somebody.

And then they both heard Henry's distinctive Irish accent.

Chapter 48

'I really need ta speak to her, it's important,' he pleaded.

'It's okay Dad,' Ellie said, walking up the hallway. 'I've got it.'

'Are you sure?' Wardy asked, waiting for the go-ahead to slam the door in Henry's face. He could tell something had happened.

'Hello Henry,' Ellie said.

She didn't look angry or upset; she just wanted to find out what happened. Something inside her was trying to provoke a smile, after all, he did eventually turn up.

'I'm so sorry for standin ya up like dat, but it wasn't me fault, well, I didn't mean ta,' Henry explained.

Ellie stood there, listening.

'Can I come in?' He asked.

Ellie felt she should give him the chance to explain. She pulled the front door back and he stepped in.

She guided him into the kitchen.

Henry could see the rest of them, sitting at the table, unintentionally eavesdropping in on their conversation. But he didn't mind. He figured they all needed to know.

'Hello Jenson,' he said.

'Hey Henry,' Jenson replied.

'Davrin not here?' Henry asked, his eyes detailing the other strangers in the room.

The silence replied. He knew something had happened, but for now, that answer would have to wait.

'I'm sorry, I did go ta da coffee shop but ya were gone.'

'It's okay,' Ellie replied. She knew he didn't really owe her an explanation. After all, she only met him yesterday. And if anything, he had done more for them than the other way around.

'I was goin ta ring ya but I tought, seen as ya were gone, I would call round in person, to explain.'

'Explain what? What's going on?' Ellie asked. Her rapid blinking displayed a fear in her eyes.

'Well, first, me apologies, I didn't bring anytin ta stop da dreamin. Stem gave us a new so-called cure last night. We used it on a some of our patients. Dey were all found dead dis mornin.'

A flurry of gasping overtook the room.

'Stephanie?' Ellie mouthed.

'No, we didn't give it to her. But dats de thing,' Henry continued, 'can I ask what da real reason was, dat ya came to see Miss Belshaw?'

'We told you the truth,' Ellie replied. A retaliation in her tone. She didn't like Henry's questioning.

'Oh righ. Because dey came an took her away last night.'

'Who took her?' Ellie asked.

'Stem soldiers. Dey came lookin for her. And I found a photo of her when she was younger. Davrin must have brought it wit him an left it der?'

Henry retrieved the folded photo from his pocket.

'Dey asked me all deese questions abou her. An den dey took her. Dey mentioned Davrin. Do you know where he is? I tink he's in a whole lot of trouble.'

They all sat there. An uncommunicative dumbness shrouded them.

Jenson's phone suddenly rang,

'Excuse me,' he said, retrieving it from his pocket and answering it while on the move out to the hallway.

'No-one has seen Davrin since yesterday,' Ellie continued.

'They can't get away with this!' Chloe demanded. Her frustration showing as she banged her fist down on the table. She then held onto her hand in pain, wincing, and looking at her bandage as the blood began to soil the plaster.

She continued. Her anger increasing,

'Davrin is missing, they killed his grandmother and now his Mum has been taken just like Jenson's family. We're all being picked off one by one. We have to do something. They'll never stop!'

'And what do you suggest?' Callum snubbed.

But before Chloe could answer, Jenson's voice resonated loudly from out in the hallway.

'Mum, please calm down, what's wrong?'

An unexpected silence released a tense feeling in the air as everybody listened in on Jenson's conversation. By the sound of it, another revelation had transpired. Another dire dissolution to this powerless pursuit.

'Mum please, just tell me?' Jenson begged.

Seconds later, he softly lowered his phone. A lifeless expression appeared on his face.

'What is it?' Ellie asked, stepping out into the hallway.

Jenson was numb. He didn't say a word.

'Jenson what is it?' She asked again. 'What's wrong?'

'It's Robyn. She never woke up this morning........she's dead!'

Chloe immediately ran over to hug him.

'I have to go,' he said, shrugging her away.

The tears began to appear, but he had no time to stop and break down. All he could think of was his little sister, lying there in her bed this morning. His poor sister who, after all his efforts, he could not save. That same sister he had promised to protect from now on as he slept beside her. Jenson's true world had just crumbled right beneath his feet, just when he thought everything was going to be okay.

The burning in his chest returned, fuelling an anger from the pit of his stomach. His whole body began to tremble.

'Oh Jenson I'm so sorry,' Ellie said. I'll drop you home.'

But Jenson seemed oblivious to her offer. He simply opened the front door and ran out.

'Jenson hang on,' Ellie acknowledged.

'Leave it Ellie,' Wardy requested, holding his hand firmly on top of his daughter's shoulder.

'But dad?'

'I'm afraid he doesn't want us now my dear. Let him go, and when the time is right, we'll be there for him.'

They all stood back in complete horror, all thinking the same thing; Robyn was yet another victim in Stem's search to find a cure, just like the thousands of others before her. They wondered if a cure was ever possible. And if so, how many more innocent people would have to die to find it?

Jenson kept going, his speed increasing with every gallop. And unlike last night, his run was erratic. He was all over the place, whipping in and out of the moving traffic. He needed to get home. He needed to see her.

He could feel his whole body overheat. The exertion began to burn. He wanted every muscle to ache. He needed the physical exhaustion to replace his emotional pain, but this transition was never going to happen. Robyn was gone forever. And the sorrow inside would never bring her back, no matter how fast he went.

He began to wipe back the flood of tears as his body stung. The fatigue causing his mind to refocus. His guilt and devastation, even though it would haunt him for years to come, had somehow shifted momentarily. Robyn's image was diffusing with every strain. His thoughts now projecting to anger. His grief fluidly changing to blame. He needed Stem to take accountability. And right there and then, he made a promise to himself, a promise he knew he could keep. The words repeating over and over in his mind,

'I'm going to take down Stem, even if it's the last thing I do!'

Author's Note

First and foremost, I would like to thank **Jennifer Maher** for her vision. Her selfless dedication and imagination in creating the cover for 'Jenson and the Dreamers' was unbelievable! It is everything I could have ever hoped for and more! A true talent!!! Any of you out there looking for a children's book to read to your child, to allow their young imagination to wonder free, please check out Jennifer's first book 'The Happy Half-Moon Girl', out now on Amazon. So proud of you Jen! May our future be bright with books!

Thank you to my twin, **Ross**. You never gave up on me, always encouraging and believing in me. You were the first person to read 'The Jenson Rose Trilogy', and your feedback helped me incredibly.

To **Paul**, my partner. Thank you for your help throughout, and for giving me the insight to what my book would one day look like. And for always making me smile through this process, even when times were tough, and I was second guessing myself.

To **Karen**, thank you for your feedback, advice, and last-minute pick me up, in a time I felt myself slipping, but your words of encouragement reinstalled the confidence in me.

To **Publish Nation**, thank you for helping me on this journey, especially **David**. Your patience and transparency, in a world full of "too many options", was like finding the perfect needle in a haystack.

To my **Mam** and **Dad**, my **brothers**, my **family** and **friends**, every single person who had an input, no matter how great or small, I sincerely thank you!

And last, but not least, to **YOU, the person reading this**. I thank you for taking the time out to begin Jenson's journey. I thank you for spending your money on it. I truly do hope you enjoyed the start of it, just as much as I had in creating it!

Please feel free to follow me on any of my other Social Media. Let us continue this journey together!

Facebook – Alan Hendrick
Instagram - alanmhendrick
Tiktok   - @alanhendrick1

Keep your eyes out for the sequel. Book 2, coming soon…..

'The Jenson Rose Trilogy'

The Last Gateway

Printed in Great Britain
by Amazon